The Trail of Lost

Also by Tracey Garvis Graves

On the Island

Uncharted (On the Island, 1.5)

Covet

Every Time I Think of You

Cherish (Covet, 1.5)

Heart-Shaped Hack (Kate and Ian #1)

White-Hot Hack (Kate and Ian #2)

The Girl He Used to Know

Heard It in a Love Song

The Trail of Lost Hearts

Tracey Garvis Graves

ST. MARTIN'S PRESS
NEW YORK

First published in the United States by St. Martin's Press, an imprint of St. Martin's Publishing Group

THE TRAIL OF LOST HEARTS. Copyright © 2024 by Tracey Garvis Graves. All rights reserved. Printed in the United States of America. For information, address St. Martin's Publishing Group, 120 Broadway, New York, NY 10271.

www.stmartins.com

Designed by Jen Edwards

The Library of Congress Cataloging-in-Publication Data is available upon request.

ISBN 978-1-250-28027-5 (hardcover)
ISBN 978-1-250-28028-2 (ebook)

Our books may be purchased in bulk for promotional, educational, or business use. Please contact your local bookseller or the Macmillan Corporate and Premium Sales Department at 1-800-221-7945, extension 5442, or by email at MacmillanSpecialMarkets@macmillan.com.

First Edition: 2024

10 9 8 7 6 5 4 3 2 1

The Trail of Lost Hearts

Chapter One

It rains a lot in the Pacific Northwest.

It's not like I didn't know this before my plane touched down in Oregon and I walked out of the airport into a steady drizzle. I know all about the area I've chosen to visit, because I've prepared for it.

I've studied the weather and topography.

Looked at endless hours' worth of coordinates on a map.

Memorized the daily high and low temperatures.

Nearly all the clothing I packed is waterproof, and my handheld GPS is state-of-the-art. I shoved an umbrella into my carry-on, too, which is a total tourist move, but that makes sense because I live in Dayton, Ohio. I also didn't feel like getting wet to prove that I know all about the natives' disdain for umbrellas. And I wouldn't call myself a tourist, either. Explorer, maybe, or whatever it is you call a woman who's on a solo quest and will fly home when she's finished doing what she came here to do.

That's me, Wren Waters. I'm the woman.

Now, as I stand at the trailhead entrance of the Wild Iris Ridge Loop in Eugene, Oregon, the rain has tapered off and the late-September air feels cool. I'm wearing a long-sleeved T-shirt and hoodie and have tucked my gray leggings into a pair of hiking boots. I've threaded my ponytail through the opening at the back of my nylon cap. Lastly, I've swapped out my regular eyeglasses for polarized prescription sunglasses.

The Wild Iris Ridge Loop is a three-and-a-half-mile lollipop route, which means I'll hike up the stem, go around the loop, and come back down the way I went up. Checking my Garmin, I make sure I'm heading in the right direction and begin.

I walk under a spreading oak just past the gate at the trailhead. The trail's namesake irises are absent, but I can picture how it must look when the ground is covered in their purple and white petals. The large gravel trail goes straight uphill and runs alongside a power-line corridor that clashes with the nature surrounding it. There is a fenced llama pasture to my right, which delights me, and a smattering of large, newly constructed homes to my left that look as out of place as the power lines. I could have hiked in from a different entry point, but I'd rather get the uphill part out of the way at the beginning versus the end. Wild blackberries line the trail; many of them are withered, but some are plump and juicy, still thriving in the last gasp of the summer growing season as it winds to a close. I pluck the biggest one and pop it into my mouth. The flavor explodes on my tongue, and before I can stop myself I eat at least ten, wiping my lips on the back of my hand. The berries are better than anything I've ever bought in the supermarket at home.

Largely deserted on this late Monday morning, the trail offers exactly the kind of solitude I've grown used to and prefer. At a band of tall trees near a creek, I pick up a narrower trail. I'm breathing harder now as I continue my uphill trek through a meadow and into a woodsy area full of oaks, and sweat trickles in a light rivulet down my neck; I take a quick break to shed a layer and tie my hoodie around my waist.

I cross a footbridge, and then at the fence, I walk under the power lines and through more woods. Finally, I make a left at the junction that concludes the stem of the lollipop and transitions into the loop part of the hike.

I stop to drink some water. Hearing footsteps not far behind me, I move farther off the side of the trail, pulling my Garmin from my waist pack under the pretense of studying its screen while I wait for the hiker to pass me.

Out of the corner of my eye, I can see a man approaching. As he draws closer, I notice that he looks a little older than me—closer to forty than my thirty-four. He's tall and broad-shouldered, but lean, like maybe he enjoys rock climbing or distance running. He's wearing hiking pants and a lightweight blue nylon jacket. A cap hides most of his hair, but enough of it peeks out that I can tell it's dark.

He looks nothing like my medium-height, blond-haired ex-fiancé, Rob.

Technically, Rob is my *late* fiancé, but that makes it sound like he's just running behind or got stuck at work, which is also sort of true. He was on his way home from his company's headquarters in Dayton when the driver of the other vehicle blew a stop sign and obliterated Rob's company car in a way that was not conducive to survival.

All I'm saying is that "late fiancé" sounds weird to me.

Instead of passing me, the hiker stops. He smiles and it's the kind of smile that probably melts hearts when it's at full wattage, but it doesn't extend to the far corners of his mouth, and there is something guarded behind it. I only notice the guardedness because his smile looks a lot like the one I've been giving everyone since Rob died. The one that says, *I'm fine. Nothing to see here as long as you don't look too closely.* He's wearing a waist pack, and his sunglasses are sitting on the bill of his ball cap. He's got a pen behind his ear, and the Garmin in his hand looks a lot like mine. His long-sleeved T-shirt is faded, and the pants and hiking boots are well-worn.

"Hi," he says.

I pinch the bridge of my nose and sigh inwardly. Since Rob died, I've often wished men could see the spiky armor I've metaphorically donned and would therefore know not to waste their time trying to penetrate my thorny exterior. Hoping he'll get the hint that I'm not interested in a trailside chat, I nod in response to his greeting, my expression pure granite.

"I'm Marshall," he says. "Great day for a hike."

"Yep," I say. Maybe my one-syllable effort and the withholding of my name will get my point across. I'm not getting a creepy vibe or anything, but voluntarily chatting with any man sounds about as appealing as a root canal.

"I see that you found the blackberries," he says with a grin.

I'm about to ask him how he knows about the blackberries when it dawns on me. I take off my sunglasses and try to use the polarized lenses as a makeshift mirror. It doesn't really work, but I wipe my mouth repeatedly with the cuff of my shirt, staining the light gray fabric.

"It's still there," he says.

Fantastic.

Here's something you should know about me: I hate being embarrassed. Like, truly hate it. I've always been this way. My friends tease me mercilessly about my inability to trip or fall and laugh it off instead of turning a mortifying shade of red. If I dribble splotches of cabernet on my favorite top, I'll spend the rest of the night sweating under a borrowed layer so that no one will know. One night, my best friend Stephanie tripped and farted loudly in front of a table full of men. Without missing a beat, she turned to them, bowed, and said, "And now for my next trick." A guy named James was sitting at that table, and he later *married* her. The best man included the story in his speech at the reception, and Stephanie laughed so hard she cried. "I would move to another state if that ever happened to me," I told Steph. "Straight up just get the hell out of Dodge."

"I have some antibacterial wipes in my pack," the hiker offers.

I hold up my hand. "Thanks. I've got some too."

He takes in my Garmin. "Fellow geocacher, by chance?" His guarded smile broadens in genuine delight.

"Yep," I say again, but unlike him, I'm not smiling. *Can't you sense my spiky armor? It's sharp and pointy and I guarantee you're not getting past it, so don't even try.*

"Looks like we might be searching for the same cache," he says. "Want to team up?"

"There are lots of caches here. We're probably not searching for the same one." I give no further comment or explanation, and an awkward silence ensues.

"Well, good luck," he finally says, moving a respectable distance away. He continues up the trail, and I watch until he's out of view, then reach into my waist pack for the wipes. I pull out my phone, open my camera, and flip the screen to turn it into a mirror. There it is. Big purple smudge on the corner of my mouth. I look like a six-year-old. In addition to the smudge, my teeth are stained a faint purple, and my lips look as if a drunk woman lined them with red wine and forgot to fill in the rest. I scrub at my mouth vigorously until I've removed all traces of the stain.

The only saving grace is that I won't have to move away, because I don't actually live here.

Chapter Two

I'm alone with my thoughts as I resume the hike. The cache location is right before—but slightly off-trail from—where I'll pick up the lollipop stick to head back down. And because I let that guy go ahead of me on the trail, he's going to get there first. According to my geocache app, there are at least fifteen active geocaches hidden here, but I'd bet we *are* looking for the same one. It's a newly listed cache placed only yesterday, and I want the FTF—the first-to-find.

Because here's something else you should know about me: I am competitive as all get-out. I will not lie or cheat, but I will do everything in my power to win. Game night with my friends is not just an excuse to have drinks and eat appetizers.

At least it isn't for me.

"You get scary on game night," Rob said to me shortly after we started dating. He was smiling when he said it, but I didn't see what the big deal was.

"I play to win," I said. "That's the whole point of playing a game."

"I think the point is to have fun with your friends," he teased.

"Two things can be true."

"You can spin it any way you like, but I'm pretty sure if we were running a race and I fell, you'd step on my head and keep going."

"Maybe don't fall then," I said, and then Rob chased me into the bedroom and tackled me onto the bed. The tackling turned into tickling and the tickling turned into kissing and I need to stop thinking about that day because it was one of the good ones.

Still walking at an incline, I hike three consecutive switchbacks through a meadow, walk past a cluster of ponderosa pines, and spot a kiosk for one of the other trailhead entrances. I've seen a few people, but I've mostly been one with nature, and the physical exertion and fresh air have my heart pumping and my mood improving along with it.

According to my Garmin, I'm getting closer, and I enter a denser forested area to my left. It's a good thing I'm looking down at my feet, because otherwise I might have missed the arrow on the ground fashioned from sticks. It points toward a small clearing in the distance, and my excitement builds. The fact that it looks undisturbed tells me there's a chance no one else has made it this far, including the geocacher who stopped to talk and whose name I've already forgotten. Miller? Matthew? Something like that.

The cache itself is easy enough to find, and the canister is fastened with wire to the base of a narrow tree trunk directly across the perimeter of the clearing. Inside the canister is a small yet intricate wooden carving of an oak tree. After unrolling the log, I see that there are no other names on it. "Yes!" I exclaim. My personal life might be in utter shambles, but I got the FTF and that feels pretty damn good.

I sign the logbook and put everything back. I'll eat the sandwich I picked up on my way to Wild Iris, drink some water, and then head back down.

Two men enter the small clearing. They're dressed in work boots and jeans. One is wearing an untucked flannel shirt and the other is dressed in a T-shirt. No packs. There's an uncomfortable silence while they study me. Uncomfortable for me, that is. They don't seem uncomfortable at all. Unlike before, when I encountered the other hiker, these guys *do* give me the creeps, and their stony glances raise the hair on the back of my neck.

"What are you doing out here?" the one in the T-shirt asks. He's short and stout with a barrel chest and a beer gut.

"Looking for the cache. Same as you."

Beer Gut looks at his friend and laughs, but it's not a friendly sound. "Cash? We don't know nothin' about any money."

The guy in the flannel shirt sends a silent message to Beer Gut with his eyes. They look around at the empty clearing and then they look at me like a couple of opportunists who can't believe what they've stumbled upon. Surely, I'm wrong.

I want to be wrong.

I hope I'm wrong.

They come closer.

"Not money," I say. "A geocache. Hidden objects you search for with GPS. It's super fun, and good exercise. Lots of fresh air." I'm talking way too fast. It's time to shut up and get out of here.

Before I can scramble to my feet, they sit down next to me, one on each side, way too close. Their deliberate proximity sends a message that is hard to ignore: my instincts were spot-on. My heart pounds and I want to run, but my legs have turned to jelly and I don't know what to do. Will the prey be even more exciting if they get to chase and overpower it first? I'm afraid to run and I'm afraid to stay.

Think, Wren.

Very casually, I take out my phone and press the side button along with one of the volume buttons until the Emergency SOS slider appears. But before I can drag it to the right, Beer Gut, the barrel-chested one who scares me the most, yanks the phone from my hand. He looks at the screen and turns to me, something cold and dark in his eyes.

"That's mine and I want it back," I say. Beer Gut slides my phone into his pocket, taking what isn't his and sending the message that he'll have me, too, if he feels like it.

I have no choice but to run.

I shoot to my feet, hoping my quivering legs will support me, but as soon as Beer Gut realizes I'm making a break for it, he clamps his hand forcefully around the part of my leg right above my hiking boot. I yelp in pain. "Sit that fine ass back down," he says.

He's still squeezing my leg, and I lower myself to the ground in an awkward cross-legged position. Every cell in my body vibrates with fear. I scan the area, my ears pricked like an animal's, listening, and I can just make out the faint sound of hikers in the distance. I know they're too far away to hear me, but I try anyway. "Hey," I shout. "Hey!"

He grabs my face and squeezes, his fingers digging into my jaw. "Shut your mouth."

My face is throbbing when he finally removes his hand, and fear roots me to my spot on the ground. My instincts tell me to run anyway, to shake his hand off my ankle and see how far I can make it before I'm tackled and powerless to avoid the arrival of whatever comes after that. I'm in good shape and I'm fast. But am I faster than both of them? I don't know, and it's my uncertainty about the outcome that paralyzes me. Cortisol and adrenaline course through my veins and I start shaking.

"This ain't a great place for a party," Flannel Shirt says. Then, with a slight tilt of his head, he motions toward the densely forested area on the other side of the clearing. My brain sends an image of one of them with his hand over my mouth leaving the other free to do anything he wants.

What they can do in less than ten minutes will remain with me for a lifetime.

"I'm not going anywhere with you," I say, and they laugh. But I will not go with them, because I listen to too many true crime podcasts, and being moved to another location will not end well for me. I am in for the fight of my life, and rage momentarily eclipses my fear. Once they make their move, it's on. Tears blur my eyes and I steel myself for what's to come.

The sound of footsteps and the snapping of twigs break the silence. Someone is coming and I exhale as the sheer relief that I am no longer alone washes over me. But my relief is mixed with trepidation. Have Beer Gut and Flannel Shirt called in reinforcements? I blink back the tears, remaining rigid and desperately hopeful until the person comes striding into view.

And that person is the geocacher who passed me earlier, whose name I still can't recall. He's on foot, of course, but to me, he looks like a knight charging into the clearing atop a white horse.

"Howdy, folks," he says. "That arrow back there sure is handy, huh?" He walks over to the cache. Opens it and logs the find. "Dammit. Looks like someone named Skyline Wanderer beat me to it."

He approaches our little group. My tears of relief overflow, and I take off my sunglasses and dab at my eyes with the cuff of my shirtsleeve, which does not go unnoticed by him. His eyes flick to Beer Gut's hand, still wrapped around my ankle, and I watch his expression change as the puzzle pieces of my situation fall into place. He's wearing the same guarded smile, but there is nothing friendly in the hard set of his mouth.

I can run now. I can shake off Beer Gut's hand and sprint down the trail to the safety of my rental car. But that will mean abandoning the geocacher and leaving him to deal with a two-against-one situation, and I can't, in good conscience, do that.

He lowers himself to the grass and sits down as close to me as he can, legs outstretched. Takes the water bottle from his waist pack, uncaps it, and drinks. "You guys taking a break?" he asks. His manner might be pleasant and unassuming, but my rescuer cuts an imposing figure—towering in height, broad-shouldered, fit.

"Why don't you move on along," Beer Gut says. The threatening tone he uses sends my heart rate climbing again. He's not willing to let this golden opportunity slip through his fingers quite so easily. "My buddy and the wife and I are having some private time."

"Wife, huh? How long have you guys been married?"

"That ain't your fucking business, and I said it's time for you to move along."

He laughs as if he finds Beer Gut's attempt to intimidate him hilariously funny. "I'll move along when I feel like it," he says, fire in his eyes, loaded for bear, "not because you told me to but because I've got better things to do than sit around with a couple of degenerates like you."

"What did you say?" Beer Gut asks, puffing out his chest.

"Man, let's go," Flannel Shirt says.

Beer Gut elbows me hard in the ribs. "Get up. We're leaving."

"I need to check my phone before we can leave. Can you hand it to me?" Now that reinforcements have arrived, I'll be damned if I'm going to let this man keep what isn't his. I may not have the brawn to win this battle, but I'm not leaving without my phone.

"No, you *don't,* and I don't have it," Beer Gut says.

"Yes, you do. It's in your pocket. Remember?" I say it sweetly, but my words drip with poison.

My savior clenches his jaw and his fists. "I bet she's right," he says evenly. "Your wife looks smart. Way smarter than you, frankly. That's probably why you married her. Wanted to level up, I bet. She's pretty, too. How *did* you land her?" He's just kicking the hornets' nest now.

Beer Gut ignores him and turns to me. "If you're so sure I have your phone, you better reach in there yourself," he says, looking at Flannel Shirt and laughing about how clever he is to have figured out how to force me to put my hand where I'd rather not.

Fuck these men who prey on women and underestimate our

resourcefulness. I will gladly reach into the pocket of this absolute piece of human garbage and take back what's mine.

And I do.

I slide my hand right inside and wrap my hand firmly around the heavy-duty water- and shockproof case of my phone. Then I jam it straight into his ball sack with as much force as the angle and depth of his pocket allow.

In for a penny, in for a pound, I guess.

Beer Gut lets out a guttural scream and flops onto his side, writhing in pain with his legs drawn up to his chest. Flannel Shirt mostly looks stunned, with seemingly no clue how to handle this unexpected development.

"I think I'll move along after all," the geocacher says, leaping to his feet. "And I'm taking your pretty wife with me." He stretches his hand toward me, and when I grasp it, he pulls me up from the ground with significant force and says, "Go."

Gone is his oh-shucks tone, and in its place is one that says, *You have underestimated both of us.*

I go.

But he doesn't.

He stays.

One of the men shouts something, and his furious intensity turns my legs back into jelly, but I don't turn around. I'm crashing ungracefully along the trail, and I feel awful when the toe of my hiking boot sends the arrow made of sticks flying in every direction. There is more shouting and then something that sounds like a primal scream of pain followed by a string of f-bombs and several very specific threats about killing. The thunder of footsteps behind me terrifies me further, but I don't dare look over my shoulder, too frightened of what—or who—I will see.

"Don't stop," the geocacher shouts, coming up behind me and grabbing my wrist to keep me steady as we slip and slide down the trail at warp speed. Beer Gut and Flannel Shirt are still screaming somewhere behind us. We might be faster, but they are not giving up on their pursuit.

"What did you do to them?" I gasp.

"Bear spray, keep going."

So, he came loaded for *actual* bear.

We don't stop until we reach the parking lot. "My car?" I ask, because I can still hear shouting from somewhere behind us and there is no question that we need to beat a hasty retreat. Scanning the lot, I try to remember where I parked it.

"Mine's right here," he says as he unlocks a blue Jeep with his fob, and we throw open our respective doors. "We'll come back for yours," he says, starting the car, throwing the six-on-the-floor gear stick into reverse, and driving with purpose toward the exit of the parking lot.

My heart rate is still somewhere in the red zone, ping-ponging unpleasantly in my chest. "That was insane," I say, gulping for air. "They could have been armed."

"They were," he says, but he doesn't elaborate, and I don't ask for details. I can't. Not right now.

He drives a ways down the road and pulls in to the parking lot of a coffee shop. We're not in peril anymore, but the emotions that overcome me are like the sweat that starts running down my body at the end of a long hike when I finally stop moving. They pour forth, beginning with a slow trickle of tears from the corners of my eyes that I try to hide. They build, gaining steam, and I eventually give up and let them flow. He says something, but I don't hear it clearly because I'm sobbing now, my breath catching in my throat as I try to synchronize the air coming in and going out.

"It's okay. They're not coming. You're safe."

But it's my safety that's allowing the pressure to release, and I cry harder and wrap my arms around myself. He reaches into the back seat and pulls a silver blanket out of a large backpack. It's the kind of blanket you wrap stranded hikers in, so they'll stay warm and not go into shock. He tucks it around me and then grabs my wrist and takes my pulse. Satisfied, he waits patiently and lets me be until I'm all cried out. "I'll be right back," he says. He locks me in the car and goes into the coffee shop, emerging ten minutes later with two cups. I've had time to collect myself, and when he gets into the car and hands me my cup, I hold it tightly in my hands.

"It's hot chocolate," he says.

"Thank you."

"You okay?" he asks.

No, I am not okay. I haven't been okay since Rob died. I don't know that I'll ever be okay.

"I'm angry with myself," I say. He starts to speak, but I cut him off before he can continue. "Women should be able to hike alone, but they can't and I took an unnecessary risk that could have gone very badly. If you hadn't come along, I know what those men planned to do to me." I owned pepper spray and always brought it with me when I geocached at home. But I couldn't bring it on the plane and then I'd just set off on my merry way like I didn't have a care in the world.

"You gonna beat yourself up over it forever?"

It seems like an oddly specific question. "I don't know," I say. "I'm still busy beating myself up over it in the present." Along with everything else I've gotten wrong in the last few years.

"You didn't know this would happen," he says.

"I know that it *can* happen. And I was defenseless when it did." For someone who'd turned overthinking into an Olympic-level sport, I'm not sure how I missed it. We sip our drinks, and the warmth of the hot chocolate soothes me. "Why didn't you run?" I ask.

He lets out a short laugh but there is nothing funny about it. "If they'd known what was going through my head, they would have been far more afraid of me." I can hear the rage and the steely resolve in his words. My trembling has subsided but a new concern takes its place. This man might have come to my aid, but that doesn't mean his intentions are automatically pure. It would be tragically ironic to escape one terrifying situation only to run straight into the next like some clueless heroine in a low-budget horror film. I don't even have my car, because it's still in the Wild Iris parking lot, where Beer Gut and Flannel Shirt might still be lurking.

"Can you take me to my car?" I ask, my voice sounding high-pitched and panicky. It feels like my tears might be gearing up for another round.

"Of course. But you're safe."

"But now I'm scared of *you*." I don't know him any better than I knew those men and yet here I am sitting in the passenger seat of his car. Utter fear put me here rather than any persuasive action on his part, but I'm done with the loss of autonomy and agency I've endured since those men walked into the clearing. I think longingly of an island where only women are permitted to live. We spend our days reading and cooking and our nights sipping wine and telling stories about how we kicked ass and took care of *ourselves*. We don't have to look over our shoulders and we don't have to listen to the bullshit and lies of men.

At first, he looks taken aback, but then it dawns on him that I have a valid reason to be afraid. How nice it would be if women could go about their lives with the confidence a man has when it comes to safety. "I'm sorry. I didn't mean to scare you. I just meant there was no way I was going to let them get away with what they did without any repercussions," he says. "I couldn't just run away." Then he removes his wallet from the console between the seats and fishes a business card and his driver's license out of it. "Here. This is me. This is what I do."

I glance at the license. His name is Marshall Hendricks and the picture matches. Then I look at the card.

MARSHALL HENDRICKS, PSY.D.

He's a psychologist.

Oof.

Now is not a great time to let anyone inside my brain, especially someone so qualified at poking around; there's a lot in there to unpack. My friends and family would argue that now is a *perfect* time—long overdue, in fact—to let someone in, but I'm not ready. I hand both items back to him.

"Keep the card." As I shove it into the pocket of my leggings, he adds, "What's *your* name?" There's nothing judgmental in his tone, and it's a fair question.

"Wren."

Marshall starts the car and drives back to the Wild Iris parking lot. "Mine's the black Honda CR-V a few rows over," I say. After pulling up right next to it, we get out and he scans the area, looking up toward the trails that I will never hike again. It's mercifully quiet. Beer Gut and Flannel Shirt are probably at the nearest bar lying to each other about how tough they are.

"Where do you live?" Marshall asks.

"Ohio. But I'm staying at the La Quinta tonight." It's not fancy, but it's the closest hotel to the trail.

"I'm staying there too," he says. "I'll follow you to the hotel. Go straight there."

Though I bristle at being told what to do, I'm too physically and emotionally drained to push back. I want nothing more than to retreat to the safety and solitude of my hotel room, and there is nothing that could convince me to stop somewhere along the way.

I keep looking in the rearview mirror to make sure he's still behind me.

He always is.

When we arrive at the hotel, we walk up to the front desk to check in. Marshall stands patiently beside me as I slide my driver's license and credit card across the counter. "I have a reservation under the name of Wren Waters," I say. The woman behind the counter takes my information and hands me a key card. Marshall does the same and then we walk across the lobby and get into the elevator.

"What floor are you on?" Marshall asks.

"Two."

He punches the buttons for the second and third floors. It's a short ride, and the elevator dings and the doors open again. I step out but before the doors close, I turn to Marshall and say, "Thank you for today. I am eternally grateful for what you did, but I'm exhausted. I'm going to lie down for a while."

He holds the elevator doors open with his hand and looks at me. "I'm in room 316 if you need me."

I nod and the elevator closes.

In my room, I shower and then slip into joggers and a hoodie. I comb out my wet hair, but I'm too spent to dry it. Then I crawl into bed and fall into a fragmented sleep punctuated by nightmares about being chased.

Chapter Three

I wake up around six, absolutely famished, my stomach churning with hunger. Back in June, when my life was still humming along nicely with Rob, if you'd told me I would one day buy a fancy Garmin GPS and start traipsing through the underbrush looking for canisters of hidden objects put there by strangers, I would have wondered if you'd hit your head. And if you'd asked what might pull me out of the deep mental funk I found myself in a month later when Rob died and my life turned upside down, geocaching would not have made the list. I'd heard the word and had a slight grasp of its meaning, but that's where my knowledge—and frankly my interest—ended.

That changed when Stephanie made me go hiking after it became apparent to her and the rest of our friend group that I was slipping into a worrisome place. Since Rob had died, I'd lost about ten pounds. I turned down all social invitations and told everyone to leave me alone. I slept too much or not at all. I hadn't made any effort toward removing Rob's clothes from the closet or disposing of his personal property, because I had such conflicted feelings about how to handle that. On the one hand, I wished I could snap my fingers and make everything disappear. But on the other, I wanted to burrow my face into his sweaters hoping for a whiff of his cologne.

Stephanie showed up one Sunday morning and called my phone repeatedly until I buzzed her into the building and unlocked my apartment door. By the time she appeared in my bedroom doorway, I was wrapped up tightly in my covers again like the depressed burrito I'd become. "Get up," she said. She rifled through my drawers and tossed clothes onto the bed. "I'll wait while you change."

I walked into the bathroom and did as she asked because I didn't have the strength to argue, and we'd been friends long enough that I knew she'd win this round. I'd go have coffee or brunch or whatever she was making me do, and then I'd come home and go right back to bed. But after I peed and brushed my teeth and started getting dressed, I realized she'd selected the clothes I normally wore for yoga.

"I am not going to yoga," I said when I came out of the bathroom, even though I was someone who *definitely* should have been going to yoga. But I had abandoned yoga in favor of my bed and had no intention of changing that anytime soon. Yoga was awesome, but it was not the solution for *everything*.

"Neither am I. Put on your Nikes. Let's go."

She drove us to Five Rivers MetroParks and found a space in the lot. "I changed my mind. I'd rather go to yoga."

"It's just a hike, Wren. Buck up."

I wasn't what you'd call a hard-core hiker. I didn't have a lot of moisture-wicking T-shirts or special shoes or hiking poles, but Stephanie and I used to go on hikes almost every weekend before she got married and I met Rob. Stephanie's husband, James, was an avid hiker, and we could have turned it into an activity the four of us did together, but Rob didn't like hiking. Rob didn't like anything outdoorsy. We had to be mindful of how we spent our time because of his busy travel schedule, so I never pushed it. But I had always loved the outdoors—camping, floating down a river on an inner tube, cookouts, bonfires, boating. I laughed when I saw someone wearing a T-shirt that said INDOORSY, and when I told Rob I was going to look for one in his size, he laughed. "I won't wear it," he said, "but not because it isn't true. I won't wear it because I'll look like an idiot."

"That is also true," I said, laughing right along with him. But my laughter felt forced and it bothered me sometimes that he didn't seem to enjoy a lot of the things that I did. And I didn't enjoy many of the things that he did, like collecting expensive scotch, discussing the stock market, and playing poker. We both liked going out for dinner and to the movies, so we did that a lot. But Rob also loved staying home and relaxing, and that made sense because he spent his life in airports and hotels. I rarely traveled anymore save for a once-a-year girls' trip with my closest friends because if Rob was home, that's where I wanted to be, too. I was still renting because I hadn't decided where I wanted to live, and my job allowed me the freedom to work from anywhere. But I dreamed of traveling— maybe not around the world but certainly within the United States. As I got older, I knew that life had more to offer than staying in the same town I'd been born in, and I'd been feeling the urge to spread my wings. And then I met Rob. I often pondered how an outdoorsy girl with an unsatisfied case of wanderlust had fallen in love with an indoorsy homebody and chalked it up to a case of opposites attract.

It was late August, sunny and hot, the day Stephanie bullied me out of bed for that hike.

"What happened to my year?" I asked as we approached the trailhead. "I was very specific when I told everyone I was giving myself a year to wallow in my grief and then I'd get back to living."

"Because healing and grieving are not mutually exclusive, and you passed wallow quite some time ago. I get it, you're not feel- ing your best right now. Who would be after going through what you've had to deal with? But do not use this time as an excuse to sink further down into the place you already are. I don't think it's a good place, Wren. It's not a healthy place, and I don't want to watch you spiral. You need to get out of bed and do whatever you can to *stay* out of it. I don't care if you're pissed about it; I just want you upright."

My breathing deepened as I followed Stephanie, and I took in a calming breath, drawing it into my lungs and then slowly letting it back out. We walked in silence, and I listened to the birds and the chatter of other people on the trail. There were kids and dogs everywhere, and I felt the first trickle of sweat at my hairline and between my shoulder blades. We walked mostly in silence, and thirty minutes later, when I was breathing hard and covered in sweat, it didn't feel so awful to be upright.

"Break?" Steph asked.

"Yes."

We moved off the trail. Physically, I felt better, but emotionally I still felt as empty and dead inside as the old fallen log we sat down on to take a rest.

Two women walked toward us. They paused in front of the log, just out of earshot. They stared at us and appeared to be waiting for something.

"Why are those women staring at us," I asked Steph, my voice low.

"I don't know. It's unsettling."

We moved over in case they wanted to use the log for the same reason we were using it, and they came closer but still seemed to be hovering. I could hear them talking now.

"Did they just call us *Muggles*?" Steph asked, her voice as low as mine had been.

"They did. This is getting weird," I said.

"Excuse me," one of them finally said. "Would the two of you mind getting up for just a second?"

We rose to our feet, and the women crouched down in front of the log and rolled it halfway over. There was a hole in the bottom of the log, and I recoiled in alarm as one of the women pulled a yellow latex glove from her waist pack, put it on, and then plunged her hand into the opening. I could only imagine what might be living inside. Then she withdrew what looked like an old-school film canister. "Hell, yeah," her friend said.

So, I guess the log wasn't empty after all.

Just me.

The women high-fived and then popped the top off the canister, took out a piece of paper, signed their names, and put everything back. Then they rolled the log back into place and said, "Thanks. You can have your log back now."

"Excuse me," I asked. "What are you *doing*?"

They laughed. "We're geocaching. We use GPS to look for items people have hidden. It's super fun. There's an app you can download that will show you where caches can be found. You should try it."

"Muggles?" Steph said.

"Oh, that's what we call non-geocachers. We prefer not to be observed, but we weren't sure how long the two of you would be sitting there."

"That was kind of cool," Steph said when they walked away.

"I guess so," I said.

We finished our hike, and when Stephanie dropped me off at home, she said, "You know I love you and I'll do anything you need me to do, but I want you to come up with a plan. Therapy, exercise, getting out of bed every day. All good things, Wren."

"I know. I love you too and I'll try to start figuring things out."

"That's all I'm asking," she said.

I leaned across the console, and we hugged. I crawled right back into bed that day, and nothing changed for another week. Even though I knew I had to help myself by doing *something* that would get me out of bed, I couldn't come up with anything that sounded tolerable.

It was mostly frustration over my lack of a solution to my

problems that prompted me to download the geocache app. I noticed that there was a cache located half a mile from my apartment, so I set out on a walk to see if I could find it.

And I did.

It was an old Coke bottle cap tucked inside a small container hidden in a flower bed next to a Jimmy John's.

Finding the cache should have felt anticlimactic, maybe even silly.

But it didn't.

It felt good.

Geocaching is sometimes described as the feeling of purpose in the middle of nowhere, and nothing had ever summed up my current situation so completely and succinctly.

I needed a purpose, and I had finally found one.

I started walking every day, going farther, and finding more caches, and I began to seek out the ones that weren't so easy. I walked an increasing number of miles, and my head began to feel like it wasn't constantly stuffed with cotton.

I bought better shoes.

I spent all my free time walking and finding and logging my caches. Then I began to think bigger. When I called my mom to say I was planning a solo vacation so I could go geocaching in a new location, I was met with silence on the other end of the phone. Finally, she said, "Why do you need to get on a plane to do this? What about doing it closer to home the way you have been?"

"Because Rob's presence is everywhere, but he isn't. His robe is still hanging on the back of the bathroom door. The glass he drank scotch out of the night before he died is still in the sink because I can't bear to put it in the dishwasher. The empty suitcase from his last trip is still sitting on the bedroom floor waiting to be repacked." I squeezed my eyes shut to block out the images, because Rob's ghost surrounded me. "I need to get out of here." There was silence on the other end of the phone. "Please say something."

"I can't tell if you're fleeing your old life or blindly running toward a new one," she said.

"Honestly, Mom, I'm not sure either. But whatever this is, it's the only thing that feels good."

My life is still a mess, but the fresh air and the miles I'm walking might help me turn it right side up again.

It's the best I could come up with, anyway.

What happened today in the clearing makes me want to go directly to the airport and catch the first flight back to Ohio. But another part of me clings to the idea of finishing what I started so I can cross this trip off the list of Things Wren Can Do to Take Back Her Life.

However, I never got the chance to eat my long-forgotten sandwich and I can't think clearly until I get some real food into me. I grab my phone and search for the closest restaurant within walking distance. I would like nothing more than to have a quiet dinner alone, but what Marshall did today went above and beyond what most people would have done for a stranger, and spiky armor notwithstanding, thanking him properly is the right thing to do. He never asked to be dragged into the mess I'd stumbled into, but he cleaned it up just the same. I fish Marshall's business card from the pocket of my leggings, which are lying in a wrinkled heap on the bathroom floor. I type "Marshall Hendricks Psy.D." into the search bar, and the top hit confirms he's got a private practice just outside of Portland. I spend a few minutes digging around on his website. His practice must be thriving, because there's a professionally worded apology about not being able to accept any new clients.

My hair has dried in a wild clump of tangles and waves, and I brush it out and put it in a ponytail. I clean the lenses of my glasses and put them on. After giving my lips a swipe of lip balm, I gather my purse and room key and walk down the hall to the elevator. Going up instead of down, I arrive on the third floor and knock on room 316.

"Hey," Marshall says when he opens it, smiling but curious.

He's wearing gray sweatpants and a T-shirt, and I can hear the sound of a sporting event coming from his TV. "Is everything all right?"

"I was wondering if you'd like to join me for dinner. My treat. If you haven't eaten yet, that is. There's a restaurant about a five-minute walk from here. But maybe you're watching the game and you don't want to. And maybe you did eat already, like a late lunch or something." Or maybe if I shut up for a second or two, he'll have time to respond to my rambling and I'll have my answer.

"The game isn't important, and I grabbed some snacks from the vending machine earlier. I was just thinking about getting some dinner. Let me grab my key card."

We take the elevator downstairs and walk out the main doors. "The restaurant is called The Cooler," I say.

"Cool," Marshall says.

When we arrive, he holds the door open and follows me inside. The sign says to seat ourselves, and a waitress drops off a couple of menus and fills our water glasses.

"Are you feeling better now?" Marshall asks.

"Yes," I say. "Please disregard the emotional meltdown I had in your car earlier today. I'm fine now."

"Nothing to excuse. I completely understand where you were coming from."

"You said they were armed." I was too shaken to ask for details earlier, but now I want to know.

"It was a knife. The one whose balls are probably still throbbing had it in the other front pocket."

Okay, so maybe I'm not feeling so fine after all.

"I knew by the log that no one had been to the cache yet, but I wasn't sure if you were coming," I say. "There were other caches, but I wanted to find that one so I could try for the FTF."

"Skyline Wanderer. I remember," he says. "Nice username."

"I didn't put a lot of thought into it, honestly. What's yours?"

"Pink Freud."

"That's . . . really good."

"So you're here vacationing?"

"Something like that."

"What does that even mean?" he asks.

"It means I'm here to look for some caches and after I've found them, I'm going home."

"Your vacation is looking for caches in Eugene?"

"No, just the one today. The rest are in various other locations in Oregon."

"Did you make a list or something?" he asks.

"I did, actually." And today might have been harrowing, but at least I've crossed the first cache off it. "Why were *you* at Wild Iris?" I don't mention that I know he lives in Portland and that there must be a reason he was geocaching a hundred miles from home on a random Monday. "How does Pink Freud have so much free time?"

"I'm on vacation too."

"By yourself?" I know why I wanted a solo vacation, but why does *he*?

"Why are you looking at me like that?" he asks.

"Like what?"

"Like you think it's weird."

Shit. "I wasn't. I'm here by myself too."

"Exactly," he says. "So, what's next on your list?"

"Why do you want to know?" It's hard to miss the suspicion in my tone, but my senses are on full alert and everyone is a potential threat.

He raises his hands in the air, palms facing toward me. "I'm going to do some more geocaching myself, that's all. Just curious where you're heading next."

"Crater Lake, Bend, and Mount Hood. Maybe somewhere in Portland if I have time. I flew into Eugene early this morning, but I'm flying out of Portland on the way home."

"Those are great locations. I've been geocaching in all of them. Maybe we can work as a team while you're here. I've got plenty of time."

"I'm really not interested in teaming up with anyone," I say.

"Anyone in general or men in . . . particular?" He draws out that last part and I enjoy watching Marshall trying to determine if I'm gay or straight.

"I like men just fine, but I'm not interested in teaming up with a new one at the moment," I say firmly.

"If you're not interested in a new one that must mean the old one broke your heart and you're still trying to get over it."

"A sixth grader could probably figure that out. A sixth-grade girl, anyway. Regardless, I'm on a solo quest."

"So it's what, *Eat, Pray, Love* but with dirt and GPS and skinned knees?"

I sense judgment in his tone. Maybe he thinks my heartache over what he perceives to be a simple breakup is disproportionate to my actions. As if my pain is so small it doesn't warrant a quest. "What if it is?" I say. "It's no skin off *your* knees. And it's less *Eat, Pray, Love,* and more Cheryl Strayed's *Wild.*" I don't divulge that for a brief period when I was still contemplating what I wanted to do, I considered hiking the Pacific Crest Trail the way Cheryl did. And just like her, maybe I would emerge on the other side a strong and capable butterfly who now had her life all figured out in comparison to the heartbroken caterpillar who couldn't figure out a better way to help herself. But truthfully, I worried that I wouldn't last two days on the PCT, and that was before I encountered the men in the clearing today. Besides, a solo hike that took five months wasn't the kind of healing journey I had time for, and there's no way I would have put my parents through the stress. One week in the Pacific Northwest seemed like a safe compromise. Just another thing I was wrong about.

"You're right. I'm sorry," he says. His tone is much softer now. "I didn't mean for it to come out as harshly as it did."

"Are you brokenhearted too? Did someone do something un-forgivable to *you*?"

A pained look appears briefly on his face. "I'm not broken-hearted," he says. "And I am *definitely* into women." But the guarded look is back on his face and there is something wounded in his demeanor, something I don't have the desire to wade into any deeper. My hands are too full trying to get a handle on my own shit.

"I don't need anyone to team up with," I say with finality even though it sounds ludicrous. I sure needed Marshall earlier today and we both know it.

"Who hurt you?" he asks.

"Get out of my head," I say. I am not one of Marshall's clients and this is not a therapy session.

"*You* get out of your head," he says.

"It's my head. I'm supposed to be in it."

"That depends," he says.

"On what?"

"If being in there is helping or hindering."

I can't answer that, buddy, not without revealing that inside my head is a hoarder-level mess of conflicting thoughts and emotions that I fear I'll never untangle. "This is not going the way I intended," I say.

"What was your intention?"

"To repay you for coming to my rescue by taking you to dinner. You could have gotten hurt, and I know how lucky I am that you were there."

"I did what anyone would have done, Wren. Fight or flight, I made my choice. Doing nothing was not an option."

"Can we start over?" I ask, rubbing my temples.

"Of course."

"Thank you for what you did today."

"You're welcome," he says.

Our waitress breaks the awkward silence that follows by

stopping by to take our dinner orders. "What can I get you?" she asks me.

"I'd like the BLT with a side of curly fries and a cup of corn chowder. Oh, and some of those chicken and cheese taquitos." I look at Marshall. "Will you eat some?"

"Sure."

"And for you, sir?" she asks.

"I'll take the cheeseburger and fries, and whatever IPA you've got on tap."

"Would you like something from the bar?" the waitress asks me.

"I'll take an IPA too," I say.

The waitress returns with the taquitos and our beers. I grab a taquito and immediately burn the roof of my mouth. I attempt to put out the fire with a big gulp of my beer.

"Hot?" he asks.

"Scorching."

"You must be really hungry," he says.

"I'm on empty."

I get another couple of taquitos into me after letting them cool a bit, and the hollow feeling in my belly starts to subside.

"Were you able to rest?" he asks.

"Sort of. Felt like I never really fell into a deep sleep, and I had a bad dream."

"What was it about?"

"It's kinda fuzzy, but someone was chasing me, and they had a bear's head and a man's body. And just when they were about to catch me, I turned around and pulled out a lightsaber."

"Of the Star Wars variety?" he asks.

"Yes, but my light—which I somehow knew was pink—wouldn't come on and then the bear ate me."

He nods. "Yeah, that tracks."

The waitress brings our food and I attack my sandwich in between spoonfuls of chowder, burning my mouth for the second time. I take another big drink of my beer and then bite down on a curly fry.

"So, the guy. Your ex. Was it serious? It must have been to send you fleeing to another state." Marshall takes a bite of his cheeseburger and washes it down with beer.

Fleeing.

There's that word again. Can't a woman do some solo traveling without everyone assuming she's running away from something?

"He was my fiancé. And I wasn't fleeing, per se. I just needed a change of scenery."

"Fiancé. Definitely serious then. Any chance of a reconciliation?"

I let out an unladylike snort. "No."

My eyes were a tad bigger than my stomach, because I can only get through half of the sandwich, a few of the fries, a bit more of the chowder, and half of another taquito before I'm uncomfortably full. I stifle a burp and wipe my mouth. Marshall's food has disappeared, and I nudge the plate of taquitos closer to him. He makes short work of the last two, and the waitress drops off the check.

"You could still try," Marshall says after I pay the tab and we start walking back to the hotel. "If you're both willing, you might be able to work through it with the help of a trained professional, if you haven't already tried that. You'd be surprised at what can be salvaged with persistence and open communication."

I stop walking. "I know you're only trying to help, but he did something really shitty to me." I let out a sigh because just thinking about it feels unbearably heavy, and I'm so tired of shouldering the weight. "Dealbreaker-level shitty. Also, any further conversation would be impossible because my ex-fiancé is dead."

Chapter Four

I didn't find out that Rob had been in a car accident until three hours after it happened. He was late getting home, but that wasn't unusual. He didn't answer his cell phone when I called, but that wasn't unusual either. He was a busy guy, and half the time he was already talking on the phone to his boss or a colleague and couldn't click over to take my call. I tried not to take it personally.

I didn't know until much later that while I sat at home waiting for him, the paramedics were extricating Rob from his car using the jaws of life. I didn't know that Rob had arrived at the hospital via air ambulance. I didn't know that as soon as the helicopter landed, six people ran out to meet it. And I didn't know that they rushed Rob into surgery for a multitude of reasons, most notably his severe head injury and massive internal bleeding.

I was still waiting for Rob to arrive when my phone rang, and I fully expected to see his name pop up on the screen. Instead, it was my friend Shannon; she mostly texted and seldom called me, but I figured she must have a good reason for it, and I answered.

"Hey, Wren, is Rob home right now?" she asked in place of a greeting. Rob and I often met Shannon and her husband, Neil, for dinner and drinks. Sometimes they joined us at the movies.

"No, he's late." My heart started to pound. "Why?"

"I passed an accident on the way home. It looked like Rob's car."

There were so many questions I wanted to ask, but all I said was "I need to call the hospital," and then I hung up on her knowing she would understand.

My hands shook as I Googled the hospital's phone number and hit the button to make the call. The only thing the person who answered the phone would confirm is that they had admitted a patient named R. Robert Stephenson. Rob would never give someone his name that way, which meant they'd obtained it from his driver's license and not him. I rushed around looking for my purse and car keys. I couldn't find my phone and then realized I was still holding it.

Though I shouldn't have, I drove myself to the hospital, barely remembering it later. I started at the information desk, and through a series of frantic inquiries I finally learned what had happened and wished I could unhear what came out of the doctor's mouth when he found me in the waiting area two hours later. He sat down next to me so that we were at eye level and told me Rob's injuries were catastrophic and that there was no detectable brain activity. He was as kind and gentle as could be, but it didn't matter how gingerly he conveyed the news. The outcome wasn't going to change, and Rob wasn't ever going to wake up. A member of the hospital staff came out fifteen minutes later and asked if Rob had a living will and if I knew whether he was an organ donor. "I don't know," I said.

It was hours before they let me see him. I passed the time by crying and calling my parents and my closest friends. I kicked myself for not knowing how to get ahold of Rob's family, but I'd never met any of them and didn't have their numbers stored in my phone. Rob had always felt like a man whose life was mostly his own, devoid of family ties and obligations because that's how he presented himself to me. He was an only child, and his parents were both deceased, but he had an aunt—his mom's sister—who lived in upstate New York and still expected him on Thanksgiving and Christmas Day. He said it was awful—too many cousins he didn't get along with and lots of family drama he didn't want to subject me to. He only went out of guilt, he said, and the holidays simply weren't a big deal to him. He always seemed mildly agitated until January, when he would perk back up again. Rob still owned a house not far from his aunt's, but he was there so infrequently he'd finally rented it out.

I usually spent Thanksgiving with a close group of friends, and then Rob and I would spend Christmas Eve together at my parents' place in Florida. He would have to leave by the crack of dawn on Christmas morning and hop on a plane to arrive at his aunt's house by midafternoon. He'd warned me that there might be years when he couldn't join my family's holiday gathering because he'd be out of the country, traveling internationally for business. Such a bummer but completely out of his hands, you know? Once we were married, I assumed his aunt would understand that he'd want to spend the holidays with me, or I would finally join Rob at his aunt's and meet the rest of his family. I decided I would call Rob's employer in the morning, track down his boss and see if he knew how to get ahold of Rob's aunt, and go from there.

Finally, someone called my name and told me I could see Rob. He'd been moved to the ICU by then, and the nurse standing outside the door tried to prepare me by explaining about the machines and the tubes that were keeping him alive until someone decided to remove him from life support.

I walked to Rob's bedside. The machines and the tubes bothered me at first, but then I stopped seeing them. Tears ran silently down my face as a profound sadness overcame me. To see him in that hospital bed, knowing his life had come to an end, left an indelible mark on me. On his deathbed, Rob had no flaws, and my grieving brain clung to the happy memories of the man I loved, conveniently forgetting about the sacrifices I'd made in the name of being a patient and understanding partner, the kind who didn't rock the boat too much because his job was so much more stressful than mine. I thought about how he'd always bring me a souvenir from the airport gift shop, the more ridiculous, the better. I replayed our first kiss and how it had taken us a few times to find our groove. But once we did, we always kissed the same way: our heads turned to the left, which took some getting used to on my part because I'd always turned to the right.

When my exhaustion grew too pronounced to ignore, I moved from Rob's bedside to the chair next to it. I sat there all night, knowing there were decisions to be made, and that I might be the one making them. I would need to confirm with his aunt that she was his next of kin. Maybe we could make the decisions together even though we'd never met. Would she want to hold his funeral service in New York? Rob had never told me where his parents were buried, but maybe he'd want to be buried near them.

Every half hour or so, I would go back to Rob's bedside and hold his hand in mine, talking to him in soothing tones in case he could hear me. Then I would return to my chair. Somehow, around dawn, and despite the noise of the machines and the medical personnel coming in and out of the room, I fell asleep. A few hours later, a woman's voice out in the hall woke me up.

"His what?" I heard her yell. Then an attractive woman who looked to be in her late thirties or early forties, with short blond hair, rumpled clothing, and bloodshot eyes, charged into the room, a nurse hot on her heels. She spotted me and said, "Who the hell are you?"

I leaped to my feet. "I'm his fiancée. Who are *you*?"

"I am his *wife*," she screamed, taking in the diamond ring on my left hand, which made her eyes grow even wider. Too many emotions to parse overwhelmed me. This was the kind of thing that happened on soap operas, where the audience was primed to expect—and accept—highly unrealistic plotlines in the name of drama. But this trainwreck was my honest-to-God *life*. My brain refused to believe it even though the apoplectic expression on the woman's face told me it was true.

Two more nurses rushed into the room. They looked at us and froze. "Only one family member at a time. And lower your voices immediately," one said.

The woman's anger found a new target as she whirled around to look at them. "I am Shayla Stephenson. *His wife.*" She pointed at my chest. "You are nothing. Get out."

And there it was. Nothing about my relationship with Rob had been real. Not his declarations of love. Not his promises for the future. None of it. I was just the fool who'd fallen for all of it.

I walked to Rob's bedside knowing this was it, the last time I would see him alive—if only technically so—and the only goodbye I would get. Our relationship might not have been real, but no one could take away my memories of Rob, and that was a good thing because memories were all I would have left. "I love you," I whispered. And then I walked away from what remained of Rob's life forever.

In the hallway, a woman who looked like an older version of Rob's wife stood holding the hands of two children. The boy was older, eight or nine, and the girl was probably a few years younger. Both had tearstained, shell-shocked faces and were crying. It was one thing for Rob to have a wife, but two children? That was too much for my battered psyche to handle and I vomited right on the floor of the hallway, the splash narrowly missing the shoes of the woman who was holding the kids' hands. It was only later that I realized it was probably their grandmother.

I no longer had to worry about tracking down Rob's boss, his aunt. Weighing in on the next steps; organ donation; funeral plans.

Any claims I might have laid to Rob had reverted to their rightful owners.

His wife.

His children.

That was the moment I realized that Rob hadn't rented out his home in New York, because his real family was living in it.

I was in such a fog when I drove to the hospital that when I walked back out of the same doors I'd entered the night before, Shayla's words ringing in my ears, I had no idea where I'd parked my car. It took twenty minutes of tearful wandering to find it.

Then I went home and crawled into bed, where I mostly stayed until Steph dragged me out of it to go for that hike.

Chapter Five

"You didn't kill him, did you? After the dealbreaker-level shitty thing," Marshall asks after we start walking again. The blunt, unfiltered query renders me speechless and yet there is something about the way he asked—not tiptoeing around my feelings or worrying about my reaction—that I find refreshing. He's the only person who hasn't treated me like I'm made of glass. Part of me wants to say that, yes, I killed Rob and then fed his body into a wood chipper. Give this geocacher-slash-psychologist something truly meaty to chew on. Another part wants to tearfully admit that I miss Rob horribly and would do almost anything to have him back, except that he was never mine to begin with. But all I say is "Of course I didn't. Someone ran a stop sign when he was half a mile from my apartment. And then I discovered the deal-breaker thing."

He stops short. "Jesus. I'm truly sorry. My comment was in extremely poor taste. I was having trouble getting a good read on you, and for some reason, I was under the assumption that he broke up with you, and that's what prompted this quest." He blows out a breath and looks away. "I'm not at the top of my game these days. Seriously, I don't know where that came from."

"No breakup. No murder. No worries," I say. I'm too worn out to care, and getting a good read on me meant he was trying to get into my head again, but this time I let it slide. It's probably an occupational hazard, and I imagine it's hard to turn off.

We walk through the front door of the La Quinta and head for the elevator. "Listen," he says before I can punch the button to summon it. "I've got an idea. Hear me out, okay?"

"Okay."

"I know this quest you're on is a solo endeavor, and I get that. Sounds like it's an important step in the closure you're seeking after losing your fiancé. And I know you can take care of yourself regardless of what happened today. You were simply in the wrong place at the wrong time. It happens." He pauses, looking pained as if something weighty has wormed its way into his thought process. Whatever it is, he shakes it off. "Two heads are better than one, and if we team up, we could be better *together*. I'll even drive. We can take my Jeep and you would be safer, and that's not me being a condescending asshole when I say that. It's simply a fact. Some of your planned locations will have caches that are even more isolated than today. I would hate for something to happen to you."

His seemingly genuine concern hits me hard. Was there ever a time when Rob acted in my best interests instead of his own? I'd ruminated on that after I found out about Shayla and the children, and I couldn't come up with a single example (or reason for why I'd allowed it).

Marshall's proposition means I wouldn't have to look over my shoulder every time I hear the sound of footsteps behind me. I wouldn't have to scrutinize every person I encounter and speculate about how likely they are to hurt me. If I'm alone, that's exactly what I'll be doing. And let's be real—the traumatized part of me still wants to head for the airport first thing in the morning to catch the next flight home.

But I really don't want to abandon my quest. Flying back to Ohio with my tail between my legs after failing at the plan no one understood or seemed enthusiastic about in the first place sounds about as appealing as telling Marshall about Rob's secret family. Then again, I'm also not willing to lay down my life in the name of a quest that crashed and burned before it even got started, and doubling down on the risk to my safety seems like a particularly dumb idea. "What's in it for you?" I ask.

He seems to be choosing his words carefully before he answers. "To be honest, I could use a traveling companion. It's more fun that way. Otherwise, I'm left alone with my thoughts and I'd rather talk to someone." Honesty, that's a refreshing change. But how do I know he isn't lying, too?

"What kind of knife?" I ask.

"Excuse me?" he says, momentarily confused by my random segue.

"The one Beer Gut had. Was it a pocketknife? One of those Swiss Army ones with all the tools?"

He hesitates. "It was bigger than a Swiss Army knife. It unfolded the same way, but it had a serrated blade that curved at the end." I get the distinct impression he's chosen his words carefully, but it doesn't matter. I'd like to think that the men would have let me go after they'd had their way with me, but I'm not *that* dumb.

"That's a very chivalrous offer," I say. "I'd like to sleep on it." My not agreeing immediately—if only from the standpoint of my safety—probably seems ludicrous to Marshall, but all he does is nod and say, "I'll be downstairs at eight o'clock tomorrow morning. If I don't see you, I'll head out without you and maybe we'll meet again someday."

"Okay," I say. I push the button and the elevator chugs its way down to us, the door opening with a ding. Marshall pushes the buttons for 2 and 3.

"Thanks for dinner," he says when we reach my floor. "Sleep tight."

"You're welcome. I'll try my best."

Chapter Six

I crawl back into bed, taking my laptop with me so I can catch up on work, and ponder Marshall's offer. I can't stop reliving the massive feeling of relief that enveloped me when he came strolling into the clearing, and frankly, I don't want to. I'll never be able to put into words how incredible it felt to realize that my situation wasn't as dire and hopeless as I'd feared. That I wasn't facing it alone.

Safety has always been a concern, but now I have to decide if it's safe to ride shotgun in Marshall's Jeep and go traipsing around in isolated areas looking for caches with *him*. If this is some elaborate ruse on his part, he's gone all-in on the long game, but I don't think it is. Ours was a chance encounter on the trail, and he showed no hesitation in coming to my aid even though it was two against one and there was a real chance he could have gotten hurt if things hadn't gone the way they did. And it's not like I give it more than a few moments' thought when I call an Uber and get into the car of a total stranger who, nine times out of ten, is a man I know nothing about.

If I team up with Marshall, maybe I can camp. Lodging was one of the things my mom had asked about right away when I told her I was thinking about going geocaching in the Pacific Northwest.

"Where will you stay?" she'd asked.

"In an Airbnb or hotel. Maybe a campsite." I'd made lodging reservations for every location on my list, but I was hoping to camp at least once if I felt comfortable enough to do so.

"A campsite? No, Wren. You can't do that. It's foolish." Even over the phone, I could tell how nervous I was making her, which stung a little. I wasn't a foolish person, and I'd never given my parents a reason to think otherwise.

Until now, that is.

"I don't even know if I'll camp, Mom. I'm going to play it by ear."

"But you must be safe, Wren. As your mother, I need to know that you'll be okay."

As usual, my mother was right. And sadly, I no longer felt comfortable geocaching solo, let alone sleeping in a tent, where I'd be completely vulnerable.

If I want to finish what I started—and I do—I need a safety net, which is the only reason I'm contemplating Marshall's offer instead of rejecting it outright. Time for a deeper dive into Marshall Hendricks's life.

Twenty minutes later, I know that he is thirty-six and will turn thirty-seven on December seventeenth, making him a Sagittarius. He went to the University of Oregon for his undergrad, and Pacific University for his master's and Psy.D. He owns his own home in a town near Portland and has lived in it for two years. His only social media accounts are LinkedIn and Twitter, and he rarely tweets save for a few that have to do with sports. No marriage licenses; no divorce decrees; no bankruptcies.

I've done all this before—it's the standard operating procedure after meeting a new man—and I don't know a single woman who hasn't taken at least a cursory spin around the internet looking for intel. It's not because we're nosy gold diggers interested in a man's earning ability or finances; it's because we don't want to get human-trafficked or killed. However, R. Robert Stephenson—with his common last name—had been a trickier search. He'd had a LinkedIn account and you could find his name on his company's website. But that's where the trail had grown cold. Rob hated social media and informed me that online platforms were a waste of time.

"You do remember that social media is my bread and butter, right?" I'd joked shortly after we started dating. I was a freelance social media manager who'd discovered there were lots of businesses that had no interest in running their social media accounts or creating content for them, and they were more than happy to outsource it to me. I was more than happy to accept the money they keep throwing at me every time I raised my rates. Take that, everyone who shamed me for majoring in communications and saying that my chosen field of study wasn't going to get me anywhere. It transported me straight to my couch, where I worked on a laptop all day sipping tea and wearing my comfiest clothes while the balance in my bank account grew.

"Yes," Rob had said, "and I bet you're damn good at it. I just don't have any interest." Fair enough. A lot of people, men and women both, eschewed social media for a variety of reasons.

When Rob wasn't on the road, he stayed at an extended-stay hotel in Dayton on the company's dime, but he hated how cramped and impersonal it was. By the time we'd been dating for a year, he was mostly living at my place. He still had the house in New York, but he never spoke of it, and it never occurred to me to ask for the address. I think about that a lot. If Rob's meager online footprint had given me even a hint about the kind of secrets he was hiding in New York, my life might have gone in a completely different direction, and I would not be in an Oregon hotel room scrutinizing Marshall right now.

Next, I spring for a criminal background check that comes up clean. I check the sex offender registry just to make sure the background check didn't miss anything.

Finally, I FaceTime Stephanie. "Hey," she says, smiling widely as our images fill the screen. Then her smile fades. "Have you been crying? Your eyes look tired or swollen or something."

"I have shed many tears today. Things have not gone according to plan."

"You couldn't find the cache?"

"Oh, I found it. I even got the first-to-find."

"Then what's wrong? Are you lonely? Bored?"

It shouldn't be this hard to tell my best friend what happened to me, but while I'm more than happy to relive the part where Marshall showed up, I don't want to relive the rest of it. I just want to block the whole thing out. But I tell her anyway, sparing no details, and watch as her concerned expression turns to horror. I'm crying by the time I finish.

"Wren, that's terrifying."

"Yep. Just one more lapse in judgment in a sea of many others." It's easy to hear the anger and self-loathing in my voice.

She gives me a look of reproach because I'd promised to stop being so hard on myself, but what happened today stoked my insecurities regarding my inability to make smart choices and not be taken advantage of. "Please be kinder to yourself," she says. "This wasn't your fault. And Marshall. Wow."

"Tell me about it. It almost seemed like he had a score to settle and he never seemed remotely concerned or afraid for his safety despite being outnumbered. I can't believe neither of us tripped over his giant balls while we were running down that trail because the man certainly has them."

"He sure does."

"Do not share any of this with my mother," I warn. "She's sent three texts since I landed asking about my flight and the weather and if I like my rental car which is code for 'Are you alive?' I've responded to all of them, but there is no way I'm telling her about what happened today."

"I won't, but mostly because I love your mom and I don't want to see her head explode. What are you going to do? Are you going to cut your trip short and come home?"

"That was my first instinct, but now I'm not so sure." I tell her about taking Marshall to dinner to repay him for what he did today and about his offer to team up.

"Is he attractive?"

I shoot her a look. "Seriously? You do remember that men are abhorrent to me, right? They're either pathological liars or they want to assault me. I bet some of them would even be cool with both."

"I am definitely aware of your current stance on men. I'm just gathering information. Painting a picture in my mind."

"He's not hard to look at," I say. When I first encountered Marshall on the trail, mostly I'd noticed how few physical characteristics he shared with Rob. And then, when we were in his car, I'd been far too consumed by what had happened in the clearing to give two shits about whether he was attractive or not. But at the restaurant, when he was sitting directly across from me, it was hard to ignore that he was a handsome man. I might be romantically broken, but I'm not blind. "He's got a real Pacific Northwest vibe," I add, throwing Steph a bone for the picture she's painting. Then I tell her everything I know about him.

"So he's a psychologist," Steph says, stroking her chin. "Hmm. That's very interesting."

"I suppose," I say.

"Wren? What is something you like to say? Specifically, a worldview that you're *known* for. Like, all of our friends are aware of this certain belief you hold and that you frequently *remind* us of as we're going about our lives."

I sigh. "That if you pay attention, the universe will send you exactly what you need."

"Yep, that's it. That's the thing you like to say."

"First of all, the universe sent me Rob, so I'd like to have a *word* with someone. Secondly, I don't need a psychologist," I say.

"Riiiiiiiight," she says. "No, you absolutely don't." She gives me an exaggerated eye roll.

"Sorry to burst your bubble, but I will not be letting this guy into my head." She opens her mouth, but before she can say what I *know* she's about to say, I cut her off. "Or my pants."

She looks at me, all wide-eyed innocence. "That's not what I was going to say."

"Yes, it was." Steph means well and she wants me to be happy, and to open my heart again someday. But it's going to be a good long while before I feel comfortable trusting a man enough to give him access to *any* part of me.

"So he's on a solo vacation too?" she asks.

"It appears that way."

"This rom-com is just writing itself," she says.

"It's not a romantic comedy. Not romantic. Definitely not funny."

"I think you should take him up on his offer," she says, ignoring my protest.

"I'm not done with my due diligence yet," I say.

"Have you looked him up?"

"I have." I share everything I know so far.

"Want me to loop Lisa in?"

"That would be great." Lisa is the real MVP in our friend group. The amount of information she can dig up never fails to astound us. "Just tell her I met someone on the hiking trail. No need to share the rest right now."

"Family, friends, colleagues?"

"Just him."

"Okay. I'll get back to you as soon as I can."

I start on the to-do list for my clients and work steadily for the next couple of hours, taking a break only when Steph FaceTimes me to announce that Marshall Evan Hendricks is clean as a whistle. "Good," I say, relieved.

"Are you going to say yes?"

"I'm still deciding." Marshall is the devil I sort of know compared to what I encountered on the trail today, and what I could encounter again. What if I'm not so lucky next time?

"He might be the key to accomplishing your goal."

"That's the only reason I'm considering teaming up with him. This trip was supposed to be my first step in taking back my life, and so far, that's not happening. I'm going *backward*, Steph."

"One more thing," she says. "If you think this isn't romantic, you're kidding yourself. He literally swooped in to rescue you. I'm half in love with him myself. I would binge this rom-com in *any* form."

"It's *not* a romantic comedy," I say.

Her forehead creases as she ponders this for a second. "You're right. Romantic dramedy makes much more sense. Your situation is a bit . . . heavy."

My situation is an anvil that fell from the sky and flattened me. I thought it couldn't get worse than loving a man who had been hiding a secret family for the better part of three years and then died, but the men in the clearing showed me there was always something worse waiting just around the bend.

"Also, there won't be any further romance."

"There could be," she says pragmatically.

"Absolutely not." I tell her about my island-of-women idea. "No men. Doesn't that sound nice?" I ask, my tone full of wistful possibilities.

"When I'm pissed at James it certainly does. Look," she contin-ues, "I agree that the timing isn't perfect."

"Timing is the least of my worries. I am trying to heal. I'm try-ing to figure things out. But right now, my biggest concern is finding out if Marshall is who he *says* he is, and if I can trust him."

"I understand. Keep me posted, okay?"

"Will do."

We hang up and I work for another half hour. Then I power off my laptop and get ready for bed. I lie there in the dark, trapped in the kind of analysis paralysis I fear may be present from now on when it comes to believing men, no matter how stellar their back-ground checks are. Maybe this quest was a little rash, impulsive even. But I want to take back what Rob's duplicity robbed me of. I want to finish what I started and for it to work out the way that I planned instead of having the rug yanked out from underneath me again. And I'll probably be safe with Marshall, or at least safer than I was today in that clearing.

I decide to team up with him, and though I'm not as confident as I used to be when choosing the appropriate course of action, I don't think I've miscalculated.

It's time for me to enter a new era, the one where I stand up for myself and decide what *I* want the rest of my life to look like. It's time for a little less giving and a bit more taking. It's way too early to know if Marshall is one of the good ones, but what I do know is that he'll make an excellent bodyguard.

Chapter Seven

The next morning, I go down a few minutes before eight but Marshall's nowhere to be found. I'm still nervous about traveling with him, but mostly because it will feel awkward for two people who don't know each other very well to head off down the road together. But I've already decided that if I feel even a hint of concern about my safety or his intentions, I'll ask him to pull into a gas station under the pretense of needing to pee—and then I just won't get back in the car. I walk toward the front desk to ask if he's checked out, wondering why he changed his mind and left early when it was his idea. But then he walks back into the lobby from outside, and when he spots me, a hopeful smile appears on his face. "Does this mean you're coming?" he asks.

"Yes," I say.

"Background check come back okay?"

If you only knew. I look him dead in the eyes and say, "It did and you passed." No man will ever hide anything from me again, and if he does it means he's not the right man for me. I want someone who doesn't mind being an open book that I'll never get tired of reading. Marshall is a traveling companion, nothing more. But that doesn't mean I won't be paying attention to the things he tells me and even more attention to the things he doesn't. It'll be good practice so if I ever feel like dating again, I won't be so slow on the draw.

"I wasn't worried," he says with a grin and a shake of his head. "So, I was outside talking to the bellman about your rental. If you decided to come with me, I figured there was no reason for you to keep paying for the car to sit in the parking lot. He told me the hotel can make sure it gets returned if you want. Who's it through?"

"Hertz and that would be great," I say. I'd planned on having Marshall follow me to the nearest Hertz location to turn it in, but if the hotel can take care of it, that's even better.

We walk to the parking lot together and Marshall stows my tote bag and suitcase in the back of his Jeep. Then we transfer the rest from the trunk of my car. I don't have much—a large backpack that holds considerably more than my waist pack, including the tent I might now be able to use, and a few grocery items that don't need refrigeration.

"Can I have the keys?" Marshall asks.

"You don't have to do that. I can run them in."

"I don't mind, and I can give them directly to the bellman I spoke with earlier."

His thoughtfulness throws me a little and my first instinct is to push back and let him know I can handle the details myself. But then I remember my new era and that it's okay to be on the receiving end of thoughtfulness for once. I lock the rental and place the fob in his palm.

"Mine's unlocked," he says, and heads back inside.

I climb into the Jeep's passenger seat and buckle up. When Marshall returns he says, "You're all set. The bellman said to watch for a confirmation email."

"Thank you," I say.

"In case you were wondering, your background check came back squeaky clean too."

He grins when he sees the shocked look on my face, but then I shrug and say, "I wasn't worried either."

We head south on I-5 after grabbing coffee and breakfast sandwiches from a nearby drive-through. Our destination: Crater Lake. I didn't pay much attention yesterday when I was having my emotional meltdown, but now I take a look around the interior of Marshall's car. It's clean, and it smells good, like maybe there's a pine air freshener somewhere.

"What made you want to go so far from home to look for caches?" Marshall asks. "Did you already find all the ones in Ohio?"

"I've found a lot of caches in Ohio, but I've always wanted to explore this part of the country and decided this was as good a place as any for my *Eat, Pray, Love* quest as you've so succinctly coined it." Visiting the Pacific Northwest is the first in a series of trips I plan on taking. If this one goes well (hahahahahaha), I plan on visiting other parts of the country. I want to Airbnb myself from place to place like it's a verb, zigzagging across the country according to my whims. Winter in Florida where my parents moved a few years ago in anticipation of their retirement years. Fall in Portland or Seattle. Spring in the Carolinas. Summer near an ocean, preferably the Atlantic. Then I'll decide which location spoke to me the loudest and maybe I'll move there. Rob's death has given me a blank slate for what the rest of my life could look like, and I have every intention of making the most of it.

I anticipate Marshall's puzzled inquiry about why I chose geocaching as the framework for my quest. It's not like I haven't heard it already. I could tell by the expressions on my friends' faces that they were confused by my decision to leave town, and my mom didn't get it at all. While I understood that a solo quest was supposed to be bigger and bolder, at that point I hadn't fully come out of my mental health spiral, and I think everyone was afraid to upset the apple cart any further by asking if I had a better idea. Good thing, because I didn't.

"A change of scenery can be very beneficial after a loss," Marshall says. "Getting out of your comfort zone can shake you loose from any rut you might have fallen into and help you feel like you're making a fresh start. It's good for healing."

His objective and nonjudgmental interpretation of the reason behind my quest is not only a welcome surprise, it also makes me want to cry. It feels good to be heard. It feels good to be understood.

This is *my* life and I get to choose how I'm going to live it.

"I like it here so far," I say. "Not what happened yesterday, obviously, but generally speaking."

"Yesterday was not good. You're definitely entitled to a do-over. I just hope you like clouds," he says.

"I do." I don't mind a sky that looks perpetually bruised, because it complements my mood. Mentally, I am not ready for the clouds to part. Like the sun, my happiness will return someday. But for now the weather seems to be saying, *Take your time. There's no hurry.*

"What do you do for work?" he asks.

"I'm a social media manager."

"Do you like it?"

"I do. I seem to have a knack for it, and I've got a lot of freedom because I can work from anywhere." I've already scheduled my posts for the next couple of days so I won't have to worry about finding a Wi-Fi signal or a place to plug my laptop in.

"Sounds like it's working great for you. Music?" he asks.

"Sure." Music will fill the awkward silence when our polite small talk finally runs its course.

"You can be the DJ. I'm not picky."

I pull out my phone, Bluetooth it to the Jeep's stereo, and cue up my favorite playlist. "One of These Nights" by the Eagles fills the car, and when I glance at Marshall, he smiles and nods his approval. I don't have the stereo up very loud and the music fades into the background at a soothing volume. "You said you've been geocaching at Crater Lake before," I say.

"Several times," he confirms.

"What's it like?" I ask.

He takes his eyes off the road for a second and looks over at me, smiling. "You'll see."

I catch my first glimpse of Crater Lake—a truly breathtaking sight nestled in the Cascade mountains—when we enter the park's rim via the north entrance. The stunning blue color of the deepest lake in the United States takes my breath away. Located in a volcanic basin, it's fed almost entirely by snowfall and rain, and because there are no sediments or minerals, it's one of the clearest lakes in the world. Even so, my Google Earth search did not adequately prepare me for this.

"Look at that water," I say.

"It's something, isn't it? There's a reason they nicknamed this place Lake Majesty," Marshall says.

"I've always wanted to find a cache in a lake. Have you ever looked for one here?"

"No. That water is *cold*."

The park is open year-round, twenty-four hours a day. None of the roads are closed due to snow yet, but October first is only a few days away, and then the countdown will be on. I press my face as close to the passenger-side window as I can without actually touching it, and gawk at the scenery. I can already sense how cool the air is outside, but if it were warmer, I'd hang my head out the window like a dog and let the breeze blow through my hair.

The outdoorsy girl in me has come *alive*. It's disheartening to remember that I was fully prepared to ignore my passion for the outdoors because the man I was in love with preferred to stay inside.

Never again.

"Do you already have a room reserved somewhere?" Marshall asks. "I checked this morning and found several places that still have rooms available. I'm planning on grabbing one if you don't want to camp."

"I've got a room reserved at the lodge. But if camping is an option, I'd rather do that." I might have to cough up a cancellation fee for bailing on my reservation, but that's a fair trade for being able to crawl into my sleeping bag and lie down in my tent at the end of an evening spent sitting around a campfire and looking up at the stars. I'm not sure what my mother would think about this arrangement, but she'd undoubtedly be thrilled that at least I wasn't camping alone.

We follow the signs for the Mazama Campground. It's tucked away in the forest several miles south of Rim Village, just beyond the park's south entrance. Marshall pulls up to the little kiosk at the entrance and we snag one of the last available campsites. A few minutes later he pulls in to the spot we've been assigned, and we get out and stretch our legs. "I didn't want to mess with a cooler, but I've got some snacks and there's the campground store and several restaurants in the park," he says as we unload the car.

"Is this what I think it is?" I ask, pointing to a small metal box on four legs near the perimeter of the campsite.

"If you think it's a bear-resistant food locker, then yes," Marshall says. "All of our food and water and even our toiletries need to be put inside. Anything that has a scent needs to be locked up."

I've got some crackers, nuts, and a few protein bars that I place inside the locker. Marshall adds his supply of nonperishables, mostly chips and nuts, and a couple of candy bars. Some freshly ground coffee. I put my small bag of toiletries inside, and Marshall does the same. Then he closes the door of the bear locker and makes sure it's secure.

We set up our camp. It's not as warm as I thought it would be, and I can really feel the chill in the air now that we're not in the car. I check the temperature and it's hovering around fifty-five but feels colder. Marshall puts a jacket on and I pull gloves and a hat from my backpack. The whole thing feels weirdly intimate, like we're on a romantic camping trip for two instead of whatever the hell this is. I don't know what to say to make things less awkward, so I don't say anything at all.

"Do you need any help with that?" Marshall asks after pitching his tent in about two minutes flat.

I've pitched a few tents in my lifetime, but the one I brought on this trip is brand-new and I can't get the pole into the little sleeve. "Thanks, but I've got it." I jab the end of the pole at the fabric, but it won't go in.

"I'm not sure that you do," he says pragmatically.

"I'll get it in there eventually," I say, finally shoving the end of the pole into the sleeve with about as much finesse as someone who's never *seen* a tent before, let alone pitched one.

We finish setting up camp and then sit down at the picnic table. There's also a fire pit dug into the ground and covered with an iron grate. The bathrooms are a short walk away.

"We have some options for the day," Marshall says. "I checked the geocache app and there are a few caches in the Pumice Desert that we can look for, or we can drive the thirty-three-mile scenic route if you're in more of a sightseeing mood. There are several lookouts and some awesome views as well as a couple of virtual caches you might like. Then we could have an early dinner at the restaurant."

The Pumice Desert is a dry meadow that formed when pumice blanketed the valley after the volcanic eruption of Mount Mazama. As interesting as the location sounds, the deep blue lake has captured my curiosity and attention. "The scenic drive sounds good," I say.

After making sure we aren't leaving anything of value—or

anything interesting to a bear—at the campsite, we hop back into Marshall's Jeep and head out.

We begin our sightseeing tour on Rim Drive, the road we came in on. Fifteen minutes later, Marshall turns the car in to the Phantom Ship Overlook. I open my door as soon as we come to a complete stop, and he follows me to the stone wall. "Wow," I say. Down below, jutting up from the magnificent blue water is an island with rock formations that resemble a sailing ship. There's a sign, and I learn that the island, when viewed in different lighting or weather conditions, seems to appear and disappear, giving it its ghostly name.

We take in the scenery for a few more minutes. "There's a virtual cache not far from here. Ready to navigate?" Marshall asks. A virtual cache refers to something you discover visually versus a physical container you search for.

"Absolutely," I say.

Back in the car, I consult the app. "Pumice Castle?" I ask.

"That's the one."

Two and a half miles down the road, I instruct Marshall to pull into an unmarked turnoff and we get out of the car. "I don't get it," I say. "The cache is supposed to be right here, but there's nothing around us but the lake." And then I spot it. In the distance, jutting out from the steep wall of the volcano that collapsed and formed Crater Lake, is an orangey-brown pumice rock that looks like a castle. "There," I exclaim, pointing at it with glee. "It really does look like a little castle."

We log the find and Marshall holds up his hand. Without thinking, I smile and high-five him with a satisfying smack. This wasn't exactly a challenge and nothing to write home about, but it's the first cache we've found together and I'm caught up in the thrill of tangible proof that I'm doing what I came here to do. It's like the rusty gears of my life have finally started moving. It feels good.

"What's next?" I ask.

"The Watchman observation area. It's also where we'll find the next virtual cache, called Wizard Island."

It takes a little under half an hour to reach our destination. We get out of the car and the GPS points us toward the overlook's stone wall. "Look down below," Marshall says once we reach it.

I do, and there's another volcanic island, this one protruding from the water in the shape of a cone. "Wizard Island," I say.

"If we'd come a month earlier, we could've taken a boat out to the island and hiked to its summit," Marshall says. Now, *that* would have been amazing. Maybe next time.

We open our apps to log the find. "We're supposed to include a picture of ourselves," I say.

"Hand me your phone," Marshall says. "I can get us both in the frame."

I give it to him, and he holds one outstretched arm in front of us and rests the other lightly across the top of my shoulders, leaving a few inches between us. My arms remain awkwardly at my side. The weight of his touch sends a frisson of something throughout my body that I can't identify, not butterflies, but a vibration of sorts that I want to lean into. It's strange that I'm reacting this way considering my libido died right along with Rob, and I can't fathom being touched romantically—I still have those sharp spikes covering me, after all. But it feels like a lifetime since I've been touched by anyone, and I can still feel the warmth of Marshall's arm on my shoulders like a phantom sensation.

After he takes the picture, he hands me my phone and I upload the photo. "Send that to me, will you?" he asks. "So I can finish logging the find."

"Sure. What's your number?"

He gives it to me, and I create a contact for him and send the photo. It's a good one and we're both smiling.

We continue along Rim Road in comfortable silence. Since we began the drive, the constant anxious chatter in my mind that I could only banish while walking or geocaching remains mostly at bay. It's nice, this reprieve from my swirling thoughts. Maybe someday, my mind will be a quieter place and I won't always feel like I'm drowning.

Marshall's voice pierces my musing. "Wren?"

"What? I'm sorry. I was lost in thought. Did you say something?"

"Are you warm enough?"

"Yes." I'm also somewhat relaxed and content. How strange. A month ago, I wouldn't have thought it was possible. And after what happened yesterday, Crater Lake probably wouldn't have been possible either. Without Marshall's offer to team up, my quest would probably have ended, because I'm pretty sure I would have slept on it and then thrown in the towel and flown home.

"What were you thinking about?"

"I was thinking about how nice this is. If I'd come by myself, I might have ended up just driving around the lake and leaving my camping gear in the trunk, if I made it here at all."

"Sharing activities with someone can be helpful during the healing process," Marshall says, looking over at me, and I see him, really see him for the first time. Not through the mindset of my grief or my anger over what Rob did to me. I see him as the tall, dark-haired, good-looking guy who seems happy about having a companion, not for safety, but for reasons he hasn't shared yet.

A few minutes later, I shrug out of my coat. Suddenly, I'm a bit *too* warm. I'm also feeling queasy because I've spent too much time staring down at my phone as Marshall drove us in a circle around the lake, and my brain can't decide if we're stationary or moving. I swallow a couple of times and breathe slowly in and out, trying not to panic. Then, almost without warning, my nausea goes from a two to a ten, and the contents of my stomach announce their impending arrival when my mouth fills with spit. "Marshall, pull over," I shout.

He whips the car to the side of the road, and I unclick my seat belt and throw open the door with so much force I nearly tumble out and would have if Marshall didn't grab the back of my jacket to hold me steady while I heave. Thankfully, there isn't much in me, and the episode subsides quickly. I reach for my water bottle, take a big drink, and swish it around in my mouth. Then I spit it out on the ground as covertly as possible before folding my body back into my seat and shutting the door.

"Better?" he asks.

My stomach feels better, but I'm absolutely mortified. Puking is something I have never done outside the privacy of my own bathroom and I want the ground to open up and swallow me. This makes the blackberry smudge on my mouth look like child's play.

"A little. I just need to get something in my stomach so it can settle." I also need to wipe my mouth, but my tissues are in my toiletries bag, which is in the bear locker. "Do you have any napkins or anything in here?" I ask.

Marshall opens the center console and rifles through it but comes up empty-handed. "Check the glove box. There might be something in there."

I press the button and it pops open. Relieved, I spot a travel-sized pack of tissues, pluck a few, and mash them against my mouth. I finish wiping and take a few deep breaths.

And then the rest of the glove box's contents come into focus. There are several tubes of lipstick and mascara. A hairbrush and a hair clip and hair ties. A rollerball of perfume. Several of the tissues have been used to blot a woman's red lipstick. There's a photo booth snapshot of Marshall with his arm around a woman, presumably the owner of the lipstick, her long dark hair piled on top of her head and her lip color a perfect match. She's smiling up at him.

I turn my head toward Marshall. "Do you have a girlfriend?"

"No, I don't have a girlfriend." Sure, that's what they all say, and the next thing you know they're dying in a hospital bed and you're feeling like the world's biggest idiot when the girlfriend you assumed they didn't have shows up and is actually their wife.

"Because if you do, you *definitely* shouldn't ask another woman if you can come along on her quest."

"I don't," he says. His firm tone has an "I'm telling the truth, end of story" kind of feel, but for the first time since I met him, he won't quite meet my eyes and looks back at the road as if the ex-girlfriend is a subject he doesn't want to talk about. Maybe he *is* telling the truth, but I have no way to know for sure. It doesn't concern me personally because we're not dating. But lying about your relationship status is an affront to women, and I'll be damned if I'm going to let an opportunity to stress how important truthfulness and monogamy are pass me by.

We continue on in silence for another five minutes. "The restaurant is closer to the campground, which is still about half an hour from here. Will you be okay until we get there?"

My stomach might be empty, but it's no longer roiling and I can wait a little longer for food. Mostly I'm just worn out from the exertion. "I'll be fine. I'm feeling better now."

Marshall turns the music back up but keeps the volume low. Exhausted, I lean against the headrest and close my eyes. There is nothing quite like being on the other side of throwing up, and my relief is immeasurable. But it feels way too intimate to drift off in Marshall's passenger seat like he's my boyfriend and we're on some romantic road trip. I snap to attention and try to focus on the scenery outside my window, but I'm struggling.

"You've got time for a short nap," Marshall says. "I wasn't planning on stopping at any other observation points between here and the restaurant."

"I don't need a nap," I say. Oh my God, a nap sounds heavenly.

"Wren, seriously. I can see that you're fading and you don't have to fight it."

I look at the capable man beside me, and my eyelids flutter and shut as I give in and let the fatigue pull me under. The last thing I remember is the Rolling Stones singing "Wild Horses," which soothes me like a lullaby, and then everything goes dark.

Chapter Eight

Marshall wakes me up with a gentle shake. "Wren, we're here." He holds the door for me as we walk into the restaurant. The welcome smell of hot food envelops me as a hostess leads us to a table and sets down menus.

The waitress swings by to take our orders a few minutes later. "I'll put those in right away," she says, scooping up our menus.

"I did have a girlfriend, but we broke up," Marshall says, as if he's been thinking about this while I slept.

Our drinks have been delivered and I take a sip of my Sprite. "Why did you break up?"

He takes a drink of his beer, stalling a bit, which tells me that my theory about it being something he doesn't want to talk about was correct. "I lost my younger brother very suddenly, and I couldn't be the fun and happy guy she was used to. That she still needed me to be."

I'm as surprised by this unexpected gut punch as he probably was when I told him Rob had died. "I am so sorry," I reply. I can't help but wonder what kind of ghosts Marshall's trying to outrun because I can see them now, nipping at his heels, almost as if they were real. A woman trying to escape ghosts of her own can spot them more easily when they're chasing others. "When did it happen?"

"About five months ago. She moved out a couple of months later." That seems like an awful thing for her to have done, but I don't know all the facts. I get the impression Marshall doesn't feel like enlightening me at this point in our journey, in the same way I haven't provided some key details about my relationship with Rob.

Our food arrives and I dig in. Marshall seems lost in thought and hasn't so much as picked up his fork. There's a look of vulnerability on his face that is in stark contrast to what I've observed in him so far. "What was your brother's name?" I ask.

"Graham," Marshall says with a sad smile. "His name was Graham."

Despite the point Stephanie made, maybe the universe wasn't trying to send me a psychologist.

Maybe the universe sent a psychologist who appreciates the company of another person while he's working through his *own* grief and pain.

Two birds, one stone.

I'm paying attention.

Chapter Nine

Marshall pulls in to the campground's gas station located next to the little store, but I don't see any attendants. "I thought you couldn't pump your own gas here," I say.

"They changed the law so we can pump our own everywhere now," he replies.

"I can run in while you're waiting for the tank to fill."

"No," he says somewhat sharply. "I'll go in." He gets out, and the pump's nozzle clanks as he puts it in his tank. He comes around to my side and opens the door, and I assume he's going to ask if I need anything. Instead, he puts a hand gently on my knee to move it out of the way, and the touch-starved side of me roars to life again. Just as quickly, I stuff it back down where it belongs. Maybe I'll book a massage when I get home so I can fulfill my need for touch in a healthy, no-strings-attached kind of way.

Then Marshall opens the glove box. Methodically and devoid of any emotion that I can see, he gathers everything his girlfriend left behind, removes it from the glove box, and tosses it into the garbage can between the pumps. He returns, sweeps his hand along the inside to make sure he got it all, and then closes it.

"It's understandable that a woman would want to know if I was already dating someone. But sometimes we just forget our ex-girlfriend's shit is in the glove box."

"We're not dating, so you don't owe me any explanations. I just meant that, in general, it's bad form to tag along on a woman's quest if you've got someone waiting for you at home."

"I agree," he says. "It *would* be bad form. Do you need anything inside?"

"I'm good. Thanks."

The flow of gas clicks off and Marshall hangs the nozzle back on the pump. He goes into the store and emerges carrying a bundle of firewood under one arm, and a can of lighter fluid in his other hand.

Back at the campsite, I excuse myself after Marshall unlocks the bear locker and I take my toiletries to the bathroom to brush my teeth. I feel human again now that my stomach is full and my mouth is clean.

We sit at the picnic table and wait for the sun to set. "Skyline Wanderer," Marshall says. "Did you choose that username because it fits with your desire to get away?"

I hesitate. "Yes. That's why I chose it."

He gives me a look like he doesn't believe me. "Is that really why?"

Is he always this observant? Probably. "I do like skylines and it's true I'm doing some wandering. But that's not exactly where my username came from."

"Where did it come from?" he asks. It's all very conversational, and I'm guessing he's simply used to digging deeper.

"So, um, there's this place back home called Skyline Chili."

He looks at me and shakes his head. "No."

I can't help but smile, and I nod. "Yes."

"You have time to make something up. Something better. Something really meaningful and impressive."

"It's just really good chili. Like, it's something Ohio is *known* for."

"Wow. I'm so sorry," he says, cracking up, which makes me laugh, too.

"You can't pass judgment until you try it," I say. "I bet you'd love it."

"Really. Well, maybe the next time I'm in Ohio I can try this awesome chili for myself. If you're so sure I'd love it, maybe I'm missing out."

He builds a fire, and the smell of woodsmoke—which I love—fills the air. "You must camp a lot," I say. "You got that fire going in record time."

"Not as much as I used to," he says, returning to the picnic table as the sky grows darker.

"Did you and your brother go camping a lot?"

"We did when we were younger, before I went off to college. After that, I was pretty wrapped up in my studies." A look of regret flits across his face, but there's no need for him to go deeper, for us to sit around the campfire trading stories about heartbreak; I've only known him for slightly longer than twenty-four hours, give or take. Instead, we trade stories about some of our favorite caches, and later when I yawn, he walks to the bathrooms with me so we can get ready for bed. Then he locks our toiletries and the chips we were snacking on back in the bear locker and extinguishes the fire.

"If you hear something in the middle of the night, don't get out of your tent. Just text me. I'll have my phone beside me."

"Like a bear?" I ask.

"Like anything." Our tents are only a couple of feet apart, and I feel safe. But I promise I will text him.

"I'm glad I didn't fly home," I say into the quiet, peaceful night. It slips out before I can censor myself, but I *am* glad. The trip that started on such a rocky and uncertain note seems to have leveled out a bit, and it gives me hope that maybe everything will be okay. At the very least, it's looking more likely that I'll be able to accomplish what I've flown here to do.

It's too dark to read his expression when he says, "Me too. Night, Wren."

Chapter Ten

The next morning, I stir when I hear Marshall's voice outside my tent. "Wren? Are you up?"

"No." I burrow deeper into my sleeping bag. I can't believe how warm it kept me. It feels like a cozy nest.

"I made coffee," he says.

"Be right there," I say, and I hear him laugh.

I unzip my sleeping bag and pull a sweatshirt and pair of pants over the thermal top and leggings I wore to bed. I find my glasses and put them on along with my jacket, gloves, and hat, then join Marshall at the picnic table. The campfire is burning brightly, and the flames flicker and glow in the predawn darkness.

Marshall hands me a Styrofoam cup of coffee. "Sorry, there's no milk."

"That's okay," I assure him, and take a drink. "I know this is going to sound like hyperbole, but this is the best cup of coffee I've ever had."

"Campfire coffee always is. How did you sleep?" he asks.

"Surprisingly well." I take another sip of my coffee. "What time is sunrise?"

He glances at his watch. "About ten minutes from now. Come over to my side so you can see it better."

I do, and now we're both looking to the east. We drink our coffee in silence and as the sun begins to rise, tears fill my eyes. Not because I'm sad but because I am so overcome by nature's immeasurable beauty that it's almost more than I can wrap my brain around. I'm sure there's a nearby ridge we could hike up for an even better view, but sitting at this table with a cup of coffee in my hand is all I really need.

This is what I wanted.

This is why I came.

I'm in dire need of experiences that will help put my rage and sadness behind me. I want to find my way back to the woman I was before I met Rob, and this hopeful sunrise is my first glimpse of what that could look like. And, more importantly, how it might *feel.* I'm no longer restricted by the things that weren't working in my life, because they're gone, and it's incredibly freeing. As clichéd as it sounds, the world really is my oyster, and there are so many pearls just waiting for me to discover them.

"Look at that," I say. It's cold enough that I can see my breath.

"Amazing, isn't it?"

I glance over at Marshall, and if he notices the tears, he keeps it to himself. "Yeah," I say, because the earth's beauty will always remind me that there is something bigger, something more significant than my problems.

An hour later, after campground showers and a breakfast of nonperishable food from the bear locker, we break down the tents and load everything back into the Jeep. Then we leave Crater Lake behind and head for Bend.

Chapter Eleven

Now that we're back on the road and I've got a good cell signal, I spend a few minutes refamiliarizing myself with our next destination. The Deschutes River runs through the small high-desert city, and it's a popular vacation spot. Lots of fresh air, mountain views, and skiing.

"You said you've been to Bend before," I say. "Is there a place you like to stay?"

"Not really. I stayed at a resort the last time I was here. Holly and I came with a big group."

"Oh," I say. "Sure."

Holly, Marshall's ex-girlfriend.

Owner of the red lipstick.

The woman who left him because he wasn't fun anymore. Our situations aren't exactly apples to apples, but I can empathize with Marshall's because it hurts to discover that someone didn't love you for who you were, only what you could bring to the table to be enjoyed by *them*. Did Marshall feel similarly? Once Holly realized

Marshall wasn't fun anymore, did she discard him? Make him feel less like a boyfriend and more like someone who was only there to keep her life humming along at a lively and exciting pace? *Are you brokenhearted too,* I'd asked when he first floated the idea of teaming up. *Did someone do something unforgivable to you?* He'd brushed off my query, choosing instead to let me know that he was definitely into women. But the bottom line is that Marshall has a past, and maybe he's not as unscathed by it as he's let on.

"I have a reservation at the Days Inn. Seemed kind of foolish to book something nicer since I was only planning on being here for one night. You can stay wherever you like."

"Days Inn is fine with me as long as you're okay with it," Marshall says.

"Yeah, sure," I say with a shrug of my shoulders. It makes practical sense for him to pass on the resort or a higher-end hotel, and I'm not going to make a big deal out of it. Marshall and I have established our roles as traveling companions, and I'm trying to be chill and not get all tangled up in my thoughts. The roles are clearly defined: two geocachers teaming up so that I don't get killed by man *or* beast and Marshall gets . . . Well, I don't know exactly what's in it for him, but it's working so far and that's all that matters.

The ringing of my phone startles me. The music cuts out and I look at my screen. Not a phone call; it's a FaceTime from Stephanie. I hit the button to answer it. "Hi," I say, looking at her with my *why isn't this a text* face.

"Oh, hi," she says. "Are you in a car?" She knows damn well that I am.

"As I explained in my text, Marshall and I are on our way to Bend."

"Hi, Marshall," she says.

"This is my friend Stephanie," I say, angling the phone screen toward him so he can respond.

"Hey, Stephanie," he says, giving her a quick smile and then turning his attention back to the road.

"It's very nice to meet you," she says. I quickly turn the phone's screen back to me before she gets any ideas and starts blabbing on about romantic dramedies or something. *Oh my God,* she mouths, and then starts fanning herself.

"That'll do," I say, shooting her another look. This one says, *Please stop losing your shit.*

"So, Bend and Mount Hood, and then back to Portland maybe?" Stephanie says, as if she doesn't know *exactly* where I'm going. I'd already sent a quick text to her and my parents letting them know my itinerary for the next several days, and this is the real reason behind Steph's FaceTime call. She's super nosy and jonesing for a look at Marshall.

"That's correct. Please tell my mother you've made visual contact. If she was open to learning how to FaceTime, she wouldn't have to rely on you as the middleman."

"I tried to walk her through it. It's like she has a block or something."

"She can text just fine, but that's where she draws the line. She thinks FaceTime is weird." For once, I'm happy that my mother is a bit of a Luddite, since she doesn't know about Marshall yet.

"I'll be sure to check in again," Steph says.

"There's no need for that," I say.

She ignores me. "Bye, Marshall!"

Once again, I angle the phone toward Marshall, and he grins. "Bye, Stephanie. Nice to meet you."

"Sprinkles and crinkles?" Steph asks just as I'm opening my mouth to say that I'll talk to her in a day or two. I shoot her another look, and this one says, *Oh my God you did not just say that.* For one, her whisper isn't as soft as she thinks it is, and two, I can tell Marshall's interest has been piqued because he looks toward me like he was trying to figure out what in the hell that meant.

"Gotta go," I say, and disconnect the call.

My girlfriends and I call our crow's-feet crinkles and spend way too much money on special creams to combat them, but they turn us into mush when we see them on a man, which is so unfair. Marshall has crinkles, and I noticed them the first time he smiled at me because I have two eyes. He also has flecks of gray in his hair, and sprinkles are what my girlfriends and I call those flecks. Over the years, crinkles and sprinkles have become shorthand when asking about someone's new love interest. One of us would start a group text about the guy we met, and someone would immediately respond with: *crinkles or sprinkles?* Rob was forty-one and had the crinkles, but his hair was blond like mine and there were no sprinkles that I could ever see.

So Marshall has both. Big deal.

I send Steph a quick text:

Stop trying to make this a thing!

Way too late for that. Just sent a group text. NOW EVERYONE KNOWS. And maybe it's ALREADY A THING?

Do you hate me? Have you forgotten what the last couple of months has been like for me?

Of course I haven't forgotten. But wasn't the whole point of this quest an attempt to put THOSE VERY THOUGHTS AND FEELINGS behind you and GO FIND YOUR NEW LIFE?

Well. She does have a point. Stop shouting, I text, because I'm running out of rebuttals that will work on her.

We took a vote in the group chat. I've told
them everything and we're all SO FIRED UP.
Stop looking the universe's gift horse in the
mouth. Have a fling. GET LAID. Do something
that feels good for a change. You deserve it.

I HATE YOU ALL, I text, because two can play the shouty game. Then I put my phone on Do Not Disturb.

"Everything okay over there?" Marshall asks. There's no way in hell he didn't know exactly what I was doing. My thumbs were flying over the keys with both speed and ferocity, and I was obviously trying to have a side conversation on the down-low.

"Totally cool," I answer brightly. Thankfully, the music starts up again and Pink Floyd's "Wish You Were Here" begins. "Hey, Pink. They're playing your song," I say. Anything to shift the focus from my frenzied texting that was *clearly* all about him.

He winks at me and says, "It's one of my best."

Something inside me stutters, and I replay that wink in my head for a good long while. Every friend in the group text would lose their minds if they knew, which is why I won't be sharing my reaction with anyone.

Especially not Steph.

We roll into Bend, grab some lunch at a Wendy's drive-through, and then pull in to the parking lot of the Days Inn. After securing a room for Marshall, we take our food and belongings and go our separate ways, making plans to meet up again in an hour or two. I work steadily, and I'm able to put a good dent in my to-do list. I'll finish the rest tonight.

I text Marshall.

I can be downstairs in about
ten minutes. Are you ready?

Ready. Dress warmly and for rain. I
thought we could look for that cache I
want to find if you're up for the task.

Marshall told me about the cache in the car on the way here
and now I want to find it, too. It won't be easy, but a challenge is
exactly what I'm in the mood for.

Absolutely. See you soon.

One look outside my hotel room window tells me the weather
has taken a turn. It isn't raining—not yet anyway—but the sky has
grown darker, and the temp has dropped from the low sixties to
the mid-fifties. It's a good thing that the REI salesman pegged me
as an easy upsell, but who's winning now, I think, as I take the rain
pants he convinced me to buy out of my suitcase and pull them on. I
grab the rest of my gear, lace up my hiking boots, and join Marshall
downstairs.

Chapter Twelve

There are only about three hours of daylight remaining when Marshall and I arrive at Tumalo State Park, which sits on the banks of the Deschutes River. Trees—pines and junipers and alders—dot the area. The parking lot is mostly empty. "I think we can find the cache before the sun goes down," Marshall says.

"It's a level four on both terrain and difficulty," I say. "But I admire your faith in us."

He parks the Jeep, and before getting out we pull on our gloves and put on hats. Grab our Garmins and turn them on. In addition to the cloud cover, it's also a bit foggy, giving the whole area a spooky vibe. There is no way in *hell* I'd ever set foot in a place like this alone; I can almost hear the theme song to the movie *Halloween* playing in the background.

We set off, heading in the direction we're being pointed in. The trail we're following runs parallel to the river, but we're heading upward on a gradual incline, glancing periodically at our devices to make sure we're going the right way. The spooky clouds and the fog only increase the difficulty of the search, as do the tree branches overhead that plunge parts of the trail into an inky semidarkness.

We come to a fallen log, and the tree branches on either side of it are too thick and tangled for us to go around. The only way we can keep moving toward the cache is to climb over it.

"Need a boost?" Marshall asks.

"I think I can do it," I say, turning around so that the log is behind me, and bracing my hands on it. I hop up and my butt lands squarely on top of it, allowing me to swing my legs over and turn back around so I'm facing in the right direction. Marshall does the same, and we continue.

Now we're picking our way through the trail at an even steeper incline. I'm breathing harder, but it's nothing I can't handle. Of course, I could do without the light rain that begins ten minutes later.

"Keep going?" Marshall asks.

"Keep going," I say.

The tree cover shields us from the brunt of it, but enough of the frigid droplets are falling on us to make me thankful for the insulated waterproof beanie on my head. But my hair is in a braid down my back, and it's absorbing water like a wick.

The last twenty feet are off-trail and downhill in loose dirt, and we have no choice but to scoot on our butts because there are cliffs with steep drop-offs on each side of us. If the visibility were better, we'd have ourselves quite a view. But all we're able to make out is the hazy outline of the river below.

I look at my Garmin, which tells me we're basically on top of the cache, but there's nothing here. Marshall pats the ground in a circle ten feet from me. "Any luck?" I say.

"No. It's supposed to be right here."

I scan the surrounding area, but I don't spot anything that looks like the container we're searching for. It doesn't help that the rain is fogging up the lenses of my glasses, and I can hardly see.

Marshall starts digging at the ground with the heel of his hiking boot, while I use my gloved hands to sweep piles of ground debris aside. Sometimes, the needle-in-a-haystack aspect of geocaching is fun and exciting. Right now, it's wet and cold and frustrating.

"Found it," Marshall says. As much as I would have liked to be the one to spot it, I'm happy because now we can log the find and get the hell out of here. The container is a white twelve-inch pipe with a screw-on cap that is partially obscured by fallen needles, and not at all where it's supposed to be. Inside it is the disposable waterproof camera listed in the cache's description. It's in a ziplock bag, and as instructed, we smile for the camera and take a selfie, our heads squished close together. Marshall pulls a pen out of his jacket, and we take out the logbook and sign it. Then he removes a little metal motorcycle from another pocket, the kind that reminds me of a child's Hot Wheels toy. I put my hand on Marshall's arm. "Are you leaving a trackable?"

"Yes. My brother had a bike just like this one," Marshall says, dropping the miniature version into my hand. It's a red, white, and blue Honda sport bike, and it's got a tag called a Travel Bug attached to it that will allow its journey to be tracked via the app.

"He was six years younger than me—there's a sister in between us," Marshall says. "I'd take him geocaching with me back in high school when I didn't have anyone better to go with. He was probably eleven the first time we went together, just the two of us. I went off to college and never seemed to have time for it anymore, especially after I opened my practice. But Graham still went out almost every weekend even when I said I was too busy to go with him. We were able to go out together one more time before he died and it's something I think about a lot."

We sit there in silence for a few minutes, getting wetter and colder. Marshall's heartache and regret over not spending more time with Graham feels palpable. His exterior might not be covered with sharp spikes like mine is, but he's been guarding the interior since we met on that hiking trail. I didn't realize that getting to know him would be like peeling an onion, each layer revealing more than the one that came before it. Probably because I didn't *want* to know him. I focused more on the safety he could offer and not on how he might be feeling inside. And back then, that was fine.

Normal.

Expected.

Not everyone will know what it's like to discover their partner has been hiding a secret family because that's a truly batshit thing, but most people know what it feels like to lose a loved one. We're mortal, it's inevitable. And Marshall is still churning around in his grief and has chosen to take a solo vacation, maybe to get his head on straight.

Just like me.

If I had to guess, Marshall's not spending his vacation resting or decompressing or doing vacationy things. He's trying to figure out what the rest of his life will look like without Holly and Graham. This may not be the romantic dramedy my friends are hoping for, but two lost souls trying to find the light is something I can get behind.

"What's the trackable's final destination?" I ask.

"Home. Graham will never return, but maybe this will." Marshall looks into my eyes, and I look into his. They're shiny with unshed tears and I'm shocked that he's letting me see the effect this is having on him. My brain doesn't quite know what to make of it.

Without thinking, I clasp his hands in mine and squeeze, hoping the pressure will convey how much I want this for him. "I hope it makes its way back to you."

"Thanks, Wren." Then he slides his hands from my grip, drops the motorcycle into the container, and screws the lid back on.

"Let's hope we can get back down without breaking a leg," I say. It's raining harder now and the needles covering the ground are as slick as ice in spots. Visibility has reached an all-time sucky low. Twice, my feet nearly fly out from under me and the only thing that saves me from wiping out are the tree branches I manage to grab on to. Marshall slips a few minutes later but employs the same tree-branch method I used to arrest his fall.

My right foot lands on a stick that might as well be coated with grease, but instead of falling forward, I fall backward and land on my ass. Marshall stops, whirls around, and crouches in front of me. "Are you okay? Is any part of you hurt?"

"Just my pride."

He helps me up and then takes my gloved hand in his, holding it tightly and not letting go as we make our way slowly down the hill while the rain intensifies. Maybe he's doing it without thinking, the same way I did when I reached for *his* hands. He's a rescuer, after all. A chivalrous man who takes safety very seriously. No one is falling on their ass again on his watch.

We reach the fallen log, and I'm relieved because it won't be long before we're back in the dry warmth of the Jeep. "Hold on," Marshall says. He climbs over the log and then turns back to me, reaching up to slide his hands under my armpits so he can lift me up and over it.

It's the moment when something shifts inside me. The path to my heart is paved with honesty, intelligence, and selfless and tender actions. When Rob died and I found out about Shayla and the children, I filtered our entire relationship through the lens of his deception and realized there were many times when he treated me badly that had nothing to do with his secret family or his lies—it was just who he was. Rob never acted selflessly, it was always all about him—how tired he was (I'll bet!), how hard he worked (all the time!), how he never wanted to go anywhere because of his grueling travel schedule (which included balancing visits to his real family in between work trips). But he did attempt to woo me, at least in the beginning. There were romantic gestures—flowers that would regularly show up at my door and candlelit bubble baths for two that he'd initiate. Maybe if there had ever been a fallen tree in my way, Rob would have lifted me over it the way Marshall did. He threw down just enough bread crumbs to hide the fact that he was an awful person hiding an awful truth—that he would never care about others as much as he cared about himself. And for some un-fathomable reason, I scooped up those bread crumbs and bragged about them to my friends. Maybe Marshall is bread-crumbing me, too. Aren't we all on our best behavior at the beginning?

Marshall reaches for my hand again, and we make our way back to the same spot where we began. His Jeep is the only vehicle in the parking lot, no surprise there. He doesn't drop my hand until we reach it. The hand-holding goes way beyond my touch-starved issue. Holding someone's hand shows that they mean something to you and that you're cool with that sentiment being on display for anyone to see. Granted, no one is here to see it besides Marshall and me, but still.

Holding hands in public was something Rob and I never did because he had an almost visceral hatred for public displays of affection, no matter how G-rated they might be. Once, about six months after we started dating, I'd turned and kissed him on the street while we were waiting for an Uber. He'd told me he loved me for the first time the night before, and I was still replaying it in my mind. I wanted to kiss him, so I did, his face held firmly in my hands, not a care in the world about who might be watching. You would have thought I'd dropped to my knees, unzipped his pants, and started blowing him by the way he'd yanked my hands away and broken the kiss. A few weeks later, he'd asked why I didn't initiate anything physical more often. I'd turned to him and said, "The last time I tried, you shot me down and it hurt." He claimed he didn't remember and told me I was making a big deal out of nothing. He remembered it just fine and he loved it when I initiated, but only when we were within the walls of my apartment where no one could see it.

"I think we got more than we bargained for," Marshall says as we climb inside the Jeep, snapping me out of the painful memory.

"Maybe, but crushing a cache with that level of difficulty and in those conditions was worth it," I say. Harrowing or not, what we just finished doing feels like *living,* and I'll take this over lying in my bed all day, wondering if I'll ever be happy again the way I did in the weeks after Rob died. I wish I could go back and tell that grieving girl that, yes, you will get through this, and, yes, you will smile again.

The way I'm smiling now.

"I'm looking forward to a hot shower, dry, comfy clothes, and a big sloppy pizza," I say.

"Want company?" Marshall asks. "To be clear, I meant the pizza. Not the shower."

I meet his eyes in the glow of the Jeep's dome light. There's something mischievous in them now, less emotional, and not so real and raw even if some of the heavier stuff has already leaked out on its own. "Ha, ha," I say, because I know how to handle the teasing, which is closer to the surface. "And sure, we can share a pizza."

I'm still at war with my regrets, but I'm getting better at silencing them. What Marshall and I are doing exists in a vacuum of our creation, and in this vacuum, there are no rules other than the ones we make, and which make us happy. It's just the two of us, outrunning ghosts, delaying what's to come as we try to eke out the smallest measure of enjoyment when everything else has gone to hell. It isn't meant to be permanent, but we can wring out every last drop if we feel like it.

And maybe I do.

It's way too soon to contemplate falling in love again, but maybe there's room for something else. Something that doesn't need a label other than it feels good. This isn't just about a shared pizza; it's the promise of a bigger peek behind the curtain than I've allowed him so far.

He puts the Jeep in gear, and we head back to the hotel. "What kind of pizza?" he asks as we enter the hotel lobby dripping water behind us like a couple of ducks.

"Sausage or pepperoni is fine," I say.

"What kind do you really want?"

"Canadian bacon and pineapple."

He groans. "Oh, God, you're one of those. That's so gross."

"You mean it's the best, right?"

"I mean that half of the pizza will have the horrible combo of meat and fruit, and the other will have the superior toppings of sausage and mushroom. I'll put in the order and text you when it arrives."

Our rooms are on the same floor but at opposite ends of the hall. "Awesome. Thanks. See you soon," I say as we go our separate ways, surprised at how much I'm looking forward to his return.

Chapter Thirteen

My hot shower feels incredible, and I finish drying my hair and slipping into my joggers and sweatshirt a few minutes before Marshall texts to say the pizza is here.

I text him back. *I'm ready.* But for what, exactly? Someone to split a pizza with? Someone to talk to? I mentioned wanting pizza and a shower, and he offered company.

Does he think this is a hookup?

It's not like I'd said, *Sure, we can share a pizza, and then afterward you can ravish me,* so I may be overthinking this. Then I picture Marshall *actually* ravishing me, and I'm flushed when he arrives, pizza box in hand.

Steph would love this.

Steph would be *thrilled* to know that I'm having these thoughts.

It's all very confusing.

He's wearing the same gray sweatpants he was wearing in Eugene, and he's paired them with a long-sleeved red Henley. The sleeves are pushed up, exposing the forearms I notice every time he shifts gears in the Jeep. A man's bulging biceps do absolutely nothing for me, but forearms are my kryptonite. If I want the pink to fade from my cheeks completely, I need to think about something else immediately.

We put the pizza box on the dresser but quickly realize that without plates we're going to make a mess, since the pizza place only threw in a measly couple of napkins. There are two queen beds in the room. My laptop is sitting on one of them along with my phone. "Put it on my bed," I say. "We can set it between us and eat over the box." Really, Wren? Is turning your bed into a dining table the best way to divert your attention away from forearms and being ravished? Because I think most people would say that no, no, it isn't.

Marshall sets the box down and we stretch out, our backs up against the headboard. He must be as hungry as I am, because neither of us says anything while we wolf down our first slices. Eating pizza on my bed with Marshall should feel awkward—talk about mixed signals—but the weird intimacy that threw me at the beginning of our time together doesn't seem to affect me as much now. It's still a bit strange, but then again, I'm in a strange phase of my life, so it's somewhat fitting, I guess.

"Would you like a slice of my half of the pizza?" I ask when I reach for another piece.

"Absolutely not," he says, which makes me laugh.

We eat in companionable silence. It feels good to have someone to split a pizza with. There were many similar domestic evenings spent sitting on the couch with Rob, a pizza in front of us on the coffee table. I miss those nights, even though, in hindsight, I realized that eating dinner at home was simply the safest option for Rob. I had imagined growing old with Rob, and that someday we'd move from the couch to the rocking chairs on the porch that we'd sit in side by side while our grandchildren played on the lawn in front of us.

Now that I'm back to square one, I don't know if I have the

"Steph convinced me to give online dating another try. It's not like I hadn't tried it already. I'd download an app now and then but wasn't having much luck there either. Steph suggested that I come right out and state on my profile that I was a sapiosexual so that the smart men would automatically know we were compatible. That sounded perfectly reasonable to me after we'd each drunk half a bottle of wine."

"I know where this is going," Marshall says. "Please do not disappoint me."

"So I worked up a new profile that informed potential suitors about the kind of man I was looking for. If I recall correctly— because I've kind of blocked it out—I *led* with that. But still, I figure it's an awesome vetting tool, right?"

Marshall winces.

"The number of men who had no clue what the word meant but wanted to hook up immediately and rather graphically was off the charts. Who's the idiot now, Marshall?" I ask, cracking myself up. "It's like I rang the dinner bell for dummies. They had no clue what the 'sapio' part meant, but they sure as hell noticed that the word had 'sexual' in it and all the blood left their brains—where there wasn't much to begin with—and migrated farther south."

He can't stop laughing. It's spontaneous and unrestrained, and it lights him up in a way I haven't seen on this trip. He's always been rather subdued, not like he's afraid to let loose, but like nothing has surprised or delighted him enough to crack through his exterior and get to that spontaneous, squishy, *unguarded* spot inside. The smile he gave me on the trail at Wild Iris, the one I thought didn't reach the far corners of his mouth, is now at its full, heart-melting wattage, and I can't stop looking at him.

"Hey, you gave it a try," Marshall says. "I mean, it was a total *fail*, but still."

"I deleted my dating profile immediately, and a week after that I met Rob. He was filling his car up at the pump next to mine, and we

stamina to look for a partner again, to start over know

hard it will be to put what happened with Rob behind me

drag all my messy insecurities into the next relationship.

I'll skip it altogether in favor of staying single, but that mea

ting go of those rocking chairs and grandchildren, and that

me sad. *You wouldn't have to look too hard to find Marsha*

voice inside my head tells me. *You've already found him.* Bu

as quickly, I dismiss that little voice. I'm not ready to dive

anything. I'm not even sure I'm ready to stand on the platform

look over the edge at the water below. And who knows if Mar

even thinks of me that way. Men can be nice, they can even flirt,

it doesn't have to mean anything.

As if he can read my mind, Marshall says, "Where did you m

Rob?"

"At a gas station. How's that for random? It happened rig

after I made the grand announcement that I no longer cared abo

meeting someone. I'd had a series of short-term relationships tha

failed to launch because they'd either fizzled out on my end or his

I wasn't desperate by any means, but I was getting frustrated and

hoped that, eventually, I'd meet someone I clicked with." I'd also

been a bridesmaid in seven weddings by that point and was starting

to wonder if taking my own walk down the aisle was even in the

cards for me.

"What didn't you like about the guys you weren't clicking

with?"

"How much time do you have?" I ask.

"Well, I'm on vacation so, a lot."

"I don't know if that's enough time, sadly. There were a variety

of reasons, but a lot of the men seemed to be lacking a certain . . .

how should I say this? They were dumb, Marshall. They were all

super dumb."

"Intelligence is such an underrated quality," Marshall says.

It is, I think. And you have it in spades.

were standing there doing that awkward thing when you're waiting for your tank to fill and wondering if you should say something when he introduced himself. We made small talk, and I remember the pumps clicking off and wishing they hadn't. I got back in my car and was about to leave when he tapped on my window and asked for my number." I liked to think that the sixty seconds between me getting back in my car and Rob tapping on my window were when he contemplated the decision he was about to make.

Did he think about Shayla? Did he think about his children?

The answers were something I ruminated on no fewer than fifty times a day, especially in the weeks after he died. Was any of our relationship real? It was to me, but what was it for him? Did he struggle with the choice he made that day and the duplicity that followed? I hate that he died before I could demand the answers; I'll never have them now.

Marshall looks appropriately somber. I've given him the origin story of my relationship with Rob, but without the rest of it, he probably thinks I'm just a woman in mourning. And I am, in a way. But not for Rob specifically; I'm pining for the life I thought we were going to have together before I found out about his other family.

"We went out for coffee the next day and lunch the day after that," I say. "He mentioned that he traveled a lot for work and was heading to the Netherlands in two days. I asked him what it was like trying to do business when you don't speak the language, and he mentioned, very casually, that he'd taught himself how to speak Dutch to get the position he currently held. My little sapiosexual heart expanded three sizes just like the Grinch's." Smart was hot, and it had always been something that attracted me to a man even more than his physical attributes, although I liked the way Rob looked almost as much as I liked his big old brain.

"Sounds like you found exactly what you were looking for," Marshall says.

"Rob set the hook that day for sure. Then he just reeled me on in." Rob *was* smart, but he used his intelligence to dupe me, and no one has ever made me feel as stupid as he did. Maybe Rob tried finding other women to cheat on his wife with, but he settled for me because I swallowed the bullshit he fed me and asked for more. Maybe Rob wanted to *avoid* smart women; I don't like what that says about me.

I'm full now, and I lean back against the headboard, slightly embarrassed about everything that just came pouring out of my mouth. "What about Holly? Where did you meet her?"

"Some mutual friends set us up on a blind date."

"How long were you together?"

"About six years."

My eyes widen a bit at the revelation. "Any chance of a reconciliation?" I ask. It's a fair question and the same one he asked me before I told him that Rob died. "I'm assuming Holly is still among the living."

"Yes, she's alive, and no, there's no chance of a reconciliation." He doesn't offer anything in the way of an explanation, and I consider pointing out that he once suggested that relationships could be salvaged with open communication. But I don't, because if anyone is aware of this, it's him. It's possible they already tried it, and it didn't solve their problems.

Or maybe Holly is still around, waiting in the wings for Marshall to become fun again and patiently hoping for a reconciliation. Who knows.

One thing I *do* know is that I've spent almost as much quality time with Marshall this week as I spent with Rob in the entire month before he died. I went back and read the entries in my journal, using them to tally how much time we spent together during Rob's last thirty days on earth, and it barely equaled seventy-two hours. He was always in a rush, flying into town approximately once a week. He'd arrive like a whirlwind, swooping in to tell me he missed me so much that he couldn't concentrate on his work. "I love you, Wren," he'd say. "I hate that we're apart so much. Someday things will slow down, and we can spend more time together." I can only hope that most of the hours he didn't give to me at least went to his family, especially his children.

That's enough of memory lane for today, I tell myself. Reluctantly, I announce that I need to get some work done, give my hands a final wipe, and pull my laptop onto my lap.

"Do you want me to go?" Marshall asks.

"Do you *want* to go?"

"You said you've got work to do," he says.

"You don't have to go. You can watch something if you want."

"Are you sure it won't bother you?" he asks. Perhaps my concern about sending the wrong signal was unfounded; maybe Marshall is wondering if *I'm* the one looking for a hookup.

"No, not at all."

"Okay," he says. He stretches out beside me again, grabbing the remote from the nightstand and clicking on the TV. He surfs the available channels and settles on a football game. I work for another hour and then stifle a yawn with the back of my hand. "Tired?" Marshall asks.

"A little. Also full of pizza."

"Mount Hood is about two and a half hours from here. Should we sleep in tomorrow and then head out after lunch?" There's something animated and enthusiastic in his demeanor that wasn't there initially. Maybe Marshall miscalculated how much he'd enjoy vacationing solo and appreciates having someone to talk to and make plans with, because I'm not the only one who seems to have come out of their shell.

"You seem happier," I blurt instead of answering his question.

He smiles, looking as if he's contemplating my words. "Maybe I am."

Better together, Marshall said when he pitched the idea of us teaming up.

I think he might have been right about that.

His phone rings and he takes his eyes off me just long enough to decline the call, perhaps because we're having a *moment.* It rings again and his thumb hovers over the button for a couple of rings as if he's deciding whether to answer. Then he finally does. "Hey," he says. There's a long pause like the person on the other end had a specific reason for calling and is letting Marshall know exactly what it is. "I know," he says. "I'm sorry. I'm in Bend."

Every fiber of my being is on high alert, because it's painfully obvious that someone is looking for Marshall and that he doesn't particularly want to be found.

"Calm down," he says mildly. "I am not *missing in action,* and I have not *gone rogue.* Seriously. Do you hear yourself? I was busy earlier, and I haven't had a chance to get back to you yet."

Yes, he has. He could have called whoever this is while I was working or during a commercial, or, well, anytime he wanted. He could have called them when he was in his hotel room showering and waiting for the pizza.

The person on the other end must be giving him another earful, because it's a good thirty seconds before he speaks again. "I was *geocaching.* The weather deteriorated, and it took me longer than I'd planned. I'm at my hotel now having something to eat."

With me, I think. *You went geocaching with me and then you split a pizza.*

Again, with *me.*

I would think that the person he's been geocaching *with* might at least garner a mention unless he didn't want the caller to know because they wouldn't be cool with it, for a variety of reasons. The biggest of which is because maybe he's not supposed to be with anyone at all.

"What I need is for you to stop *hounding* me, Jill."

Wait. I know who Holly is, but who is Jill?

"You don't have to text me fifty times a day, and I don't want you to start calling me either. This is better than what I was doing, right? You can't possibly find fault with this."

What was he *doing*? I'm leaning toward him slightly in an attempt to hear better.

"I'm sorry," he says again. "I'll do better at responding to your texts. I just need some time to clear my head, okay? Can you give me that?"

Apparently, Jill can, or at least she must have promised him she'd try, because he thanks her and disconnects the call.

I start typing away on my laptop, trying to make it look like I wasn't following along with every second of his conversation. "That was my sister, Jillian."

"Oh," I say. I'm supposed to feel relieved. Isn't that how this works? I thought it was a girlfriend, but it turns out that it was only his *sister*. Whew! Thank goodness for that! This is the point where the romantic dramedy Steph is desperately hoping for gets back on track.

But *who* Marshall was on the phone with is not what I care about. The whole time Rob and I were together, I thought we were building something. To find out I was nothing more than a side piece, hidden away in Ohio with no chance for the future I'd been planning, nearly destroyed me. Listening to Marshall's conversation has scratched at that scab and it's bleeding again. A simple "I'm with a fellow geocacher named Wren" would have sufficed. He doesn't have to include the part about holding my hand or splitting a pizza next to me on my bed. Just a quick mention to allay the fears I have about not being worthy enough to exist out in the open.

Marshall's not smiling anymore, and he says, "I'm gonna head back to my room. Just text me when you're ready to go tomorrow."

"Sure," I say, walking him to the door. "Thanks for the pizza." Then I close it and lock it behind him.

I don't think Steph was on to something after all. And it's still too soon to open myself up to anyone.

Chapter Fourteen

Marshall might have been able to sleep in, but I spend five hours the next morning completing enough work to keep me caught up for the next several days. We get back on the road around two thirty, after a late checkout and another drive-through lunch. Whatever magic I felt before his sister called last night has dissipated further. For Marshall, too, I think, because we are oddly formal with each other now, our conversations mostly a polite exchange of information about how we slept (so awesome, we assure each other, even though I kept waking up throughout the night and he's got dark circles under his eyes) and where to eat (anything is fine, we say).

It's a cloudy, dreary day, and it's raining again. "I booked a room at the lodge last night," Marshall says. "Thought it would be easier if I found something at the same place you said you were staying."

"Sure," I say. "It probably is easier that way." The Lost Lake Resort Lodge rooms all have kitchenettes, which is ideal because we're planning on spending a couple of nights in Mount Hood.

The café is closed for the season, but there's a general store that has groceries. We don't have to eat our meals together if we don't want to. We're not joined at the hip, we can go our separate ways if we feel like it. It's fine.

It's raining harder now, which is why I smile when Creedence Clearwater Revival's "Have You Ever Seen the Rain" comes on. I hum along, quietly singing bits and pieces of the verses and part of the chorus even though my voice is merely passable. My shoes are off, and I'm sitting cross-legged in the passenger seat, lost in my own little world that Marshall doesn't feel a part of since we've mostly listened to my playlist instead of talking since we got back in the car.

"*I wanna know, have you ever seen the rain?*" I sing softly, not sure Marshall can even hear me. But then he says, "All the goddamn time, CCR," which cracks me up and we look at each other and start laughing. It breaks the tension we've been wrapped in since we met up in the lobby this afternoon.

"*Coming down on a sunny day,*" I sing, a little bit louder and with more enthusiasm as the song winds down and ends. Before the next song starts, I turn to Marshall and say, "I like the rain," and he looks over at me as if what I said means something to him and says, "Good."

We arrive at Mount Hood a little before five. We've left fall behind; everything around us points to winter. It's no longer raining, and the air is crisp and cold. The snowcapped peak of Mount Hood stands tall in the distance.

I give the woman behind the counter my reservation number and wait for her to complete the check-in process. "I'm sorry, I don't see that reservation," she says.

"I booked it online. That's why I have a confirmation number." I scan through the email inbox on my phone. "Here," I say, showing her the message I received after booking it.

"You definitely received confirmation, but it's not pulling up now. There must have been a glitch in our system when it was made. We're completely booked. I'm truly sorry."

"You don't have anything available? Nothing at all?" I ask, feeling panicky.

"Wren, it's okay," Marshall says. "We'll figure it out. Can you pull up my reservation?" he asks.

He gives her the confirmation number, and a few taps later she looks at him and smiles. "Yes, Mr. Hendricks. It's right here."

It's fitting that I've chosen the Pacific Northwest for my quest, because the rain cloud of failed dreams and disappointment that's been hanging over my head since Rob died probably feels right at home here. Can't anything go right for a change? Meanwhile, I am without somewhere to sleep tonight.

"You're welcome to share my room," Marshall says. "I'm fine with it if you are. Or we can find a room in a different hotel for you." The woman behind the counter leans forward as if she's super invested in our lodging drama.

"I really did make a reservation," I protest.

Marshall looks at me, puzzled. "Of course you did. I'm also pretty sure this mix-up is on their end," he says, pointedly shooting the woman a look. She straightens and starts typing again, but I can tell she's still listening. "This is not some ploy to get you to share my room. I just want you to know it's an option."

"The rooms have separate sleeping areas," the woman says, perking up. "If that helps."

Well, yes, it does. But this is a new level of togetherness. I thought this trip couldn't get any weirder from an intimacy standpoint, but I guess it can. And it has.

"Do the sleeping areas have doors?" I ask.

"Yes, they do," she says.

"And you're sure you don't have any other rooms?"

She shakes her head. "I'm sorry. We're full."

I exhale. "Your call," Marshall says.

"It seems like overkill to look for another room or for both of us to pay full price when the beds are in separate rooms with a door."

"Again, I'm fine with it if you are," he says.

I look at the woman—she's leaning over the counter toward us again—and say, "I'll share with him."

"Lovely," she says, handing Marshall two key cards. "Enjoy your stay."

Steph's brain is going to explode. The group chat is going to lose their *minds*.

We unload our belongings from the Jeep and bring them to the room. It's nice. The kitchen and bathroom are tiny, but the living area has two couches that face each other with a coffee table in between. There's even a balcony with a couple of wrought-iron chairs and a truly spectacular view of the surrounding forest.

Both bedroom doors are closed, and we open the first one. It has a triple set of bunk beds because of course it does. The other bedroom has a king-sized bed. "I guess we can make it work," I say. "But how will you fit in a bunk bed? Won't your feet hang off the end?"

"Absolutely they would. But they won't in a king." He sizes me up. "You're what? Five three?"

"Five *four*. But I can jack myself up to five seven with the right shoes," I say, gesturing with my thumb toward the sky.

"I bet you'd fit perfectly on one of those bunk beds."

"I want to argue, but I've got no leg to stand on here. Not long ones, anyway. You and your six-foot-three-inch body can have the big bed. It's *your* room. I'll be okay with one of the bunks. Like a ten-year-old."

"That's very accommodating of you. And just so you know, I'm six four."

I try to keep a straight face, but I can't, and I don't really want to. The levity we shared in the car is back and I like it better this way. It makes things less awkward and takes some of the focus off of the whole room-sharing thing. "Fine. I'll give you the inch."

Marshall laughs, giving me a friendly poke in the side that tickles. "And I'm gonna take *it*." I feel like a young girl on the playground who's just discovered that a boy's teasing isn't all bad. Maybe it can even be kind of nice.

We leave the room in search of the general store, and when we find it, we each grab a basket. I pick up a box of crackers and some cheddar cheese, then grab some apples and a loaf of bread. Marshall reaches for butter, jam, and some bacon. "Eggs?" I ask.

"Definitely. I make a mean omelet," he says, grabbing some diced ham. We add a box of pasta, some jarred sauce, a six-pack of beer, a loaf of French bread, and a salad kit to our haul, along with some chocolate chip cookies, bottled water, another bag of coffee, and some half-and-half. I always wanted to do domestic, mundane things like grocery shopping or running errands with Rob, because they seemed like things two people in a committed relationship might *want* to do together. But I did those things during the week when he was gone. Rob treated our apartment like a hotel he visited regularly where the sheets were always clean, and there was an in-house concierge to make things more enjoyable. Maybe Rob did those things with Shayla when he was home.

We're walking back to the room when my phone rings, but it's in my back pocket and my hands are full. No one but my mom ever calls me, and I can tell by the sound of the ringtone that it's not a FaceTime call from Stephanie. The ringing annoys me, but it ends soon enough.

And then it begins again ten seconds later. "Wow, they must really want to talk to me about my car's warranty," I say.

Marshall laughs. "I *hate* those calls."

We're setting the groceries on the kitchen counter when my phone rings a third time. Now I'm more worried than annoyed, and I reach into my back pocket and pull out the phone. It's an unknown number, but the jolt of anxiety the repeated ringing has given me needs someplace to go, and I'm ready to vent it to whoever's on the other end. I slide the button to answer and say, "Hello?"

"Am I speaking to Wren Waters?" a female voice asks.

I don't like that she knows my full name.

"Who's calling?"

"My name is Terry, and I'm calling regarding an overdue balance that requires your immediate attention."

I also don't like her tone.

"I don't have any overdue balances on anything," I say.

Again, almost as if she didn't hear a word I said, she repeats that there's an overdue balance requiring my immediate attention, and this time I *really* don't like her tone.

"I pay my bills on time, and you can stop taking that tone with me. Obviously, you have the wrong person."

I look at Marshall and shrug as if to say, *I have no idea what this is about,* and he leans back against the counter, waiting.

"This balance needs your immediate attention," she repeats. "You can send in the full amount, or we can set you up on a payment plan."

"Quit saying that. What balance? From where? Wait. Are you a *bill* collector?" I ask. She neither confirms nor denies.

"The balance due is for medical treatment rendered on July twenty-third. The total is seven thousand four hundred dollars and thirty-two cents. We need your immediate attention, otherwise, we'll be forced to take further steps."

"Oh, my God," I say, because I know exactly what this is about. Now Marshall looks worried.

"That's one of my late fiancé's—" I catch myself. "That medical bill is not mine. I'm not responsible for those charges."

"Your name is on the bill," the woman insists.

"The name on the bill should be R. Robert Stephenson, who is deceased."

"It would be much easier if you could make a payment over the phone and let me set up the installments now."

"Yes, easier for *you*. But again, I'm not paying anything. I am not the responsible party."

"Until this is resolved, you are still responsible for the balance. Your name is on the bill."

"I have no idea why my name is on the bill. It should not be." I vaguely remember someone coming into Rob's hospital room and asking questions in a hushed voice and inputting things into the computer on wheels they rolled in with them. I didn't know the answers to many of them, but they asked for my name several times and I gave it to them.

"But it is," she stresses. "And the balance must be paid."

"Then I suggest you get ahold of Shayla Stephenson. She lives in New York. I'm sure you can track her down. You seem to be very good at that."

"And what is her relationship to the person who incurred these charges?" the woman asks.

"Shayla Stephenson is Rob's wife—" I catch myself again. "His widow. Do not ever call me again," I say, and I disconnect the call with a fury far greater than when I answered it.

Chapter Fifteen

"Breathe, Wren," Marshall says calmly. He doesn't look the slightest bit fazed.

I've been pacing since I hung up on the bill collector, my fists clenched and my fury radiating from me in waves that are so potent they must surely be visible. Being on the hook—even if it's in error—for Rob's treatment is too much salt in a wound that's still stinging. *I'm just the mistress,* I wanted to shout at the bill collector. *You'll have to save the big guns like insurance co-pays and medical bills for his wife!* I heed Marshall's directive, stop moving, and take several deep, long breaths. It helps but not enough. "I need fresh air," I say, heading for the door that leads to the balcony.

"Do you want to be alone?" he asks.

"No," I say, and he follows me outside. I want to talk about Rob. Now that Marshall knows what really happened, I want his insight, knowledge, and feedback. I keep thinking that if I can somehow make sense of what Rob did and why he did it, I might heal faster. Rob was a puzzle I can't solve on my own, and I'm tired

of banging my head against a wall. If anyone can help me understand, it's Marshall the geocacher-slash-psychologist. It's wild that
the man I didn't want in my head is about to be granted free rein to
come on in and start poking around.

The wrought-iron chairs are hard but not uncomfortable, and I
take another deep breath. Outside, the air is crisp and clean, and the
sky has grown darker as dusk approaches. I start at the beginning,
and I tell Marshall everything. He listens with the same unfazed
expression he's been wearing since I hung up the phone. "I'm truly
sorry for what you've been through," he says. "I'm sure it was painful and a lot to wrap your head around."

"How are you not shocked?" I ask. "What Rob did was some
Jerry Springer–level shit."

"There's not much that surprises me anymore given the stories
I've heard over the years," he says.

I can see that. Marshall has probably heard things that are even
more shocking than men with secret families. He's desensitized and
unfazed by my situation, which puts me at ease, because it's night-
and-day different from what I experienced with my friends and
family when they heard the news. You should have seen Steph's
face when I dropped the giant bomb of Rob's wife and kids in her
lap. She came over immediately after I'd returned from the hospital
because I'd sent her a two-word text saying only *he's gone*, and then
I'd turned off my phone. I hadn't broken the news of Rob's death
to anyone but her at that point, not even my parents, or maybe
especially not them because I was deeply ashamed about the mess
my life had become. That I'd allowed it to become. Steph's jaw
had nearly unhinged like a snake's when she realized the scope and
depth of the shit that had just hit the fan. "No," she kept saying.
"Yes," I said. "This can't be real," she said. "I wish it wasn't," I'd
replied, and it went on like that for a while.

And telling my parents is not a hell I'd wish on anyone. It's a
good thing my mother *doesn't* like to FaceTime, because the phone

call I made to her had been difficult enough, and I could only imagine how much harder it would have been if I'd had to see the look on *her* face. There had been a long silence on the other end of the phone after I broke the news, and finally, she sputtered, "How, Wren? How did he keep up with the charade for so long? You never suspected anything? You didn't have a clue?"

And there it was, the crux of all that ails me, and the burning question everyone wanted to ask (and many did): *How* could you not know?

What they really meant was: How could you be so stupid?

I don't blame my mother for asking. I don't blame my father, either, but at least that conversation was a bit easier, since my mother had mostly brought him up to speed by the time we talked. I can't blame anyone. Why *didn't* I suspect anything?

Why didn't I have a clue?

The only thing I can offer for my defense is that Rob was really good at covering his tracks. I never caught him in a lie. He never messed up his story about where he'd be or who he'd been with. He was a busy guy with a busy job, and I assumed things would change at some point. He'd get tired of traveling and would cut back if he could. We'd get married and buy a house together. Get settled.

"I understand why you have such strong feelings about what Rob did to you," Marshall says. "Strong feelings" is the understatement of a lifetime. If Rob hadn't died, part of me would want to rip him to shreds with my bare hands, but the other part might want to cling to him, relieved that he'd pulled through. When I was still trying to convince myself that Shayla and those children in the hallway had been some sort of fever dream and were not real, I half expected Rob to emerge from his comatose state to explain their existence in a way that made total sense, despite how delusional that sounded.

"I'm just so angry," I say, "but also heartbroken and I'm trying to work through the conflicting emotions, and I don't feel like any of them are valid because he's dead. How can I be furious with him? I loved him. I loved him right up until the moment he died. I can't simply turn those feelings off like a faucet."

"Anger is just sadness coming out sideways, Wren."

His statement renders me speechless, and tears fill my eyes. It is the most profound and relatable explanation of grief that I have ever heard. Until now, I've mostly brushed my grief under the rug in favor of my anger, because how could I be sad about losing something that wasn't real? But the grief didn't stay where I'd shoved it. It got tangled up with my anger and it's been oozing at the seams this whole time. The tears filling my eyes become a torrent, and there's no emotional dam powerful enough to hold them back. Marshall waits quietly, patiently, as I surrender and let them stream down my face. If we were in his office, this is the point where he'd probably nudge the Kleenex box toward me. Instead, I make do with my sleeve, dragging it across my eyes, cheeks, and nose until the fabric is soaked. Eventually, my tears subside, and I take a big hitching breath.

"Everything you're experiencing is normal, Wren. Your feelings are bound to be complicated, but they're valid because they're *your* feelings. Of course you're angry. I'd be angry, too. I can't imagine anyone who wouldn't be. And you're right. You can't turn off your feelings for Rob and how much you loved him like a faucet. It doesn't work that way."

"On a logical level, I know that. But emotionally, I want people to justify my anger, to shake their fists and say, 'Yeah, Wren, I totally get why you feel this way. You sure did get screwed.'"

"Did anyone do that? Did they shake their fists and say you got screwed?"

"No. Everyone just wanted to know how I'd missed so many red flags. I wish I had a time machine so I could go back and undo the stupid choices I made."

"Do you really think your choices were stupid?"

"Yes," I shout. "And so did everyone else. I could see it on their faces. I could hear it in their voices. Poor, stupid Wren."

Marshall looks over at me, and on *his* face I see nothing but kindness and empathy. "A person's level of deception is not an indicator of your intelligence. It just means they were willing to take drastic steps so that it could continue. Your belief that Rob's duplicity reflects poorly on you isn't fair, Wren. You were one of the victims here, and you certainly didn't deserve what he did to you."

His words and their meaning make me feel like I've been wrapped in a warm hug of understanding. Maybe it's because he's not a part of my inner circle and can maintain his objectivity, or maybe it's because he's good at what he does. Whatever the reason, Marshall has pulled back the curtain and examined this for what it was: a shitty situation in which there were no winners. Not Rob, not Shayla, not me, and certainly not those children standing shell-shocked in the hallway with their grandmother.

And it feels so much better than being judged.

"Thank you for that," I say, my voice barely more than a whisper. We sit in silence for a few minutes, and I get the sense that he's giving me time to absorb everything. But now that I've broken the seal on all the thoughts and emotions I've been stuffing deep down inside of me, there are more still clamoring to come out. "I flew here because I wanted to take back control of my life. I thought maybe if I took this trip, I could prove to myself that Rob didn't break me and that I could be fine on my own. I could concentrate only on what I wanted and not worry about the rest. But my friends and family didn't really understand that, either."

"It wasn't their decision to make. It was yours and you made it and you're here. They don't have to like it. They don't have to understand it."

"Yes, but maybe it *was* another stupid decision because the first hurdle I encountered was those men in the clearing."

"Is that why you told me you were angry with yourself when you were sitting in my car?"

Marshall's recall is amazing. "Do you remember everything I've ever told you?" I ask, looking into his eyes as if they hold all the answers.

His eyes lock with mine. "I remember a lot. And I can assure you that the malevolent actions of bad men are not your fault or your responsibility to bear." I nod because I know he's right. But women will always be called to defend their actions even if all we're trying to do is go for a hike.

"Rob's deception shredded me. I was angry, but I also felt immense pain and heartache when he died." It feels good to set these feelings free. Sharing them with Marshall has already lessened some of the power they have over me. I never realized until now how much they were poisoning my life, and I guess we really are only as sick as our secrets.

"You got your heart broken twice, Wren. Once when he died, and once when you discovered that the man you were in love with didn't actually exist. It's important to grieve, not only for the person you lost but also for the life you're not going to have with him."

"I really wish you'd stop making perfect sense." I smile to show him that I'm not serious, but it's a sad smile.

He smiles back. "I've had a lot of practice."

"I know that I should have gotten help. Everyone wanted me to talk to someone, but I was too embarrassed. I didn't feel comfortable pouring my heart out to a stranger and admitting the situation I'd gotten myself into."

"You didn't get yourself into it alone, Wren. What Rob did was inexcusable."

"I hope you don't think I'm trying to get a free therapy session out of you," I say.

"I'm not your therapist and I didn't think you were."

But what is he?

It's safe to say that Marshall is not only my protector—he's also become a friend. But what else do I want him to be? I'm not sure yet, but I feel something building with each wall he knocks down.

"It must be hard to listen to people talk about their problems all day. To carry the weight of them," I say. It's not like Marshall didn't suffer a horrible loss of his own when Graham died.

"Yes," he says. It looks like he might want to elaborate, but then he just says, "It's hard."

"Thank you for listening to mine," I say.

He looks at me with just a hint of a smile. "Anytime."

Chapter Sixteen

Marshall and I go inside to make dinner, and it feels good to focus on something that doesn't require a lot of mental energy. I put a pot of water on the stove's single burner and dump the pasta in after it comes to a boil. Marshall assembles the salad kit and slides the bread into the tiny oven. The small galley-style kitchen doesn't have a lot of elbow room and there's some bumping of body parts as we maneuver around it. Marshall places his hands on my hips and gently moves me a few inches to the left before he opens the oven door. His moving me out of harm's way makes me feel cared for, which isn't surprising considering that Marshall is clearly a very caring person. My impromptu therapy session on the balcony cemented that. He cares about people, listens to their problems, and offers his thoughts. But the actual touch, the feel of his hands on my body, makes the touch-starved side of me pipe up again. *Doesn't that feel good*, it says. *I bet more touching would feel even better.*

The two responses separate like oil and water. My brain controls one layer; my body oversees the other. And my body feels that

Marshall's hands on my hips are merely an appetizer and could I please bring on the main course? *We're hungry over here but not for food,* it shouts.

My brain is more rational. I feel close to Marshall in a way that has nothing to do with touch and everything to do with how safe he makes me feel—and not just from bears and bad men. I feel emotionally safe, and the force field of that security radiates from Marshall like heat from the oven, drawing me closer to its warmth.

He grabs two beers from the fridge, uncaps them, and hands me one. We clink bottles and take a nice long drink. I can almost feel the remaining stress leaving my body, and I'm completely drained in the best possible way.

It doesn't seem so weird to be sharing a lodge room with Marshall now and preparing a meal alongside him in companionable silence. In fact, I'm more at ease with our domestic situation than I've been since its inception. Why wouldn't I be? We have settled into an easy rhythm that feels natural. When our dinner is ready, we dig in and I'm surprised to discover that I have a hearty appetite.

After we're done eating, Marshall asks if I'd like to take a walk. "If you're up for it, that is," he says.

Most of my exhaustion is mental and a walk sounds good to me, so we grab our coats and head out into the darkness.

We pick up the walking trail that encircles Lost Lake. "You're not too cold, are you?" Marshall asks.

"Nope," I say. The temperature has dropped and it's in the mid-forties by now, but I find it invigorating. The area isn't well-lit, but there's enough light from the nearby campground to illuminate the trail.

"Why do you think Rob did it?" I ask after we've been walking for a few minutes. I've let Marshall into *my* head, but now I'd like to dive into what might have been going on inside Rob's.

"It's hard to say. He might have felt that his emotional needs weren't being met at home. You said he traveled a lot, which meant his wife was probably holding down the fort by herself. Maybe they both felt like they were doing more than their fair share, which can build resentment over time. He might have thought it justified going outside the marriage to have his needs met. Divorce is expensive and stressful, but a secret love affair is exciting. It's the perfect antidote for what might have been missing in his life."

"That makes sense," I say. "Looking back, I can remember there being a few times I found his reactions puzzling. Frustration over a canceled flight that seemed disproportionate to the circumstances, or an extra work trip thrown at him after he'd told me he was looking forward to being home for a while. I assumed that meant *my* home, but maybe Shayla needed him, or one of the kids did, which required him to pivot. I can just picture him in an airport, a phone in each hand. Texting his mistress on one and his wife on the other. What a juggler!" Marshall and I share a laugh. Nothing about what Rob did is funny, but despite everything he put me through, I hope that someday it won't have so much power over me, and laughing might help me take some of it back. It makes me feel better, anyway.

On our left, we pass a campsite where a very informal wedding reception is taking place. Everyone is wearing jeans and coats, including the groom, who is spinning the bride around the campsite to the music playing on an outdoor speaker. But the bride is wearing a gorgeous lacy white dress. She's probably freezing, but I bet she doesn't care. Who would want to cover up such a pretty dress on the only night you get to wear it? "They look happy," I say, glancing wistfully at the couple as we drift by, virtually unnoticed.

"That must poke at some wounds," Marshall says after we've left the wedding revelers in the distance.

"It does," I say. I'm not someone who's been dreaming about her wedding day since she was a little girl. I don't have a Pinterest board full of pinned rings and dresses and venues. I could get married in the backyard in bare feet while wearing jeans and an old T-shirt as long as I can trust the man standing beside me and that there are no secrets between us. There was nothing authentic about Rob's proposal, which feels humiliating to me now, a nuptial mirage. "I'm happy I never got too attached to the idea of marrying Rob."

"You didn't want to marry him?" Marshall asks.

"No, I did. I wouldn't have said yes if I didn't. I was in love with him, and I was at a place in my life where I felt ready to settle down. I wanted a family, and I got excited thinking about the one we'd build together. But it was only after he died—when I looked at our relationship from a completely different angle—that I could be honest with myself, and I realized ours wasn't as perfect as I'd led others to believe. As I'd led *myself* to believe. Marrying Rob would have been a horrible mistake."

Hindsight might be 20/20, but it also has a way of shining a light on how gullible someone was. How gullible *I* was. It's hard to play the victim when I made it so easy to be victimized.

"I asked Rob several times if I could accompany him on one of his business trips. We spent so little time together and because I could work from anywhere, it seemed like an ideal solution."

"And?" Marshall asks.

"Boy, did he shoot that idea down quickly. He told me he'd be tied up in the evening with clients and that no one ever brought their significant other. He'd said he'd be working late every night and that I'd be bored cooped up in a hotel room. I eventually stopped asking and figured it was just something he wasn't open to. Now I know those business trips allowed him the freedom to take calls from his wife. Talk to his kids and tell them he couldn't wait to get back home to them. For all I know, Shayla might have accompanied him on some of them. Or maybe he had a girlfriend stashed overseas, too. I missed so many signs. Now they all feel like a blinking neon trail leading straight to a man who was conning me the whole time. Our relationship was perfectly contained within the city limits of Dayton but once Rob cleared the city's perimeter, I disappeared from his life like some clueless sister wife who didn't know she was sharing her partner."

"You didn't know because he didn't *want* you to know," Marshall stresses.

"Maybe so, but I sure did miss a lot. He was emotionally absent at times. I'm sure the ins and outs of maintaining relationships with two women were complicated and took up a lot of brain power. Maybe that's why I sometimes felt like he wasn't there even when we were sitting right next to each other. But he was smart and I was attracted to him, and we had good chemistry. My friends and family seemed to like him. He checked more boxes than he didn't. Do you know what I mean by that?"

"Absolutely."

"This isn't going to paint me in a great light, but I'd invested a lot of time in the relationship. Too much to throw it away because something was missing that I couldn't put my finger on."

"Lots of people stay in relationships hoping things will improve," Marshall says. "Your heart still wanted a future with Rob even though your gut was telling you that things weren't quite right. In time, your gut might have won out."

I think about that for a moment.

My heart did want it.

My heart *ached* for it.

If he hadn't died, would I still be waiting?

"I'm not sure if Rob was even aware that for me, something was missing. I should have tried harder to articulate it, and I should have talked to him about it. Or maybe Rob did sense it but didn't care and put a ring on it anyway. Maybe he was planning to divorce

Shayla and figured he could get it done by the time he had to marry me. We did seem to be having some trouble nailing down a wedding date." I laugh because it's so absurd to me now, but maybe my laughter means the threads of healing are starting to knit together.

Marshall laughs, too. "I bet you were."

"He blamed his work schedule. I was waiting for whatever was missing to finally reveal itself so we could work on it. I was still waiting when he died. Once Shayla arrived at the hospital, everything made sense, and I had my answer. I just don't understand why he would try so hard to preserve something that couldn't possibly come to fruition."

"You'd invested your time, but Rob was splitting his and probably hoping that his double life could continue in some capacity. Maybe he was in too deep by then and the issue of marrying a woman when he was already married to someone else might have been a problem for another day."

"Staying in a relationship that isn't checking every single box is not something I'll settle for ever again. It seems unfathomable to me now."

"That's because despite how traumatic this experience was, you learned from it. It's one of the gifts we're left with when something doesn't work out. The next guy will know how strong you are and that you won't stand for any unchecked boxes."

"Is that what happened with you and Holly? You said you'd been together for six years." See? I remember things too, Marshall.

"No," he says evenly and without elaboration.

"You said she left because you weren't the same fun guy she was used to. Did that mean everything else was okay?" I've divulged plenty of painful and humiliating details about my relationship with Rob, but what prevented them from taking their walk down the aisle? It doesn't sound like Holly had a secret family or some other skeleton in her closet, but six years is a long time to date. Maybe Holly was waiting for Marshall to put a ring on *her* finger.

"Everything was fine," he says, and he doesn't sound despondent or like there's anything significant to divulge. Maybe Holly truly did get tired of waiting for Marshall to snap out of his grief, which doesn't paint *her* in the best light either. But whatever it was, he's not saying and I'm trying not to roll the baggage of mistrust that Rob left me with into every conversation I have. I've poured my heart out. I've bawled my eyes out. But I can't demand that Marshall spill every juicy aspect of his relationship with Holly, good or bad, and maybe they simply grew apart. Sometimes I forget that relationships can come to an end with a finite thud versus a shrapnel-spraying explosion.

"Should we turn around and head back?" Marshall asks. The moon has risen but the trees are blocking most of the light and it's becoming difficult to see the path under our feet.

"We probably should," I say. "It's all fun and games until someone sprains an ankle." We walk back the way we came, and when we pass the bride and groom's campsite, the music is off, the revelers have dispersed, and the happy couple is nowhere to be found. They've probably gone inside to get started on the honeymoon. Who can blame them?

We're almost back at the lodge when I skid on some loose rocks. Marshall grabs for my hand to steady me, and without thinking, I lace my fingers with his and hold on tight. It's Tumalo State Park all over again, and a warm feeling blooms inside of me.

Except that maybe it isn't Tumalo State Park all over again, because now I'm not sure if Marshall wants to hold my hand or if he was just making sure I didn't fall. There's no need for him to keep holding it because the path is now ablaze from the lights of the lodge, which is just up ahead, and we can see fine. And he's not really holding my hand; it's more that our fingers are awkwardly half laced, as if I'm the one holding Marshall's hand and he's letting me but not actively participating. Mortified, I casually withdraw my hand.

Once we're back in the room, my embarrassment builds and all I want is to burrow under the covers of my bunk bed and act like the whole thing never happened. Thankfully, it's late enough by then that we take turns in the bathroom, say our good-nights, and retire to our private spaces.

Chapter Seventeen

I wake up around three in the morning and can't get back to sleep. It's not because the bunk bed is uncomfortable—it's fine. But everything that happened yesterday, from spilling my guts on the balcony to my misjudgment over the hand-holding thing, is still swirling around, and it appears my brain would like to stew over it a little more.

Maybe Marshall didn't want to hold my hand because he isn't thinking about me romantically. It's possible the hand-holding at Tumalo was purely chivalrous, and that's fine.

That is all very fine.

But it's confusing, too. My ability to interpret a man's signals may be a bit compromised these days, but my friendship with Marshall is growing and expanding, and we're standing on the precipice of whatever comes next. I can feel it and thought he could, too.

But Marshall didn't take the plunge, so I don't know what would have happened.

Unfortunately, not only am I wide awake, but now I have to pee. I pad softly toward the bathroom, pausing in front of Marshall's closed bedroom door on the way. He has been patient. He's been caring and supportive. But instead of making a rush toward the end zone, he stayed firmly in the *friend* zone.

I continue on my way to the bathroom, and when I crawl back into my bunk bed, I'm more awake than ever. What would a fling with Marshall even look like? I consider how strange it would feel to open myself up to another man. To trust him. To believe him when he tells me what he's thinking.

Can I do it again?

Do I want to?

Also, the timing is all wrong.

Isn't it?

I manage to fall back to sleep until six thirty and then get up to make the coffee. Marshall's bedroom door is still closed. I take my cup back to my bedroom, plug in my laptop, and work for a couple of hours, stopping only when Steph FaceTimes me.

"Good morning," I say. "Should I stop sending the detailed text updates if you're just going to FaceTime me anyway?" I'd finally broken down and admitted to Steph that Marshall and I were sharing a room, and then bound her to secrecy. Please do not inform the friend group or my mother, I'd typed, issuing a stern warning that included several angry emojis to show that I meant business.

She squints. "Is that a twin bed?"

"Even better. It's a twin *bunk* bed."

"So, is it weird?" she asks.

"It's actually pretty comfortable."

"Is it weird sharing accommodations with *Marshall*?"

"Oh. No, it's fine. This began as the weirdest road trip ever, but now we're like seasoned travel companions with a side of awkward sexual tension that is mostly occurring in my head. But he's really easy to talk to. So easy that I told him all about Rob."

Her eyes widen and she holds up a finger. "Put a pin in the sexual tension thing. We'll come back to that in a minute. But first, you told him about the secret family stuff?"

"Every last sordid detail," I say, explaining about the bill collector and how Marshall was standing there when the call came in.

"And?"

"If his clients find him half as helpful as I did, then he's really good at what he does. He helped me make sense of things in a way I hadn't been able to. It was cathartic and emotionally exhausting, but it cleared out a lot of the psychological junk I've been hauling around up here," I say, pointing to my temple.

"I'm so glad you finally talked to someone. That couldn't have been easy for you."

"It wasn't as hard as I thought it would be. Once I got started, I felt like I could have talked for days."

"You're obviously very comfortable with him," Steph says. "Now let's get back to the sexual tension part. Does this mean you're open to Marshall becoming more than a travel companion?"

"Maybe? This is where the awkwardness comes in because I have no idea if he feels the same way." I tell her about my hand-holding gaffe and that maybe I simply misread Marshall's chivalry at Tumalo. "Plus, his brother recently passed away and he told me that he and his girlfriend of six years broke up because he couldn't snap out of his grief, and she left. We've both suffered significant losses and probably don't have the greatest headspace for starting something new. It's quite messy."

"What happened to his brother?"

"I don't know. He hasn't offered much in the way of details, and I haven't asked." I hated when people I wasn't close to asked me that question after Rob died. Nothing about their morbid curiosity consoled me, and it often made me feel worse. "I'd be lying if I said I wasn't curious about what happened to his brother because I am. I'm curious about his ex-girlfriend, too. And he's on vacation this week, but his sister called the other night, and it seemed like his being out of town was something he hadn't shared with his family. She was really grilling him."

"But you *like* him," Steph says. "You like him in a way that's allowing you to open yourself up to the possibility of taking this up a notch. That's what I'm hearing."

"I like him. I thought he might be interested in me romantically, but now I don't know. But he's a great guy, and I might be open to it."

It's only after the words come out of my mouth that I take a few seconds to think about what I just said. Marshall *is* a great guy, and I visualize what "taking this up a notch" might look like. And it mostly looks like Marshall and me making out like a couple of horny teenagers, and I don't hate it. Falling into temporary lust with Marshall might be exactly what I need.

Steph's expression is hopeful. "That's wonderful."

"Don't get too excited. It's complicated."

"Complicated is very on-brand for you, Wren."

"Not by choice."

"It doesn't have to be a big deal. If I know you—and I do— you're probably overthinking it. So maybe just don't, okay? Let it unfold. See what happens. Seize the day."

"I've gotta go," I say. "I have work to finish, and we'll probably head out to look for a cache after we finish breakfast. Make sure my mom knows that I'm safe despite all the detailed texts I send to both of you. I don't want her to worry."

"Who do you think prompted this call? Try and have some fun, okay? You deserve it."

"Will do. Talk soon."

Fun has been in short supply lately, and this time, Steph and I are totally on the same page. I deserve to have some fun and if I'm lucky, maybe Marshall will help me find some.

Chapter Eighteen

I work for fifteen more minutes and then shut down my laptop to get started on breakfast; Marshall's not the only one who makes a mean omelet. After a quick pit stop in the bathroom to brush my teeth, I put on a bra and head to the kitchenette. The omelets turn out perfectly and there's toast and bacon and a fresh pot of coffee. I lay it all out on the small table and tap lightly on Marshall's door. "I made breakfast," I say.

"Be out in a minute," he says.

His door opens and then I hear the water running in the bathroom. "Wow," he says, joining me in the kitchen a few minutes later. "Look at this spread."

We're both sporting bedhead and Marshall isn't clean-shaven, but it feels comfortable and like we've been doing it for years. The awkwardness I felt the night before has dissipated and is not worth dwelling over. So I misread the signals and thought we were going to hold hands. Big deal.

He must be as hungry as I am, because neither of us says anything for a few minutes. Then Marshall spreads jam on his toast and holds the jar out to me. "Thanks," I say, spreading a layer on mine.

He takes another bite of his omelet. "Okay, your omelets are even better than mine," he says, getting up to help himself to more bacon, placing another slice on my plate, too. "Have you been outside?" he asks.

"Not yet."

After we've eaten our fill, Marshall refills our coffee cups. "Breakfast was great, Wren. Thanks. Grab your coat. I want to show you something." We pull on coats and shoes, and Marshall opens the door to the balcony. The sight of the sprawling forest and all those tall green trees shrouded in fog takes my breath away. It looks like something out of a fairy tale, beautiful but foreboding, as if supernatural creatures lie in wait, obscured by the mist.

"Wow," I say.

"Amazing, isn't it?" Marshall says.

"We need a picture," I say. I dash back inside for my phone, and when I come back out, Marshall joins me in front of the balcony's railing, the fairy-tale forest behind us. I hand him my phone and he holds one arm out in front of us and slides the other around my lower back instead of resting it lightly on my shoulders. His hand is under my coat and his fingers curve so that they're encircling my waist; I can feel the weight of his fingertips through the thin fabric of my T-shirt. I slide my arm around him, and the cracks in my armor widen. Marshall takes the photo and hands the phone back to me, so I can text it to him.

"There's a cache high up on Oak Ridge Trail about thirty minutes from here," he says. "Looks like the trail has a pretty good incline. Feel like getting some exercise?"

"Absolutely." I need something to shake off the shackles of Rob's ghost. Thanks to the bill collector's call, it sidled right up next to me and inserted itself into *my* quest. If I work up a sweat, maybe I can purge it. "Do you want to have some fun?" I ask, remembering what Steph and I discussed during our FaceTime call this morning. My cheeks flush with warmth as I get another visual of Marshall and me kissing.

To his credit, he does not do anything off-putting or juvenile like wiggling his eyebrows or saying, "I can think of a few ways for the two of us to have some fun." Instead, he looks at me and says, "Sure," which takes a bit of the wind from my sails. I could have been asking him if he would share an order of taquitos with me again. Maybe he's truly *not* interested in my end zone and friends are all we're ever going to be. Steph will be bummed, but she'll get over it. Besides, you can never have too many friends, right?

"Good," I say. "Fun has been completely absent in my world lately. I can't remember the last time I cut loose."

"I'm not sure I can either," he says. "Let's go find some."

Chapter Nineteen

There's a small parking lot at the base of the trailhead, but it's empty save for a handful of cars. The fog has burned off and it's almost sunny; the high will reach into the mid-fifties. We've dressed in layers and are both wearing waist packs containing water and a few essentials. I swap out my glasses for my polarized sunglasses and retie my hiking boots.

"Difficulty level of five," I say. "Very challenging."

"Guess we'll find out," Marshall says, locking up the Jeep once we've readied our gear and ourselves.

"Care to make it more interesting?" It comes out flirtier than I intended, the result of my competitive nature rather than my awakening libido, but I don't walk it back.

He takes off his sunglasses and studies me; his expression has *layers*. Contemplation. Curiosity. And unless I'm reading him incorrectly—which is a distinct possibility—I see desire. Oh, how I'd love to get inside his head and do some poking around of my own. What is this man thinking?

"Definitely," he says. It's also pretty flirty, but he doesn't walk it back either. "What do you have in mind?"

"Just a friendly competition to see who finds the cache first."

"What's the prize?"

"I'll let you know when I win. Think you can keep up?"

He laughs. "Honey, I can do more than just keep up."

I falter. "Honey" is my all-time favorite term of endearment, because it can be sweet or sexy, depending on a man's delivery (and in Marshall's case, it's both). Rob preferred "babe," which honestly never did much in the revving-my-engine department. It made him sound like a frat boy.

I get ahold of myself and sprint off in the direction of the trail. Marshall laughs like *aren't you cute* and takes off after me.

It's on.

The trail *does* have quite an incline, which gets my heart pumping right out of the gate. And despite my shit-talking, Marshall catches up with me far too quickly. Then he leaves me in the dust. His legs are longer, and I've already made a rookie mistake: I can't maintain this pace or attempt to match his.

He stops and pretends like he's studying his Garmin until I catch up with him. "Okay, slight modification," I say. "The competition will not begin until we're within range of the cache. I will definitely puke if I try to beat you during the hiking portion, and I've already done that once in front of you. I think that's plenty."

"Deal," he says, and we resume the climb. Parts of the trail are quite steep and covered with loose rock, which slows us down in spots. We walk through shaded areas where the dense tree cover blocks out the sky, and other sections that are open, giving us a breathtaking view of the valley below and Mount Hood in the distance.

There are several switchbacks, the trail zigzagging from one direction to the other, and after a particularly grueling traverse, we stop to drink some water. I could stay here for days and probably not get tired of the scenery—the lush greens of the forest and the snow-white mountaintop. I can only imagine what it looks like in the spring when the wildflowers are in bloom. "It's so beautiful here," I say. "I'll always have a soft spot for my home state, but it doesn't hold a candle to what I've experienced since arriving here."

"Good reminder for me not to take it for granted," Marshall says.

"Did you and Holly do a lot of hiking?"

"Yes," he says.

"You've probably been lonely without her and your brother."

"Yes," he says again. I wait for him to open up about Graham and share a few details about what happened and how he's coping, the way I have. Instead, he pulls out his Garmin and studies it. "Ready to continue?" he asks.

My muscles are aching and I'm sweating, but the exertion is manageable and feels good. The shackles of Rob's ghost have already loosened. "Yep."

The trail ends in a T intersection. "If we take a right and walk for another mile, there's a great view of the mountain, or we can turn around," Marshall says. We've already decided to look for the cache on the way back down, since it requires going off-trail a bit. Everything on the way up is purely for sightseeing and exercise. "You up for it?"

"Sure."

I'm so glad we kept going, because when we pop out of the forest again, the view of Mount Hood—all of it, not just the glimpses we've seen on the way up—leaves me speechless. I stare in rapt wonder at this incredible sight.

Standing here with nothing but the blue sky above, I feel like the bird I was named after. My mother chose the name Wren because she thought it was beautiful but also because the wren is a harbinger of spring and rebirth.

I am being reborn.

I am beginning to soar.

I sit down right there on the hard ground, my legs stretched out in front of me, the chill seeping through my hiking leggings. Marshall sits and stretches his legs out next to me. I want to stare at this mountain and commit these optimistic feelings to memory. This quest *was* the right thing for me to do, and I'm the only one who needs to believe that.

"I wanted to hold your hand last night," Marshall says, and I look over at him, stunned. If someone had offered me a million dollars to predict what he was going to say, those words wouldn't have even made the cut.

"Then why didn't you?" I ask.

"You've been through a lot, and I didn't want you to think I was taking advantage of your vulnerability after everything you told me yesterday. I don't know what *you* want, Wren. I didn't know how you'd feel about it."

I look at the mountain again, thinking about what I want to say, and then I look at Marshall. "I wish you had been the one pumping gas next to me instead of Rob," I say. *There. That's how I feel about it.*

He looks into my eyes, comprehending the meaning of my words, and says, "So do I."

Chapter Twenty

We head down via the same route we took up, our declarations still ringing in my ears. *What does it mean?* I want to shout—at the sky, at Marshall.

At myself.

His words are like hot honey coursing through my veins—it's agonizing but in the best possible way. We've set the issue aside for now, but the pin our words have pulled might as well have been from a sexual grenade, and eventually we're going to feel the boom.

A mile from the bottom we veer to the right and enter a densely forested area. We're off-trail now, making our way through the underbrush and tree branches. Our GPS points us uphill again, which is much harder when there's no trail and no switchback to make the incline more gradual. I haven't reminded Marshall about our competition, but I can tell he hasn't forgotten by the way he's studying his Garmin and picking up the pace. Then we come to a section that is straight up. We're close to the cache now, but the only way to get there is by climbing vertically using the base of the tree trunks as handholds to heave us up. Marshall pulls ahead, but I give it some extra gas until I'm literally on his heels. Then I scramble onto his back like a toddler hitching a piggyback ride and am actively trying to catapult myself over his shoulders.

"Are you seriously trying to climb me?" Marshall asks, laughing and reaching his arm behind to wrestle me off his back like I'm a fly he's trying to swat.

"I was just trying to see over you," I say, sliding down Marshall's back until my feet make contact with the earth.

"Uh-huh. Sure," he says.

We finally make it to more level ground. The cache is supposed to be right here. I nearly collide with Marshall because there's only so much ground available, and he *definitely* hasn't forgotten about the challenge I proposed.

Seriously, game night with Marshall on my team would be *amazing*.

The cache is nowhere to be found, and we may have to dig for it again. I lean up against a tree and take a quick drink from my water bottle. It's not an ideal time to take a break if I hope to find the cache before Marshall does, but I'm seriously parched.

"Where the hell is it," Marshall finally says, sounding every bit as frustrated as I am.

"Maybe someone moved it," I say while searching the ground for a sign that it's been disturbed in some way. Once I spot something that looks out of the ordinary, I'll pounce and start digging.

Marshall takes a few steps in my direction, and I worry that he's doing exactly what I'm doing and has spotted a disturbance on the ground. But then he comes right up to me, so close our chests are nearly touching. My heartbeat quickens. We've never been this close face-to-face and I can hear both of us breathing. Then he flicks his eyes upward. "Don't move," he says.

I freeze.

He's pressed against me closer now, our bodies touching, the fabric of our jackets making a swishing sound as he shifts, reaching up. Then Marshall lowers his arm, and in his hand is a rope. The cache is up in the tree I'm leaning against.

It's retrievable by a pulley system. Marshall leans in closer still, and the smoldering look he gives me turns into a satisfied smirk as he takes a few steps back and lets the rope out slowly. The canister comes into view, dangling between us. "Looks like I won," he says. "I guess that means I get to choose my prize."

"I guess it does," I say, and the husky sound of surrender in my voice gives the words a certain *tone.*

He smiles. "Go ahead. You can open it."

I unscrew the lid of the canister and withdraw the log. Marshall takes a pen out of his pack and hands it to me. I scrawl my user-name and he does the same. After he puts the pen away, he takes a few steps toward me and uses the pulley to put the canister back in place for the next person. As it rises, Marshall comes closer, until we're right back where we started, chests touching. "Ready to pay up?" he asks, and now it's *his* words that carry a certain tone.

"Depends on the price," I say, knowing full well that the price doesn't matter because I've already decided to pay it.

"It won't cost you a thing."

For once, I don't care that I lost. Instead, I tremble in anticipation because I know what he's about to do, and I want him to do it. Rob might have died, but he also did an awful thing to me and I'm still very much alive, free to make my own choices without justifying them to anyone simply because it feels good. I can take all the time I want admiring the sprinkles of gray in Marshall's messy hair and the crinkles around his eyes when he smiles at me. I can notice his hands, big and strong, and imagine slipping my palm into his and feeling a comforting squeeze. Kissing Marshall will feel like diving headfirst off a cliff, but instead of crashing, it will be like landing in one of those soft, foam-filled pits they have at indoor trampoline parks—all of the thrills with none of the painful impact of hitting the ground at a high velocity. I bet kissing Marshall will feel like floating on a cloud, but even if it doesn't, it'll feel a hell of a lot better than anything has since the day Rob died.

This time, when Marshall raises his arm, he lets go of the rope and slides his hand behind my head, cradling it in his palm to pull me toward him. He bends down and his lips graze mine before pulling back a few inches in the most tantalizing tease. My arms move of their own volition, encircling his waist and pulling him closer as I wait for his mouth to make contact with mine again. Maybe the real price I'm paying is being driven crazy with need, because he has not kissed me fully, not yet. But he's cracked the code, because any man who comes on too strong sends me running. The ones who tease me and don't make their move right away are my weakness.

Again, his lips graze mine, but then he kisses his way down my neck and scrapes the tender skin with his teeth. I am going to burst into flames and the forest fire I start will be all my fault. We're both breathing heavier, but it has nothing to do with the hike. I can smell his skin, a mixture of exertion, soap, and the outdoors, and it's the most intoxicating combination of scents I've smelled in quite some time. I let out a barely audible whimper, but he hears it and drags his mouth from my neck up to right below my jaw.

So close.

Come on.

Now.

I pull his face toward me, aching for our first deep kiss, and then his mouth claims mine in such a brutally possessive way that I cry out, not in pain but because my sheer need has finally been met. His, too, I think. We've both turned instinctively to the right and my mouth fits his in a way it never did with Rob.

My rusty libido roars back to life.

My libido thinks making out with a man I met less than one short week ago is a *great* idea.

Marshall nudges me backward until my back is firmly pressed

against the tree. He reaches down, puts his hands under my butt, and lifts me, sandwiching my body between his and the tree. "Wow, we're just going for it right here, aren't we?" I say, laughing and wrapping my legs around his waist. Marshall captures my laugh with his mouth, and I can tell by the way his lips move against mine that he's laughing, too.

"We're outdoorsy people," he murmurs before sucking gently on my neck. "But if you'd rather wait for someplace less . . . rustic, I promise I can control myself."

"You might be able to, but I don't think *I* can," I say, and he lets out a low guttural sound that cuts off abruptly because his mouth is on mine again.

Now the forest truly is on fire.

Time ceases to exist, because Marshall has joined me, diving headfirst off the same cliff I did and landing in the foam-filled pit where anything goes as long as it feels good. His hands roam freely—up the sides of my rib cage and down the front of my chest, his thumbs skimming my nipples. Breaking the kiss so that my mouth is free to work on Marshall's neck, I begin just below his ear and make my way down his throat, sucking and scraping my teeth against his skin the way he did to me, which elicits another moan.

Marshall slips a hand under the front of my sports bra. His fingertips are hot, probing, setting my nipples ablaze and blurring the line between pleasure and pain. It feels wonderful, but it would feel even better if they were in his mouth. Then he slips a hand inside the front of my pants and strokes me. I don't even entertain the thought of stopping him. It feels too good, and I've passed the point of no return, so I close my eyes and go along for the ride, gasping and crying out when I come.

I want more.

I want him to tear off my clothes.

I want to tear off *his*.

I want to know the sounds he makes when he's right on the edge and I want to be the one who sends him over it.

"Didn't think to throw a condom in with my hiking gear," he says, because it's clear that we've reached a fork in the road and a decision must be made.

"Neither did I. It wasn't that kind of quest."

Also, we might be outdoorsy, but even if one of us had a condom, I draw the line at getting naked on the ground where any number of creepy crawlies might join the party. Instead, we go back to slow, lazy kisses, and our breathing slows.

"I just have one question, Wren," he says, his breath vibrating against my ear, sending shivers across my body. "Are you having fun?"

"Words cannot express how much fun I'm having," I say. "But you didn't get to have quite as much fun as I did." I've yet to touch him the way he touched me, and I intend to remedy this as soon as I'm able.

"Trust me, I had plenty of fun," he says.

I adjust my clothing and we make our way back down the trail. Marshall catches my hand in his once we reach the parking lot and squeezes it. This time, no one lets go. "I forgot to get a picture with the cache," I say.

"We can take one now," Marshall says.

I pull out my phone and we get into position. "Would you like us to take your picture?" a woman says. She's standing next to a man and they're beaming at us.

"That would be great. Thank you," I say, and hand her my phone.

Marshall slides his arm around my waist, and I do the same to him. But this time, I turn toward him and lay my opposite hand on the front of his jacket.

The woman hands me my phone and we thank her one last time. I open the image and stare at the picture. I'm looking straight at the camera, but Marshall is looking at me. His tender expression takes my breath away.

"What's wrong?" he asks. "Are someone's eyes closed?"

"Nope. It's perfect." I click a few buttons. "Sent it to you."

Marshall tucks me into the passenger seat, and we head back. As good as this feels, I falter when I think about the temporary nature of what we're doing. This might scratch an itch, but it's a fling, not a future. I'm flying home in a few days, back to my messy life in Ohio.

And okay, maybe I *was* fleeing.

But I could argue that I'm now more equipped to handle what I left in the rearview, thanks to Marshall. Until I get on that plane, I'm free to daydream all I want, to imagine an alternate universe where time stands still, and Marshall and I spend every second doing only what feels best to both of us, no holds barred. Scratch that itch until it's out of our systems but good.

Marshall looks over at me and smiles. "You got quiet. Where'd you go?"

"A place that makes me happy. You were there too."

Chapter Twenty-one

Marshall wakes me with a brush of his lips, startling me. "How long have I been asleep?" I ask.

"About twenty minutes. I looked over and your eyes were closed. You must be worn out," he says.

"I guess so. But I feel good now."

"Want to join me in the shower?" he asks once we've reached the sanctuary of our room.

"It's like you read my mind," I say, already untying my shoes and shucking my jacket.

"Please let me take off the rest," he says with a grin, looking at me like I'm a present he desperately wants to unwrap.

I laugh. "Have at it."

Boy, does he.

Peeling me slowly out of my clothes, he gets out of his in record time and joins me under the spray. There is a visual component that was missing in the woods, and finally, our eyes can roam, taking in every inch of each other, followed by our hands. Marshall's body is incredible, chiseled in all the right places. As we soap each other's skin, our hands exploring shamelessly, Marshall inhales sharply when I kiss him and stroke him at the same time, which pleases me to no end. I want him to feel every bit as good as he made me feel. I don't stop kissing and stroking until he cries out, pulsing in my hand, and then it's my turn again. It's only through sheer will and frequent breaks that we complete the actual purpose of the shower. When we get out, we dry each other off and Marshall takes me by the hand and leads me to his bedroom.

Our bodies are intertwined, and the kisses are hot, so hot, hotter than they ever were with Rob. I could kiss Marshall for days and not get tired of it. Then he flips me onto my back and leaves a trail of kisses down my body, not stopping until he's buried his face between my legs. His mouth and tongue bring me to the edge several times and it's only when I gasp "Marshall, please" that he stops teasing and brings me all the way there. I'm transported to a place where the past doesn't exist. It's blissful and it takes me several minutes to come back down to earth and catch my breath. I look over at Marshall, now stretched out beside me, one leg over my body, eyes closed, smiling. Overwhelmed by my desire for him, I say, "I want you to come in my mouth," mere seconds before closing it around the length of him. With his hands twisting strands of my hair, and with light moaning that builds and rises in volume and tempo, he complies.

Finally spent, we lie in each other's arms. "When's the last time we ate?" he asks.

"Breakfast," I say.

He pulls on a pair of sweats and tosses one of his T-shirts to me. In the kitchen, we put together a spread of sliced apples, cheese and crackers, and chocolate chip cookies, then sit down at the table, and eat ravenously.

"My quest seems to have taken an unexpected detour," I say with a laugh.

"How're you feeling about that?" he asks, looking as if he's searching for signs of regret.

"I came to the conclusion when we were in Bend that there are no rules," I say. "Just whatever makes me happy. Whatever makes *us* happy. I'm so tired of being sad."

"Me too," he says. Sometimes I forget that Marshall is also grieving. Maybe because he doesn't talk much about his brother and hasn't spilled his guts on a balcony yet the way I have. The guardedness I initially recognized on his face runs a lot deeper than just his expression. The NO TRESPASSING signs are clearly posted, warning everyone to stay away from his head.

And maybe his heart.

"What about after you get home?" he asks, his voice neutral, giving nothing away about what he's thinking about it.

"I don't know yet," I say. Letting Marshall into my head was a big step for me; giving him access to my body is on a different level entirely. Both are important for different reasons, mainly because in the days after Rob died, I couldn't fathom acquiescing to either. Sex isn't going to heal us, because relationships don't work that way, or at least mine don't. I'm not done recovering from the wounds Rob left me with, and I have no clue what a relationship with Marshall would even look like. I live in Ohio, he lives here. "This is a fling, right?"

"It's whatever you want it to be, Wren." That's true, it is. I get to decide. There are worse ways to get your groove back, and falling into a man's bed, especially a man like Marshall, is working out pretty well so far. He makes me feel safe. He makes me feel heard.

After we clean up from dinner, we spend the next few hours cuddled up on the couch watching TV, stopping often to kiss. It feels calming in a way that nothing has for a long time. At bedtime, Marshall leads me back into his bedroom. "The bunk bed sucks, doesn't it?" he says.

"It's actually pretty comfortable," I say, slipping under the covers. "But this is much better."

After another round of kissing and touching that leaves us spent, the exertion of the day catches up with both of us. Marshall nudges me onto my side, my back to his front so he can spoon me. He slips his hand under my jaw and gently turns my head back toward him, dropping a kiss on my mouth. "Night, Wren."

"Good night," I say, barely getting the word out before falling asleep.

Marshall's arms are still around me when I wake up the next morning. Maybe he senses that I'm awake, because I feel him stir. "I have an idea," he says. "What if we spend your last two days at my house?"

"You're not tired of me yet?" I ask, my voice rough from sleep.

"No," he says. "I'm definitely not tired of you." He pulls my body against his a little tighter, nuzzling the side of my neck with his lips.

"That feels so good and I don't want you to stop, but I have to pee super bad," I say.

He laughs and I do, too, and then I throw off the covers and take off for the bathroom in a naked sprint.

"So, is that a yes or a no about going back to my house?" he asks.

"It's a yes," I yell over my shoulder. I like the way Marshall thinks, and I like that there are no rules.

Just whatever makes us happy.

Chapter Twenty-two

Marshall pulls in to a parking lot and parks his Jeep in the spot marked with the number eleven. I can see flashes of blue, and it takes me a second to process that he lives on a lake in a waterfront condo.

We come in through the kitchen and set our things down. The condo isn't overly large, but it's an open plan and beyond the kitchen is a living space facing south with an amazing amount of natural light coming in from the wall of windows. Through them, I have a dazzling view of the lake and the deck with a row of boat slips. The one right outside his unit contains a blue and gray boat that says MASTERCRAFT on the side. "Is that your boat?" I ask.

"Yep. It's the reason I bought the place." He opens the sliding glass door, and we step onto the deck that runs alongside the building.

"Wow. Talk about easy access," I say.

"I'll take you for a ride later," he says, grabbing my hand and pulling me back inside for the rest of the tour. There's a small bedroom that's set up as a den, a half bath off the hallway that I stop to use, and then Marshall's bedroom. It has a king-sized bed flanked by two nightstands; a dresser faces the bed against the opposite wall, and a large TV is mounted above it.

"I like your place," I say.

"Thanks. I like it too. Are you hungry?" he asks.

"Nope." We snacked most of the way here on our leftover provisions. I'll be full for at least a couple of hours.

"Good," he says, and he leans down and kisses me, hard. It feels empowering to be desired by him, and I realize that I am, in fact, quite hungry. Starving even. But not for food. Everything we've done so far was merely the appetizer and I am more than ready for the main course. Marshall strikes me as the kind of man who truly worships a woman's body, and there's no holding us back this time.

I inhale that intoxicating Marshall smell, and his mouth tastes like the apple we shared, passing it back and forth between us as we rolled into town.

He walks me backward toward the bed and we tumble onto it. His hands are in my hair, and I feel him slide the hair tie from my ponytail, freeing it. There are so many kisses. Between them, he reaches for the hem of my shirt and eases it slowly up and over my head. My bra soon joins my shirt wherever Marshall tossed it. After a few admiring glances, his fingers and then his tongue tease my nipples, and I ride the line between pleasure and pain; it's almost too much for me to handle, yet I don't want him to stop.

The depth of how touch-starved I still am reveals itself with each kiss, each stroke of Marshall's hands and mouth on my body. The support of friends and family only goes so far, and this physical manifestation of mattering to someone, at least at this moment, feels wonderfully soothing. My inhibitions dissolve completely.

"I've wanted you since the very beginning," he whispers, and the words and the vibration of them against my ear send electric sensations throughout my body. It's as if he is single-handedly re-filling a well that went bone-dry months ago.

He slips his fingers into the waistband of my pants. His breath-ing has grown heavier, and he strips me of them quickly. I expect him to do the same with my underwear, but he doesn't. He slows everything down, rubbing his fingertips over every place the cotton fabric covers, which drives me so crazy I almost whip them off myself.

Just when I think I can't take it anymore, he speeds back up and strips me the rest of the way so that I am fully naked. Marshall quickly brings me to an embarrassingly vocal orgasm with a com-bination of his fingers and his mouth.

Once my trembling subsides, I want nothing more than to ravish his body, and I start by pulling his T-shirt over his head and tossing it on the floor. My hands slide from his shoulders down the length of both arms and back up again before moving to his chest. I stop to kiss him, and I press my chest against his so that we're skin-to-skin. I pop the button on his jeans and slowly lower the zipper. Looking into his eyes, I can see his desire like a blinking neon sign, his gaze never leaving my face or my body. Together, we get him out of his remaining clothes, and then we're skin-to-skin again, the entire length of our bodies pressed as close as we can get them. I'm torn between touching him and begging him to enter me because everything below my belly button is pulsing and engorged. But I can't resist running my hands and my fingertips across his skin, down the length of his arms, and back up again. I tease him the way he teased me, and then I'm not so gentle, closing my hand around the length of him. He groans and pulls away so suddenly I almost ask if something is wrong. But then he stretches his arm toward his nightstand to grab a condom, and I understand that nothing is wrong and everything is right.

He enters me slowly, and just like the kissing, we are compatible in a way that Rob and I never were. There is no fumbling, only a perfectly in-sync readjustment of speed and depth as we climb, and there is something so freeing about accepting the pleasure he's offering simply because it feels so incredibly good. I cry out and I can feel Marshall barreling toward his orgasm when I start climbing again. It must be sheer torture for him, but he holds off until I reach the summit. Then I say, "Now," and he lets out a primal sound that I'll be thinking about for days.

Our skin is slick with sweat and even though Marshall is heavy, I wrap my arms around him tighter as we try to catch our breath. The weight of him soothes me, makes me feel as if I've been claimed in the best possible way. He shifts slightly, no doubt worried about crushing me, but our limbs remain tangled. "Wren," he says, placing a slow, deep kiss on my mouth. "You felt so good."

"So did you," I say. So it seems that Rob didn't break me after all, didn't take away my ability to trust again and to make decisions based only on what *I* want. I have shaken loose from the shackles of his betrayal, but not entirely—that will take a while longer. Healing isn't always a straightforward and linear process. But I'm not as naïve as Rob's actions led me to believe. Marshall said that Rob's deception was not a measure of my intelligence, and he was right. I never had a reason to second-guess my abilities, in any capacity, before I met Rob. The equilibrium between my heart and mind has been restored, and what a joy that is. Not only am I soaring, but I can see clear above the treetops and the view is mighty nice. I might even admit that it's breathtaking. Who would have thought? Certainly not me.

We cuddle for a while, Marshall nuzzling my neck with his lips, and then take a break for the bathroom and some water. Once we're back in bed, I stretch my limbs, pointing my toes and reaching my arms over my head. Marshall pulls me into his embrace, and I kiss him simply because I can. Then he kisses me, and everything he does next is achingly slow, as the parts of my body he's already explored are discovered once again.

What we're doing isn't happening in an empty sterile vacuum at all—I was wrong about that. Maybe it started that way, but it's morphing into a rapidly expanding ecosystem with condensation running in lazy, meandering rivulets down the sides of its walls. New shoots, green and lush, are unfurling, reaching upward toward the sunlight. The first blush of color has appeared on the petals of blooming flowers. It smells earthy and fertile, a beautiful breathing thing. I allow myself to see further into the future than I once dared, and it shocks me to realize that I might want Marshall to be part of it.

But I *was* right about Marshall being the type of man who worships a woman's body, and we never do go for that boat ride.

Chapter Twenty-three

Dawn brings a repeat of what we did last night and again around three this morning when we were half asleep. I've gotten it out of my system, and it appears that Marshall has, too, at least temporarily. Now we're lazing in bed after eating the breakfast he had delivered. "I don't even know what I've got in the fridge at this point," he said.

We've spent almost every moment together since we left the La Quinta in Eugene, and this 24/7 togetherness has been as effortless and comfortable as pulling on my favorite pair of sweats, at least for me. Snuggling closer to him, I throw a leg over his body and tuck my head under his chin. He kisses the top of my head and then twirls a piece of my hair in his fingers. Lying in his arms feels natural, and there's no place I'd rather be. We rouse ourselves from his very messy bed around noon to take a shower, and once we're dressed, we grab a quick lunch on the patio of a nearby restaurant. It's overcast but not raining, and the temperature is a mild fifty-eight.

"Let's go for a boat ride," Marshall says when we get back.

I clap my hands together in delight because I can't wait to get out on the lake. "Yes," I reply.

"It'll take a few minutes to get it ready," Marshall says, gathering some rags and other cleaning supplies. We go out to the deck and Marshall removes the tarp that covers the top third of the boat. He extends a hand and helps me step onto it. The boat has been protected from the elements, but there's a lot of dust and cobwebs in the corners. He uses a small broom to brush away the cobwebs; I grab a rag and start wiping. Even with two of us working together, it takes more than a few minutes to ready the boat, and the amount of cleaning we do tells me it hasn't been used in a while. Marshall said his brother died about five months ago, which would have been sometime in May. It makes me think that the boat has been tethered to the slip since then, unused. I picture the beginning of the summer boating season and Marshall having no desire to do something he enjoys so much that he bought a place on a lake. Maybe Holly wanted to go boating, but Marshall couldn't bring himself to care.

"Is this something you want to do?" I ask. "Take the boat out? We don't have to if you're just doing it for me."

"I want to. I haven't used it much other than starting it now and then so the fuel didn't go bad, and I've missed being on the water." Marshall has a smile on his face as he fires up the engine. It sputters a bit and sounds uneven as if there are cobwebs in there, too. But then the engine settles into a steady rhythm and Marshall turns on the stereo.

We pack a small cooler bag with water and a couple of beers. Some cheese and crackers and the last two apples. We're dressed in layers—sweatshirts over our T-shirts. The autumn air feels cool and crisp but still warm enough that we don't need anything heavier. The sun nudges out from behind the clouds, and the lake water sparkles.

I sit in the seat across from Marshall as he motors us away from the slip and out onto the lake past the no-wake zone. "I'm going to blow out some of this old gas," he says. "Hang on." He increases our speed until it feels like we're flying, our hair blowing back in the wind. As we hurtle by, I check out the lakefront houses that surround the water. They're beautiful, some of them wide and sprawling, and others that are built vertically, four stories high, all with entire walls of windows. There are lots of boats on the lake on this fine Sunday afternoon, and their owners wave when they pass us. We wave back.

Marshall is beaming.

After we make a full circuit around the lake, Marshall reduces his speed and brings us closer to the shore, giving me a much better view of the homes and the people sitting on their docks enjoying the beautiful day. "Do you want to drive?" he asks.

I laugh. "Me? I don't have a lot of experience. I'd hate to crash your boat."

He beckons me toward him with a wave of his hand, and now I understand what he means. I nestle myself between his legs and put my hands on the wheel. I can't do much damage this way. Marshall drapes his arms around me and kisses my neck. "Careful," I say. "You'll distract me from the task at hand." He laughs and nuzzles his mouth into my neck, sucking gently. "Make yourself useful and take our picture." He picks up my phone and snaps one.

The speed at which we're motoring through the water might be slow and leisurely, but our time together feels as if it's accelerating, an hourglass filled with sand, each grain signifying the minutes I have left here. They're emptying at a rate that feels breakneck, urgent. I wish I could stop them.

"Well, aren't you a sight for sore eyes," someone shouts. A man who looks to be in his mid-fifties is standing at the end of his dock, smiling. Marshall places his hands back on the wheel and we veer toward him and bump up against weathered wood; the man places a foot on the boat to steady us as Marshall throws him a line. He seems surprised to see Marshall and even more so that we stopped.

"Kent, this is Wren," Marshall says after cutting the engine.

Kent leans down into the boat to shake my hand. "Nice to meet you," I say.

"Likewise," he says.

Kent turns to Marshall. "It's been a while." His wide smile and the way he clasps Marshall's hand tell me that he could not be more delighted by our visit.

"Too long," Marshall admits. He helps me onto the dock and then reaches back into the boat for the cooler. "Where's your better half?" he asks Kent.

"She went shopping. Wasn't interested in day drinking with me on this fine October afternoon. Good thing you came along when you did." Kent is still smiling, but his face is full of unasked questions. His eyes flick back and forth between Marshall and me.

"I'm from out of town," I say. "Visiting from Ohio. Marshall and I ran into each other on the hiking trail, and he suggested that we team up."

"It wasn't quite that easy," Marshall says. "Took more than a little convincing before she'd have anything to do with me."

"Smart woman," Kent says. "I like her already."

Marshall opens the cooler and pulls out a couple of beers, and Kent says, "Put that away. This calls for whiskey."

He hurries up the dock toward the house as if he's afraid we'll bolt once he lets us out of his sight. "Friend you haven't seen in a while?" I ask.

"Yep. He's just about my favorite person on this lake. His wife, too."

Kent returns with a bottle of whiskey and three glasses. He pours a few fingers into each glass, and we sit down at the small bistro table at the end of the dock. "Cheers," Kent says, picking up one of the glasses. We pick up the others and clink our glasses with his.

"Been keeping yourselves busy?" Kent asks. My face flushes because we have been very busy, in bed, but that's not what he's asking. He's looking at both of us but seems more interested in Marshall's response, which introduces a creeping feeling of doubt about how well I know Marshall. There's an underlying vibration running through Kent's side of the conversation that has piqued my interest in a way it might not have before Rob.

"Been road-tripping with this beauty for almost a week now," Marshall says with a tilt of his head toward me.

Kent seems taken aback. "You've been off work? How'd you swing that?" I see concern mixed with trepidation in the grooves of Kent's forehead and the worried look in his eyes.

"I took a leave. Shuffled some appointments and found someone to pitch in."

A leave? As in a leave of absence? As in, something in his life had gone so completely sideways he needed to step away from his job. Losing Graham would be the obvious reason for it, but there is something Marshall hasn't told me, something significant. My heightened scrutiny is another parting gift from Rob, but I'm not mad about this one, not right now anyway.

"When? And for how long?" Kent prods. It's like I'm invisible.

"About a week ago, and I don't know yet." I met Marshall on that hiking trail late on a Monday morning six short days ago. Is that why he looked so guarded? Was that the first day he didn't go to work? Because not once did Marshall mention any of this. Have I just been one giant distraction? A way for him to avoid dealing with his issues? Maybe that's why Marshall's sister seemed so upset when she tracked him down in Bend. He might have taken a leave from work, but it seems like he went AWOL with his family and friends. No wonder Jillian was mad; no wonder Kent looks so confused.

"So you picked her up and then whisked her away for a week? You must have really turned on the charm." Kent's words carry a teasing undertone that seems forced. There's something he'd rather say about Marshall's presumably out-of-character behavior, but he doesn't want to say it in front of me. Maybe he thinks Marshall and I lost our minds and eloped or something.

"Nah, just a little geocaching. That's why Wren's in Oregon."

"Oh," Kent says, visibly relieved. "That's good. I'm glad you got out of the house." I can imagine the unspoken sentence that might have gone through his head. *And that you weren't doing something alarming or reckless that would only add to my worries.*

"So am I." Marshall takes a drink of his whiskey and gives me an affectionate look that divulges nothing about whatever demons he's been battling. I give him one of my own, but it's forced and mostly for Kent's benefit because I have questions.

So many questions.

"How long are you in town?" Kent asks me.

"Unfortunately, I leave tomorrow."

"Maybe you'll be back?" he says, and I can't tell if the yearning on Kent's face stems from his approval of me or his desire to see Marshall turning a corner in some way.

"Maybe I will," I say. But will I? I don't know. Marshall and I are still very much in the moment, and while I might have visualized him in my future, *our* future and what that might look like isn't something we've talked about yet. Right now, taking things one day at a time is about all the bandwidth I can spare.

The conversation shifts to more mundane topics, and an hour later, when the sun has started sinking lower on the horizon and the air has cooled, we say our goodbyes. Kent smiles at me. "I hope it's been a good week." His eyes search my face looking for clues, something to make sense of Marshall's actions, to further ease his concerns, whatever they might be.

Marshall pretends he's busy untying the boat, but I know he's listening. "It's been a great week," I say. I don't know Kent well enough to go into detail about my past and what happened with

Rob, and right now it isn't important. But I do smile, and I look him in the eyes. "I haven't known Marshall for very long, but he's helped me in many ways. I'll miss him. He's one of the good ones."

Isn't he?

Now Kent is smiling, too. "He is."

Marshall gives me his hand and I step back into the boat. He turns back to Kent, who pulls him in for a brief hug and a clap on the back. "Seeing you on the water, pretty girl by your side, makes me hopeful that things are better," Kent says. "Are they?" So, maybe he *doesn't* mind asking Marshall these things in front of me.

"I don't know," Marshall says. "Maybe."

He doesn't look at Kent when he says it.

We motor slowly back to Marshall's place. He glides the boat into the slip and cuts the engine. Questions swirl through my mind as I help him tarp the boat, and we go inside. "I liked Kent. He seemed concerned about you," I say.

"I've just never taken a lot of time off before. He knows it's hard for me to get away. I've been threatening to do it for years and I finally did." He sits down in the large, overstuffed chair in his living room and pulls me onto his lap. The setting sun fills the sky with pink and orange; the view from Marshall's living room windows would be the thing that sold me on this place if I had been the buyer. We kiss for a while and then come up for air. "What time is your flight tomorrow?" he asks.

"One o'clock."

"That's less than twenty-four hours," he says, and the longing in his eyes carries far more weight than his words.

When I first met Marshall, I suspected that he might also be going through something, but at the time, my hands were too full trying to get a handle on my own shit. But it's time that we wade into his. If we hadn't stopped at Kent's dock and I hadn't seen the concern on his face, maybe I wouldn't have to. I might have let it go. But we did stop at Kent's, so I open my mouth and let the words tumble out. "Can you tell me about your brother and what you've been going through since he died? I'd like to know what happened."

He doesn't answer, and instead, he kisses me again. And even though I know it's his way of distracting me from the shit that now feels like quicksand, I kiss him back. Then I pull away and wait patiently.

"Graham's death was devastating for me," he finally says. "For all of us."

"Of course it was," I say gently.

"I don't like talking about it." I can only imagine the number of times one of his clients has felt the same way while sitting in Marshall's office. Oh, the irony.

I remain silent, respecting and honoring his desire not to divulge what happened to Graham. I don't expect Marshall to lay bare his deepest darkest secrets, but I've shared more with him than he has with me, and the lack of reciprocity hits a raw and tender nerve flayed open by Rob's deceit.

"He died in a tragic accident," Marshall says. "There's nothing more to say."

My body tenses from the finality in his tone, and I know Marshall can feel it because his arms are around me. On some level, I knew that Graham's passing was out of the ordinary and that the repercussions had been significant enough to send Marshall's girlfriend out the door. And now I know that it necessitated a leave of absence months after the fact. I'd wondered if Graham had taken his own life or been fighting a long and painful illness with no hope of a cure. But now I'll never know, because Marshall has elected not to enlighten me.

I remember my conversation with Stephanie when I was trying to decide if it was safe to team up with Marshall. Asking Steph to loop in our sleuthiest friend, Lisa. *Friends, family, colleagues?* Steph had asked.

Just him, I'd said. If I'd told Steph to have Lisa cast a wider net, she might have stumbled across something online, and I would have known from the beginning. Would it have changed anything? I'm not sure, because the issue isn't really what happened to Graham; it's that Marshall doesn't want to talk to me about it. Unlike Holly, I would never rush him through the process or tell him to snap out of it. But maybe he wouldn't talk to her either, and it frustrated her so badly that she finally just up and left. Marshall's silence feels like being shut out and like he didn't keep his end of the bargain— except that we never had an agreement. But I did pour my heart out to him and the reciprocity I've been waiting for has never materialized.

I pull his head toward me and run my fingers through his hair. He seems soothed by it. Marshall has a lot to work through. Possibly more than me, and I've got plenty. But I get the sense that he's not working through it, that distraction *is* his preferred method for shoving it onto a back burner, to be dealt with only when he's forced to. The diversion we jumped into with both feet offered a welcome reprieve, but the real world beckons, and our bubble is about to burst.

Chapter Twenty-four

I wake up shortly before dawn the next morning, my night of fragmented sleep leaving me tired and sluggish. Based on the amount of tossing and turning from his side of the bed, Marshall didn't sleep well either. My phone is on the nightstand, and I unplug it from the charger and take it with me into the bathroom. I do my business, wash my hands, and then type "Graham Hendricks" into the search bar on my phone's browser. The first hit is an online newspaper article from *The Oregonian,* and I gasp so loudly I freeze, waiting to see if Marshall knocks on the door to ask if I'm all right. Hearing only silence, I read it again.

> *Three people are dead after a shooting Sunday night at a Texaco station in Lake Oswego. A police department spokesperson said the incident happened around 6:30 P.M. local time. A witness at the scene observed the shooter speaking to a female employee shortly before fatally shooting her and a customer who walked in as the incident was taking place.*

The shooter then took his own life and was pronounced dead at the scene. This appears to be an isolated domestic dispute, and no further investigation is necessary.

I know without further digging that Marshall was the witness and Graham was the customer, and I'm having trouble wrapping my head around the enormity of what he's experienced. *How are you even getting through the day?* I'm more certain than ever that he's getting through it by spending a week traveling around Oregon with a woman who just happened to have time to kill. I really can't blame him. But something is festering inside Marshall and despite his years of training and the advice and assistance he regularly provides for others, he can't liberate it himself.

And there's one more thing that feels significant. I met Rob at a gas station and Marshall and Graham met tragedy at another. These random encounters set us on paths different from the ones we'd been traveling and that ultimately converged on a hiking trail in Eugene, Oregon. It's something to think about.

When I slide back under the sheets, I curl my body around him and spoon him as tightly as I can. I wish I could tell him that he doesn't have to be the strong one all the time and that I am more than willing to offer the same comfort he's offered me. But I can't, because he won't let me. I understand why he doesn't want to open up—what happened to Graham is so much worse than I'd imagined. But Holly's attempts presumably failed long before mine did, and if six years together couldn't do it, a one-week fling certainly won't. In the silence, I can tell that he's awake by the sound of his breathing, and I hug him tighter. He takes my hand, brings it to his lips, and kisses it as if to say, *Thank you. This is exactly what I need right now.*

I try not to think about our collective sorrow, because those grains of sand in my imaginary hourglass have nearly run out. It hits me that I'm going home today to pick up where I left off, and it feels depressing, like the first day back to work after one of the best vacations you've ever had. I remind myself to stay in the moment, to savor the way he feels in my arms. We remain curled together for so long that I drift back to sleep.

An hour later, Marshall kisses me awake and removes the T-shirt I'm wearing. This is it, the final hours leading to the bittersweet end of my time in Oregon. I'm going to squeeze every last drop, because there won't be any more, not after I get on that plane.

It's different from the other times, slower, more sensual. The urgency is still there, but it's tempered, as if neither of us wants to finish because that means it really will be over. Marshall looks so deeply into my eyes that I almost turn away. What I see in them doesn't support a fling; it looks more like longing, as if he has seen those same glimpses of the future and my face is the one he's picturing, which makes the pain even worse. We could have made something long-lasting out of this, and I wonder if he can see the longing in *my* eyes. And if he can, what does he think about that?

And eventually, it is over. We lie in each other's arms, the sweat cooling on our skin. "I already miss you," he says.

"Me too," I say. But what I really mean is that I'll miss what this might have become. It's not fair to expect Marshall to lay himself bare to the woman he's known for such a short amount of time, but if I had seen one single weak spot in *his* armor, something I could widen, I would have capitalized on it. I want nothing more than to remain in this living, breathing ecosystem we created, even though I know it's gasping for air and has already begun to die.

But Marshall's armor is impenetrable, so I get out of bed because we've got just enough time to shower before we need to head for the airport.

The sand in the hourglass has run out. I'm going home.

Chapter Twenty-five

Marshall insists on parking the Jeep and walking me into the airport. As we walk, he reaches for my hand and holds it tight. My mood is as bleak as the rain that started to fall on the way to the airport. I can't speak for Marshall, but I've come back down to earth and landed with a depressing crash. Our real lives are waiting, and it's time for us to return to them. I can't heal Marshall any more than he can heal me from the lingering wounds of our losses, and we both have work to do.

Marshall remains silently by my side as I check in at the kiosk and then head toward security. The line isn't long, no need to rush. Gently, he takes me by the arm and moves us out of the flow of travelers. "I don't want this to be over, Wren," he says. "I don't think a long-distance relationship will be that hard. It will take work, but it's doable." It's as if he's been mentally rehearsing his sales pitch on the way here and he's ready to back it up with ideas and solutions.

Ordinarily, I would agree that a long-distance relationship isn't a deal-breaker, especially at our age. When it's right, you don't mind the sacrifices because you know the long-distance part is temporary and merely a stepping stone to one of you relocating. It would be so much easier to nod my head, tell him that a long-distance relationship could absolutely work, and tell him how on board I am. But if there's one thing I learned from my experience with Rob it's that I will never settle for unchecked boxes again. My ideal man, whoever he is, will be as transparent as freshly polished window glass. Hindsight revealed the mistakes I'd made with Rob, but foresight cautions me not to make them again. I swallow the lump in my throat and look into his eyes because if I don't say it now, I might not say it at all.

"I made a promise to myself that I would never enter into a relationship again if I felt that something was missing. It might seem like I'm overreacting, but you of all people should understand where I'm coming from." I can tell by his surprised expression that this is news to him and that he doesn't think anything *is* missing, so I keep going. "You were right when you said I'd made myself vulnerable on that balcony and that you were hesitant to do anything that might be construed as taking advantage of it, but I never felt that way. I opened up about everything because I felt comfortable with you and what you said helped me more than you'll ever know. You're really good at what you do. But for some reason, I don't think you can see the disparity between what I've shared and what you haven't. I'm not going to chase that. I'm not going to pry things out of you. Maybe a woman whose entire life wasn't turned upside down by a man who kept things from her would be able to. But not me. And I realize that laying yourself bare to a woman you've only known for a week might not be something *you're* able to do. I don't have the training and knowledge that you have, but that's not what this is about. It's about reciprocity. And this was supposed to be just a fling, right? A 'get back up on the horse' or the bike or whatever I seemed to have fallen off of. I got back on, and the world didn't end."

This trip marched me toward the life I wanted to create for myself, and it's been good in ways I never expected or dreamed it could be. And heartbreaking in a way I should have seen coming from a mile away. Maybe it's me. Maybe I'm the common denominator. Maybe I'm destined to repeat the same pattern, falling for men who will only share a fraction of themselves with me so they can save the rest for the soulmate they haven't found yet.

"Wren," he says, taking my hands in his. "I'm not hiding anything from you."

"But you haven't been vulnerable with me. You're not trusting that I can be there for you the way you were for me and that's the wound *you're* poking at. I know what happened to Graham. I looked it up online because I wanted to know, and you wouldn't talk to me about it."

His eyes blaze, not in anger but a swirl of emotions—shock, pain, and something else I can't decipher. "You also told me you were on vacation, but a leave of absence is a very different thing. Not a lie, exactly, but an omission of the truth. I can't have that with you. I can't have that with any man." Marshall is the one who told me the next guy would know how strong I was and that I wouldn't stand for any unchecked boxes.

But what he didn't take into account was that *he's* the next guy.

It's my Hail Mary. Tell me everything, Marshall. Give us a strong foundation to hold up the structure we started framing prematurely. Convince me that it's solid and that I can trust you.

Convince me that it doesn't have to be over.

Instead, he looks down at the floor and then away, and my heart sinks. It's the moment I realize that a fling is all this will ever be. Time for me to let go of the hope that Marshall will throw the door wide open and become the open book I'll never get tired of reading. Better to know now, though. Saves me a lot of tears later.

He finally looks at me and I muster a sad smile. "This has been a wonderful week for both of us, and sometimes a fling is exactly what the doctor ordered," I say. I take his hands in mine to soften the words and he lets me. "We were really good at that."

He remains stoic, but I can see the pain in his eyes, and I know without a doubt that this is not the outcome he was so sure was coming.

My quest was never about a destination; it was always about discovering who I am and what I want the rest of my life to look like. From that standpoint, I'd say I accomplished exactly what I set out to do.

So I'm getting on that plane.

He takes my face in his hands and kisses my forehead tenderly. "Fly back to me," he whispers, his mouth now pressed against my temple. "Or I'll come to you, and we can get some of that chili you think is so spectacular."

I smile through my tears. "It *really* is."

"One last picture?" he says.

"Sure." He holds my phone out in front of him like he has so many times before. When he hands it back to me, I send the picture to him and add it to my album. He kisses me one more time, with tenderness and longing, and I don't pull away until I'm damn good and ready. Finally, I take a step toward the security line and then turn back around. "If you had let me in, I'd be half in love with you by now," I say, and then I walk away before I can see the expression on his face. I don't need to see it. I've said my piece. It's time to go.

As soon as I'm on the plane and settled in my seat, I reach under my sweater and unbutton my jeans. They've been digging into me since I put them on, and I feel like a can of biscuits whose seam has exploded. The relief is both satisfying and alarming. I only brought them because I assumed all my hiking clothes would be dirty by the time I flew home, and I was right.

Because I'm a masochist, I open the photo album on my phone titled Wren and Marshall. I look at each picture, taking my time and remembering exactly what we were doing, how I was feeling, and what I was thinking in each one of them. In the first picture, taken at Crater Lake, I see a man and a woman whose body language indicates that they aren't yet sure what to think about this unexpected union. I look at the pictures that follow, the gap between our bodies narrowing until it disappears. I notice when Marshall is no longer looking at the camera and is looking down at me and I notice when I switch from looking at the camera and start smiling up at him. The picture of us on the boat, when I'm driving, is my favorite because I look like I'm right where I want to be. Where I wanted to stay for a good long while, Marshall's arms around me and a smile on my face.

In the final picture, we look miserable. My eyes are shiny with unshed tears and Marshall looks defeated and forlorn.

Looking at the pictures makes me want to cry, and my eyes fill again. My nose starts to run, and I dig a tissue out of my carry-on, but the more I dab, the more choked up I get. My seatmate is trying desperately to capture my attention, presumably so that I'll tell her what's wrong and she can offer words of comfort or wisdom. I curl my body away from her, wipe at the tears with a balled fist, and shut my eyes hoping to stem the flow.

The pictures in that album do not tell the story of a fling, at least not any fling I've ever had. Parts of what we had were real and they meant something. But it wasn't enough, and I told him so. I put the phone away and give my eyes a final dab.

The flight attendants have begun their drink service, but I pass on a glass of wine. I do accept the tiny package of pretzels because my stomach feels both empty and nauseated, and I'm hoping they'll settle it.

My stomach feels off and my jeans are tight, I think while eating the pretzels that don't settle my stomach at all.

I've been on vacation, though. Everyone's jeans are tight when they fly home. Except that we did a lot of hiking and very little vacation eating. Food was more of the sustenance variety and not the multicourse meals from my past vacations. We even missed a couple. My jeans should be looser at the waist. I chew on my cuticles, a bad habit that surfaces when I'm stressed.

There's no way I could be pregnant, and this is probably another example of my brain catastrophizing tight pants and immediately assuming a baby is the only logical explanation. I'm on the pill. I'm covered.

I take a magazine out of my tote bag and try to read, but my stupid brain keeps returning to the thing that *absolutely* cannot be happening because I am freer than I've been since losing Rob. I have taken back my life. I'm no longer making bad choices. I'm standing up for myself and for what I need.

I'm a bird, and I am soaring.

But I'll take a pregnancy test just to shut down all this mental chatter.

I text Steph as soon as I have cell service.

> Just landed. I'm stopping at Walgreens
> and should be home in forty-five minutes or
> so. Can you come over? It's important.

Her reply comes through while I'm waiting for my bags.

> Sure! But what's the deal with
> Walgreens? Can't it wait?

> I need a pregnancy test.
> Just for peace of mind.

Steph already knows that Marshall and I "took it up a notch" because I sent a discreet text yesterday when we were in the car on our way to Marshall's place. She was thrilled.

If this is your way of telling me you had a
condom failure with Marshall, let me put your
mind at ease. It's way too early for a pregnancy
test. Grab a Plan B and some wine instead.

No condom failure and yes, it would be way
too early for Marshall. But not too early for Rob.

She sends a string of emojis in response. I've never seen half of
them, but it's obvious they're all some variation of her mind being
blown.

A second message comes through from her.

DON'T PANIC. I'm sure it's fine.

Unfortunately, I'm starting to worry that nothing in my life is
fine at all.

Chapter Twenty-six

I've talked myself down from the ledge a bit by the time Steph arrives with her two-year-old, an adorable little girl named Clementine.

Steph said it was fine. I'm sure it's fine.

"Clemmie!" I say, crouching down to her level. "May I please have a hug?" Clemmie smiles and plants a wet kiss on my mouth instead. "Why, thank you." Discreetly, I wipe off the toddler slobber. *Maybe you're going to have a toddler!* my brain says. *This is great practice.*

"Sorry, James has his basketball league tonight," Steph says, pulling a few toys out of her diaper bag and getting Clemmie set up on the floor of the living room.

"No worries," I say. "And I'm probably overthinking it. I'm on the pill. My jeans are tight, but it's not like I'm turning green at the thought of certain foods or running around puking in random garbage cans. I feel fine." Suddenly, my eyes grow wide.

"What's happening with your eyes?" Steph asks.

"I puked when we were driving around Crater Lake. But that was carsickness. Right?"

"We won't know until you go pee on this," she says, sliding the test across the kitchen counter toward me.

I slide it back. "I don't want to pee on that. I've changed my mind. I want to remain blissfully unaware here in the land of I'm not pregnant by my late fiancé who had a whole other family." *Because that shit's wack.*

"Really?" she asks. "You'd like to remain in the dark? I didn't think that was something you enjoyed, Wren. Not knowing things."

I exhale and roll my aching neck from side to side. I know what she's doing and it's working. I do want to know things. It's my life, and maybe I couldn't convince Marshall to be transparent, but I'll be damned if I'm going to start hiding things from myself.

"It's just that it's a lot," I say.

She nods. "It is."

I don't want to remain in the dark forever, but I need a minute or two to absorb the possibility that I am, indeed, with child, to filter the events of the last couple of months through a different lens, much in the same way I did with Rob's deception. I'm shocked at the picture it's painting. Yes, I was slightly nauseated for most of August and early September, but I thought it was because I was stressed out and eating only sporadically. Sure, I puked in the car with Marshall and fell asleep in the passenger seat—twice. And my boobs did feel like they were on fire when Marshall touched them, but I attributed that to the things he was *doing* to them.

Defeated, I go into the bathroom and take the test. After capping it, I sit down on the couch beside Steph and lay the test on the coffee table. It takes less than thirty seconds for the word PREGNANT to show up. Stunned, I try to comprehend how my life could go so completely off the rails in such a short amount of time.

Shouldn't there have been a reprieve of some sort before the next wave knocked me off my feet? Steph's jaw is doing that unhinged snake thing again. I can't say I blame her.

"Maybe it's wrong," I say. "I bought two tests. Should I take the other one?"

"You can if you want to, but they're pretty accurate," Steph says. "Have you missed a period? Maybe more than one?"

"No! The first one after Rob died was late, and I assumed it was because I was so stressed out. But then I got it."

"Was it lighter than usual?"

"Yes. Only one day. How did you know that?" *It still counts*, I want to shout. *It counts!*

"It was probably implantation bleeding. Lots of women mistake it for a light period. Were there any more periods after that?"

"No," I admit. "But with my cycle being all screwy, I wasn't sure when to expect the next one. Technically, I'm late again, but it should be arriving any day now. I've been feeling PMS-y for a while. If I were pregnant, wouldn't I be having symptoms?"

"That's not PMS," Steph says carefully. I rest my throbbing head in my hands. I am the biggest dumbass who ever walked the planet.

"This isn't happening. I put alcohol in my body, Steph. I put *Marshall* in my body! How did I not know!" I wail. A very unpleasant visual pops into my head, one involving Marshall's penis poking the baby even though I know that, anatomically, it doesn't work that way. I shudder anyway.

"Probably because you weren't looking for it," Steph says reasonably.

"I don't even know how far along I am." I stand, pull up my shirt, shove my jeans—which are still unbuttoned—down to my knees, and turn to face her. "Do I look pregnant?" I ask, my belly at her eye level.

"No," she says, shaking her head like I'm acting a little cuckoo.

I turn to the side. "Look closer."

This time, she gives my midsection more than just a cursory glance, but all she says is "You don't look pregnant. You look very slightly rounded like you overdid it on those Crunchwrap Supremes from Taco Bell that you love so much."

"I'm like those women on reality shows who gave birth in the toilet because they didn't know they were pregnant."

"Let's not dwell on that for now. Are you going to keep it?" she asks. We share a look.

Steph knows how much I want a baby. So much so that I'd contemplated freezing my eggs when my late twenties rolled over into my thirties. I thought about it again at thirty-one and on each birthday after that. I asked my doctor six months ago if I should stop thinking about it and move forward with doing it because I wanted to have a baby someday and freezing my eggs would increase the odds that I would. She said it wasn't a bad idea, but at my age, I still had time to conceive without taking the extra steps. "I've seen women in their early forties become pregnant naturally and deliver healthy babies, and I've seen younger women who needed considerable assistance to conceive. It's really up to you and what you're comfortable with," she said. Rob had seemed lukewarm about having kids the few times it came up, although he assured me that they were great and that he absolutely, positively wanted them someday. He was forty at the time and I thought about mentioning that the clock was ticking, but it really wasn't for him. Just me. There were so many times I should have been firmer about telling Rob what I wanted, and the issue of having children was one of the most significant. If I was worried that we weren't on the same page, I should have pushed harder for a more definitive answer. Then again, I doubt that pushing would have changed a damn thing, because I didn't know about the two children waiting at home for their dad to come back from his latest business trip, suitcase bulging with souvenirs.

I would never have stopped taking the pill until I felt comfortable that Rob was totally on board. I know birth control isn't foolproof, but I never gave its failure much thought until it failed for me.

"Yes, I'm having the baby." I've only just begun to get the derailed train of my life back on its tracks. But I also wanted a baby, and now I would have one.

Rob's baby.

A constant reminder of one of the most painful episodes of my life. His ghost isn't leaving anytime soon—it's unpacked its bags and picked out wallpaper.

"Where did you leave things with Marshall?" Steph asks, because my latest bombshell has taken precedence over everything else.

Just thinking about how things ended brings tears to my eyes. "It's over. Not happening." I bring her up to speed on everything that transpired before I boarded the plane. "I can't repeat the pattern. I won't."

"You did the right thing," she says.

"I didn't want to," I say.

She hands me a tissue. "I know."

"He wasn't oblivious to the way his actions affected me. A man as smart as him isn't going to miss something like that. He knew. I could see it in his eyes. It doesn't sound like he could talk to his ex-girlfriend about it, either, so she left. They were together for six years, so he sure as hell wasn't going to talk about it with me after one short week. He could have been the best thing that ever happened to me, Steph. Maybe I could have been the best thing that ever happened to him."

"He might come around," she says.

I shake my head. "It's probably for the best that it went down the way it did." The man I've known for a week won't want anything to do with a woman who is pregnant with another man's child. And even if he did, I still have to figure out how to have a child on my own. I pick up the pregnancy test and stare at the word PREGNANT. "Still think this is a romantic dramedy?" I ask.

"Oh, Wren," she says, because we both know it isn't. The romance might have been dead when I got on that plane, but it's dead *and* buried now. The dam bursts and my tears flow. Clemmie, adorable sweet Clemmie, chooses this moment to join us on the couch and I pull her onto my lap and bury my face in her silky hair. "I suppose you're going to tell me this is from the hormones," I say to Steph.

"No," she says.

"Then what is it?"

She puts her arm around me. "It's heartbreak."

"Well, at least I've got some experience with that." *Piece of cake,* I tell myself.

I'm exhausted by the time Steph and Clemmie go home. *Because you're pregnant!* my brain says. *Remember?* In desperation, I take the other pregnancy test, and it's also positive. I was supposed to be looking for pearls in oysters, but never, in a million years, did I think I'd find a bun in the oven.

I'm lying on the couch staring up at the ceiling when my phone chimes with a text. I assume it's Steph making sure I'm okay. But it's not Steph, it's Marshall, and despite my current predicament, my hope spikes.

Maybe he's thought about what I said.

Maybe he caught that Hail Mary pass after all.

> I just wanted to make sure
> you got home safely.

I crash back down to earth and can barely see the screen from the tears pooling in my eyes.

I did. Thank you for checking.

Then I cry for thirty straight minutes, big howling sobs. What can I say? The heart wants what it wants, and hope is one hell of a drug.

Chapter Twenty-seven

The next morning, after a sleepless night that kicked my exhaustion level into the bleary-eyed zone, I call my gynecologist's office as soon as they're open and beg them to squeeze me in. "I'm pregnant," I say. "It's a bit unexpected and I have no idea how far along I am." They've had a cancellation for nine thirty and ask if I can make it there in time. "I'll be there," I say.

I provide a urine sample as soon as the nurse calls me back, and when my doctor walks into the exam room ten minutes later wearing a big smile, the first thing she says is "Congratulations. You're having a baby!"

I respond by bursting into tears because it's my current default setting. She sits down on her little rolling stool, her smile fading, replaced by a look of confusion. "I'm sorry, Wren. But I thought a baby was what you wanted."

"My fiancé passed away," I finally manage to choke out. "He never knew about the baby because I didn't know either."

Her face falls. "I am *so* sorry," she says, getting up from her stool so she can put an arm around my shoulders. "I can't imagine what you're going through. How are you holding up?"

"I'll be okay," I say. I'm still in shock, but a baby is the silver lining of an otherwise disastrous relationship built upon lies. The essence of Rob will be present in our son or daughter, offering a daily reminder that he'll always be a part of my life and that his spirit lives on.

She hands me a tissue and waits until I've composed myself. "Why don't we take a quick look and see where you're at," she says. I'm already gowned up and ready, so I lie down on the table and she does a quick exam and internal ultrasound.

"Looks like you're about ten weeks along," my doctor says. "Conception would have taken place around July twentieth, give or take. Your due date is April twenty-eighth."

"July twenty-second," I say. "It was the night before he died." Rob had finished his glass of scotch and taken me by the hand and led me to the bedroom. He'd been gone for a week, and I was so happy to have him back.

I leave my doctor's office with a handful of prenatal vitamin samples and a pile of pregnancy handouts. I've got a lot of work waiting for me at home that I'll need to dive into immediately if I hope to be caught up by midnight, so I decide to call my mother from the car. I sent a text last night letting her know I was home and that I was exhausted and would call her today.

But first, I run a few practice conversations in my head, because not only am I the fool Rob bamboozled, but now there's been an oopsy-daisy birth control failure on top of it. My parents have mostly moved on from the shock of the whole Rob situation. I say mostly because I'm sure there have been lingering conversations I wasn't privy to. Telling them I'm having Rob's baby will be like shining a spotlight on the whole sordid mess. This conversation isn't going to be fun for anyone.

Hey, Mom! Are you busy? Guess what? You're going to be a

grandmother. Awesome, huh? Oh, the father? Yeah, about that. It's Rob. Or maybe, Hi, Mom. Have I got some news for you! Hope you're sitting down because you're not going to believe what I'm about to tell you.

My lip starts wobbling as soon as I initiate the call because of course it does. "Hi, honey," my mom says when she picks up the phone. "How was the trip? Dad and I have been waiting to hear all about it."

"It was good," I say, but I can already hear the tremble in my voice, and here come the stupid waterworks, preventing me from getting any more words out.

"Wren, what's wrong," she says. "You're scaring me."

"I'm pregnant with Rob's baby. I just found out. I hadn't stopped taking my birth control pills or anything, but something went wrong."

I'm met with silence that stretches on for a good ten seconds. It feels like an eternity. "Mom, please say something."

"I need a minute," she says.

"Yeah, okay." Taking deep breaths, I wait for her to process the latest speed bump in my personal life.

"I'm going to be a grandmother," she finally says. There is nothing judgmental in her words. She sounds like she might even be . . . okay with it. Not excited, exactly—that would be strange considering the circumstances and the fresh supply of parental worry I've just dumped on her. But whatever I'm hearing brings my tears to an abrupt end, as if she's reached through the phone and shut off the tap.

"You're not disappointed in me?"

"Because your birth control failed? No, I'm not disappointed in you. I am stunned because it seems you've got a bit of a dark cloud following you around, but you're still *my* baby and I'm not the fuddy-duddy you sometimes think I am. I'm not going to banish you to a home for unwed mothers. Give me some credit here."

She's right. I do sometimes act like she's a fuddy-duddy, but the truth is that she's a pretty open-minded sixty-two-year-old. My dad is even more so.

"You want this baby and you're having it, right?" she asks.

"Yes, I want it and I'm having it. But it's such a shock. *I'm* still in shock," I say.

"Oh, trust me. I'm shocked. But maybe also a little desensitized?" she points out kindly.

That's fair.

I've already given her the doozy of Rob's secret family to wrap her head around. She's also more adaptable than I've given her credit for.

"I hope I'm at least half as good as the mother you are to me. Knowing I have your support will go a long way toward helping me get through this. I want what's best for my child, and I know it won't be easy."

"No, it won't be easy, Wren," she says. "But it will be the hardest job you'll ever love."

Chapter Twenty-eight

I ran Rob's rocks glass through the dishwasher the day after my doctor's appointment. It felt cathartic, and my eyes were dry and my head was clear when I set the clean glass on the counter next to the other glass in the set, and the half-full bottle of Macallan that Rob kept in the cabinet above the fridge. Then I placed everything in a box and knocked on the door of the guy who lives next door. "Can you take this off my hands?" I asked.

He glanced into the box and smiled. "I absolutely can." We both felt like we won.

That was a few weeks ago, and it's time to clear out the rest. My baby is now the size of a peach, and I'm already in my second trimester, which doesn't seem possible. I guess that's what happens when you're blissfully unaware of what's going on inside your body.

I'm too overwhelmed by everything I need to take care of to let Rob dominate my thoughts, because I'm trying to get my head on straight before I face the challenge of bringing my child into the world alone. But I'd be lying if I said I'm not thinking about

Marshall, and I'd be embarrassed to admit how many times I've looked through that photo album on my phone. It's foolish of me, because if Marshall had wanted a future and not just a fling, he would have opened up and let me in. But he didn't, so the loss of the man I hoped would be part of my future is yet another man I have to heal from.

When I rented my apartment, I opted for a two-bedroom because it wasn't that much more than a one-bedroom and I wanted the closet space. Present me is thanking past me for that very prescient decision. The extra bedroom previously housed an assortment of miscellaneous items like suitcases, a set of dumbbells that I never used and often stubbed my toe on, and a pair of end tables I didn't have room for in the living room but liked too much to give away.

And all of Rob's clothes.

The suitcases are his, too. They were often left on the floor lying open, just waiting for him to throw his clothes into them before he took off again. Rob had his packing down to a science and would toss his dopp kit into whatever size suitcase the trip called for, repack it, and kiss me goodbye before flying out the door again. Unbeknownst to me, some of those suitcases weren't packed for a work trip; they were packed so he could go home and see his family.

I zip the suitcases closed and line them up by the front door where I'm putting all the items I'm donating. There's a box of garbage bags on the floor of the bedroom waiting to be filled, and one bag already contains Rob's robe that I washed and folded. It will take multiple trips to get it all into my car, but once I have, I'll take it to Goodwill and that will sever the last physical tie I have to Rob until the baby is born.

There's something niggling at me as I work, something important that has escaped me, that I should be thinking about. But with so many items on the mental to-do list that is constantly swirling around in my head, I'll just have to hope that it comes to me.

As I tackle the closet, I touch each item and embrace the memories the clothing conjures—good, bad, and everything in between. What were we doing when he last wore this shirt or those pants? Where had we been that day? His cologne lingers on several items, and I press my nose into the fabric and inhale. Despite my anger and sadness over his actions, a lingering remnant of nostalgia for the good times remains. Rob was a man I spent almost three years of my life with. It's not feasible to pretend he never existed, to snap my fingers and erase the memories we made together.

My hands touch a dark green wool sweater, and I smile. We had gone to lunch that day. It was a Saturday and unseasonably warm for November in Ohio. They were seating people on the patio, and we ate our meal outside and accepted the waitress's offer of the second round of drinks—another old-fashioned for Rob and an Aperol spritz for me—not because we really wanted them but because we didn't want to leave. "That sweater makes your eyes even greener," I said. Rob's eyes were greenish blue, and they changed color depending on what he was wearing.

"My eyes are blue," he said, laughing.

"Not today." I took a sip of my drink and looked around at the other happy couples sitting on the patio, feeling smug that I, too, had found such a good man. When I set the glass back down and looked in Rob's direction again, I caught him studying me. No, not studying. Staring. "Busted," I said.

"I love you," he said by way of explanation.

"That's the bourbon talking," I said, my cheeks flushing in delight.

He shook his head. "Nope."

We'd been dating for a few months by then, and it was the first time he'd said it. "I love you too," I said, thinking about the future and how happy I was that he'd be part of it. I believed him that day. The boxes were all still checked back then, and if they'd stayed checked, I would have married Rob with all the conviction my heart could hold.

Sometimes, I wonder if I imagined the whole thing.

With newfound stoicism, I drop the green sweater into the Goodwill bag, and my mind fills with images of another man. A tall one with crinkles around his eyes and sprinkles of gray in his dark hair.

I can't snap my fingers and erase the memories of Marshall either.

I stand back and survey my work. Slowly, the room has transformed from the place Rob used to store his clothing and suitcases into the room that will be occupied by his child. His ghost no longer feels like something I'm trying to banish or outrun. Now it feels more like a benevolent presence waiting to watch over the son or daughter who never got the chance to know their father.

The circle of life continues.

Chapter Twenty-nine

I once came across a picture of an old, abandoned shopping center. The article that accompanied it called it a dead mall, devoid of tenants and shoppers.

Devoid of life.

Amid piles of garbage left behind by squatters and vandals were empty echoing concourses and storefronts with gates that were permanently closed. It was all coated in a thick layer of dirt and dust, leaving it gray and brown and lifeless.

Vacuum, ecosystem. Even a once-thriving mall. They're all temporary. When you're inside breathing life into them you don't have to worry about what's going on outside the idyllic environment you've created and whose lush permanence was never promised.

Nothing thrives when you stop watering it.

I miss what Marshall and I created.

I've reached the halfway point of my pregnancy when I have my first pregnancy dream. I knew it was inevitable that I'd have one at some point, because everything I've read informed me of this like-lihood. It's a way for my unconscious mind to process information and attempt to allay any concerns I'm experiencing.

Good luck with that, dream brain. I'm juggling a bunch.

The dream is in color, and everything is so sharp and bright that I bring my hand up to shield my eyes. Then I realize it's not that the colors are bright, but that an actual light is shining into my eyes as a nurse tells me to take a deep breath and push with all my might. Rob's hand is holding one of my legs wide open in a room full of people, and the nurse who told me to push is holding the other one. I am not embarrassed by any of this. "You can do it, babe," Rob says, and he sounds so proud. "She's almost here. I can see her head. She's got a lot of hair."

"Your husband is right," the nurse says. "A few more pushes and you will meet your baby." I want to protest that he's not my husband, but in the dream he is. I'm wearing an engagement ring and a wedding band that look painfully snug on my swollen fingers. My hospital bracelet says that my name is Wren Stephenson.

Rob is mine. In this parallel universe that exists only in my dreams, he's not married to Shayla; he's married to me, and I am giving birth to our first child, a daughter. I give one final push and the room erupts in jubilant cheers. Rob cuts the cord and they plop her onto my chest, toweling her off as her newborn wail fills the room.

Rob and I are crying, too. "You did it. You did it, babe," Rob says.

Then I jolt awake.

For a moment, I'm not sure where I am. I'm shivering because I'm as sweaty as I was in the dream and the dampness has seeped through my pajamas and chilled my skin. Slowly, I realize that I'm in my bed and it was just a dream. Also, the dream didn't solve *anything* and only served to highlight my fear and anxiety because Rob is still dead, and I've never felt more alone. My hands go to my stomach, and that's when I feel my baby move for the first time. I think maybe it's a remnant from the dream, a flutter so subtle that I'm now second-guessing it.

Then I feel it again, stronger, as if the baby is saying, *You can do this. I have faith in you.*

Steph arrives at my place a few days later to accompany me to my ultrasound. "Do you still think it's a girl because of your dream?" she asks.

"It's a girl," I say firmly, even though I know nothing about anything. But I did Google it and dreaming of having a baby girl is a sign of optimism and an upcoming phase of life that is joyful, and if those aren't my wishes in a nutshell, I don't know what is.

My mother is heartbroken that she's not flying up from Florida to attend the ultrasound with me. And the reason she isn't is that I vehemently protested when she floated the idea. I know how excited she is. I'm her only child, so the only grandchildren she'll have are the ones I produce. She and my dad continue to roll with the punches, and for that I'm grateful.

"Save your vacation time for the birth," I'd told her. "I'll spam your phone with so many ultrasound images you'll beg me to stop. Steph will be with me. It's fine." If I can't handle an ultrasound without my mother in attendance, it doesn't bode well for how I'll do once I'm holding an actual baby in my arms. I haven't told my mom that this is something I worry about no less than fifty times a day. I don't want to worry *her.*

"Ready to go see your baby?" Steph asks.

"I'm nervous," I say.

"I was too, with Clemmie. You'll feel better once you're on the other side of it."

She's right, because as soon as I see my baby's heart beating and the shockingly clear features of its face on the screen, I am instantly calmed. My eyes take in every inch—it's surreal in the best possible way. And it only gets better when the ultrasound tech leaves the room and my obstetrician—who is also Steph's doctor—walks in and says, "Hey, Mama. Looks like you're having a girl."

"Is she healthy? What about her growth? Is she on track?"

"She's healthy and everything is measuring right where it's supposed to be," she says.

Now that I know the most important part, that she's healthy, I can admit, at least to myself, how thrilled I am that it's a girl. There is something about my daughter and me figuring out life together that uplifts me. Girl power. The female bond. A child who will hopefully feel as close and connected to me as I do to *my* mother, whom I cherish. I still have my worries—being a self-employed single mom means that finances and childcare are at the top of the list. I make great money when I've only got myself to provide for, but I'll be stretching it a bit for two. I've been budgeting, and planning, and I think I'll be okay. I won't have an extra pair of hands to relieve me, either, which is almost a bigger worry. Those are issues for another day, though. Right now, I am thankful that the baby is healthy.

In the car on the way home, I turn down the volume on the stereo. "I have something important to ask you," I say to Steph. I may love and cherish my mother, but she does have one significant shortcoming as it pertains to my giving birth.

"Sure, what is it?"

"Will you be my birth partner? My mom thinks that's her role, but you know how squeamish she is about blood. One look and she passes out. She swears she can do this as long as she stays up near my shoulders, but if I need a C-section, she'll have to tap out completely."

Steph reaches over the car's console for my hand and squeezes it. "Of course. I would be honored. None of that stuff fazes me. I can get right down there. I don't even care if you poop on the table. You know that's a possibility, right?"

I whip my head over to stare at her, eyes wide, before turning them back to the road. I do know that. I have read all the pregnancy books and spent just enough time on that particular section to add another worry to what is already a very long list of embarrassing things I will not handle well. "Why would you say that? Do you even know me at all?"

"I'm sorry. That was probably the wrong thing to mention."

"You think?" I say. "Because yes, it was. For a multitude of reasons."

"If you do poop, I won't tell you that you did. James told me later that it happened to me, but I couldn't feel anything from the waist down so I had no clue and couldn't have cared less."

"Of course you didn't. Can we please stop talking about it?" I beg. "Oh my God, now that's all I'm thinking about."

"Listen, I know how freaked out you get about embarrassing things, but it's no big deal and I assure you that you won't care about a lot of this stuff once you're in the moment because you'll be in too much—" She stops abruptly.

"You were going to say pain, weren't you?"

"No," she says, shaking her head. "I wasn't."

"Really? Okay, what were you about to say?"

"That you will be in too much *awe* over meeting your baby."

"You know what? I'm not surprised you pooped on the table because you are absolutely full of shit."

Chapter Thirty

In mid-February, when I have ten weeks left until my due date, Marshall texts me out of the blue.

It's been an eternity since the chime of an incoming text sent me running for my phone, hoping it was him and knowing how foolish—and, let's face it, futile—it would be if it was. I'd given up hope that he'd reach out, and the possibility of him doing so seldom crosses my mind anymore. If he wanted to, he would, and he didn't.

Until now.

I wish I could say that Marshall himself doesn't cross my mind anymore either, but he does. It's stupid to cling to a man who isn't interested, but sometimes I let my mind go there anyway. Mostly, I replay what I've come to think of as the Oregon Highlight Reel, which begins with Marshall striding into that clearing and taking on two men, and then moves to the two of us sitting on that balcony at Mount Hood when I poured my heart out to him. It ends strong, with the memory of every kiss he placed on my lips and every touch of his hands on my skin.

I can't help it. I miss him.

I'm so rattled by this unexpected development, and what it might mean, that I don't open the text right away. I can see the preview of the message on the screen:

> Hi Wren. I know it's been a while and I've
> got a break between clients so I wanted

So, he wanted . . . what?

To say he misses me and he's sorry he was such a closed-off idiot? To say he can't stop thinking about me? To say he thinks we can make this work?

The curiosity gnaws at me. It isn't fair. I've already put this issue to bed—or at least I've attempted to—and the smart thing to do is let sleeping dogs lie.

So that's what I'm going to do.

Let it lie.

I'll probably just delete it unread.

I'm busy trying to get some deadlines wrapped up before the end of the day, so I silence my phone's notifications. It takes every bit of focus I possess to return my attention to the task at hand. I don't even fire off an *oh my God, you'll never believe who just reached out* text to Steph.

Thirty seconds after sending my last work email, I wake up all those sleeping dogs when I grab my phone and open Marshall's text.

> Hi Wren. I know it's been a long time, but I've
> got a break between clients and wanted to let
> you know that I've been following the journey of
> the motorcycle trackable I left behind at Tumalo
> State Park in honor of Graham. It's had quite a
> ride and it's getting closer. I'm hoping it arrives

here before summer. It will feel like a part of my
brother is home. I hope you're doing well.

I read it three times, and my crushing disappointment runs deeper than the Mariana Trench. You'd think I'd be used to it by now, considering how often my expectations don't match up with reality. I swipe at my eyes with the back of my hand.

Lots to unpack here. He did not apologize for being a closed-off idiot, so there's that. He's back at work, which is a good indication that he's feeling mentally strong enough to resume his life, which is good. I'm happy for him. And he's sharing something related to his brother, which makes sense because the trackable was something he didn't have trouble sharing with me before.

He's also assuming I want this update. But do I? I swipe at my eyes again, because they won't stop filling with tears. A good cleansing cry is what I need, so I stop fighting it and let it out. It takes a while, but I breathe in deeply when it's over and exhale slowly. Before I can overthink it, I pick up my phone and send a response.

I'm good, Marshall. I've gotten my life back
on track, and Oregon feels like a distant memory.
Thanks for letting me know about the trackable.

There, I think. I've shut this down. Now neither of us will waste any more time. But it's not the time I'm worried about—it's the instantaneous jolt of hope I'll feel every time a text comes in, followed by the plummeting crash when it isn't from him. I assign a unique text tone to Marshall to subvert my yearning every time my phone chimes.

I'm still in mourning, pining for what could have been. I did the right thing in responding the way I did. Oregon is a distant memory, I said. *You* are a distant memory, is what I meant.

I've moved on.

A leftover tear plops onto the screen. I wipe my phone on my sweatshirt and throw it across the room, where it slides harmlessly across the carpet, making me even angrier.

I've gotten into the habit of doing my work in the nursery, which is complete because my mom and I went shopping when she and my dad came for Christmas. I was only a little past the halfway point in my pregnancy then, but when we saw all that baby gear on display, we lost our damn minds. "At least you'll have it all taken care of," my mom said. "You can cross it off your list." Now the room contains a crib, a changing table, a small dresser, and a glider. My mom also painted the walls a soft gray to go with the pink and gray bedding after my landlord grudgingly agreed as long as I return it to the original color when I move out.

The glider is my favorite piece of furniture. It's comfortable and it makes a great work chair. Good back support and the gliding motion soothes me. I've been working in the nursery since this morning, and at five, I close my laptop to get ready for a girls' night out.

Getting dressed is becoming trickier. I refuse to wear anything that doesn't have an elastic waist, so leggings continue to be a staple. But tonight I jazz up my usual maternity outfit by swapping the hoodie for a nice sweater and stepping into ankle boots instead of sneakers. I make zero improvements to my hair because I don't have the energy for anything fancier than a ponytail. I just want to enjoy an evening with my friends.

I arrive at Steph's to pick her up. "Any more texts from Marshall?" she asks when she gets in the car. It's been two weeks since I received his out-of-the-blue message. Marshall's smart and I don't doubt that he received my message loud and clear. *I'm not interested.*

"Nope. And I'm not going to dwell on it either." I've got more important things to worry about.

She looks like she might want to say, "Ah, but I know you *are* dwelling on it." But she lets it go and all she says is "Good."

We have analyzed Marshall's random, completely unexpected text message from every angle, and formulated a theory. He was fishing, testing the waters to see if I'd bite. But he, of all people, should understand exactly where I was coming from when I broke things off at the airport. If he were my therapist and we were having a session, he'd probably say things like, "What Rob did made you feel like you can't trust or depend on romantic partners. It won't matter how early you are in a relationship, either—those elements will need to be present from the start, so you'll feel safe connecting with someone new."

And he would be right.

But for some reason, Marshall seems oblivious to my needs, so I threw that fish back and doubt I'll hear from him again. I have, however, had plenty of conversations with him in my head, and they go something like this: *Why was it so important to shut me out, and why are you trying to worm your way back in? I've shared everything and it's your turn now. Quid pro quo, Marshall.*

"Are you ready for a night out?" Steph asks.

"I'm starving," I say.

She laughs. "Not what I asked, but our reservation is in fifteen minutes, so you should have some food in front of you soon."

"I'm ordering dessert too. The baby wants cheesecake."

It's a Thursday night, so the restaurant isn't too packed. The others are here already—there are six of us in the group chat comprised of my closest friends, and everyone could make it tonight, which is a miracle that doesn't happen often. We squeeze into the booth next to them. Steph is the only one who knows about Marshall's text, and I've already cautioned her not to bring it up. It's too exhausting to rehash for a new audience, and I really *am* trying to put it out of my mind.

When we're done eating, we move from our table to a comfortable spot in front of a roaring fireplace. I'm able to have one-on-one conversations with my friends as we split off into duos, catching up on everything that's too involved to share over text. Except Marshall. Whenever someone asks about him, I repeat that it was a fun fling that didn't work out and leave it at that.

A man sits down next to me on the large L-shaped sectional we're sharing with other patrons. He makes eye contact when I turn my head and then smiles. He's handsome, probably my age or a little older. "I'm not crowding you, am I?" he asks.

"Nope," I say.

"Out for girls' night?" he asks.

"Yep." I'm the only one in the group not wearing a ring; he's probably trying to isolate me from the herd. He hasn't noticed the bump under my oversized and very forgiving sweater. It's harder to see when I'm sitting down, the fabric loose and drapey.

The small talk continues. He's not a bad conversationalist and he's polite, telling me a few things about himself—he's a divorced forty-year-old CPA, no kids—interspersed with questions about what I do for work and if a boyfriend is here with me tonight. "I'm with my friends" is all I'll admit to. No need to encourage him by announcing that I'm single.

"Can I get you another drink?" he asks, pointing at my empty glass.

"I'm good, thanks."

"Are you sure? I'm going up to the bar anyway."

"Okay, that would be nice." The mocktails here are delicious and we're still an hour or so from wrapping up the evening. My friends are giving me big googly eyes like they think this could actually go somewhere.

"What are you drinking?" he says.

"The mocktail with lavender and hops."

His expression falters. "You don't want a real drink?"

I cup my hands around my stomach. "Consuming alcohol is frowned upon by my doctor. It's bad for the baby."

He doesn't miss a beat. "Of course. Mocktail it is. Be right back."

I'm still waiting forty-five minutes later, and the girls and I have had a good laugh. "Where did he go?" I ask. "What could have possibly caused him to leave this fine establishment so quickly?" I'm laughing so hard now I'm in danger of peeing myself. I've just had a glimpse into the future of my dating life. Sure, it's funny now. The last thing I need is a new man to complicate this shit show even further. But someday, I may change my mind and yearn for a partner. If it was hard to find someone before, I can't imagine what it will be like as a single mother. Maybe I'll skip it entirely.

We head home. Halfway to Steph's house, a text notification sounds and the unique tone I've assigned to Marshall fills the car and causes me to swerve briefly. My response is Pavlovian, and the hit of dopamine I receive shocks me with its intensity.

"What's wrong? Why did you swerve? Those *were* mocktails, right?"

"The text that just came in was from Marshall. I gave him his own text tone so I wouldn't get my hopes up every time someone messages me."

"Seriously?" she asks. "That was from him?"

"Yep. Grab my phone. What does it say?"

She plucks it from the cupholder. "It says, 'Can you please give me your email address?' What does *that* mean?"

"You're asking me? Because I think we both know I have no clue what it means other than apparently, he wants to send me an email."

"Are you going to give him the address?"

"I don't know. Dammit, he's really piquing my curiosity this time."

"Only one way to kill that cat," she says.

"If I don't respond, he'll probably stop trying."

"Would you be sad about that?" she asks.

I answer honestly. "Yes." Maybe Marshall's finally ready to open up and let me probe at the weak spots in *his* armor, and that's the outcome I'm chasing. "Not that this could possibly work out. Think of what I'd have to tell him. Can you even imagine? Oh, hey, Marshall, one quick thing before we fire whatever this is back up: I am with child." I start laughing and Steph joins in, too. If I don't laugh, I'll cry. Just when I thought my crazy life couldn't get any more complicated or ridiculous, it does!

"I know what this is now. It's a romantic tragedy!" I exclaim, and now I *do* start crying.

Steph shakes her head. "*Romeo and Juliet* is a romantic tragedy. Let's not get ahead of ourselves here. No one is drinking poison. This one still has legs."

"It *so* doesn't," I say, and then I start laughing as the ridiculousness of what she just said hits me. And just as quickly, I stop laughing, and here come the tears again.

"I'll just wait until you cycle through all of this," Steph says mildly.

It takes a good five minutes for the laughter and tears to taper off. My nose is running, and my cheeks are wet. We're almost to Steph's by then. "Write him back," I say. "Give him my email."

"Yes!" she replies, typing quickly as if she's afraid I'll change my mind. "There. Done."

Here goes nothing.

"Let me know what he says." Steph gathers up her purse and gives me a quick hug before getting out of the car.

At home, I change into my comfiest pajamas and sit down on

the glider in the nursery. The group chat is humming as everyone texts to say how much fun they had tonight and how great it was to see everyone.

Ten minutes later, Marshall's email lands in my inbox.

Chapter Thirty-one

Hi Wren,

Thanks for giving me your email address. I wasn't sure if you would because I could tell from your response to my text that you didn't seem interested in hearing from me again, and I understand why. I also understood why you said everything you did at the airport. But understanding where you were coming from and being able to say what you needed to hear was a bigger hurdle than I'd realized it would be. It caught me off guard, but that's my fault, not yours. It's a testament to how far you've come that you already knew exactly what you'd allow from a man and what you wouldn't. I know what Rob did to you and I should have anticipated how it would play out in your next relationship. I got caught up in the moment during the time we spent together because it felt good to be with you, better than anything else had for a long time, honestly. But I handled things badly, and I'm sorry. I know that it hurt you.

I went back to work the week after you flew home. And the week after that, I started seeing a new therapist. Grief is a bill and until you pay it, life puts a lien on everything else. When you shut things down in the airport, it forced me to stop trying to distract myself from losing Graham, and forced me to get help. Maybe I'm trying harder, or maybe it's easier now that I've switched to someone else. Whatever the reason, it's helping, and it shouldn't have taken me this long to figure out that a different therapist might be able to do what the previous one hadn't been able to. The person I'd been going to since Graham died was someone I knew and trusted, but we just weren't compatible. Once I realized it, I parted ways with him amicably.

Most of the sessions with my new therapist focus on Graham because there's a lot I still need to work through. I should have told you what happened to my brother. I'm sorry you had to go searching for it.

I talk to my therapist about you too. I told him how much you helped me, and how much I regretted not opening up to you. I talked about you so much that he mentioned delving into it further. So we did. And then I sent that text that probably felt very jarring to you after all this time. I'm sorry about that, too. I can assure you that it's not my intent to jerk you around.

I'd like to keep emailing, but only if it's also what you want. And if you don't, that's okay. I understand. It's your decision, and you've been through enough.

On a lighter note, I'm glad we took so many pictures together. I looked at them for a long time when I got back from taking you to the airport even though I knew I'd just let go of one of the best things that ever happened to me.

How are you? It's unfair of me to ask, but I'd like to know.

Marshall

I FaceTime Steph and read the email aloud. "Well, now you know what he wants," she says. "I think it's commendable that he's acknowledging where things went wrong and admitting that it was on him. But the bigger question is: What do *you* want?"

"I want what we had when I was there, with the addition of transparency so that I don't have to wonder about what he isn't telling me."

"Are you going to email him back?"

I blow out a frustrated breath. "I want to, from the standpoint that I'd like to hear what else he has to say. Whatever he's been keeping bottled up is so hard for him to talk about that he needs the protective buffer of an email to get it out. I commend him for finding a tolerable workaround, but my life looks very different now. He'll be as shocked as I was when he learns that I'm carrying Rob's baby."

"Are you going to tell him about that?"

"I'm going to wait and see where this goes. Making amends could simply be part of his healing and a way to clear his conscience. Maybe his therapist is the one who suggested he reach out and apologize. This might not have anything to do with us, romantically speaking." The irony of keeping something from Marshall isn't lost on me, but there's no reason to bring it up until I know more about his intentions.

"And if this is about more than opening up, if it *is* about us, I'm not sure what I'll do. I can put Rob's duplicity behind me, but the baby is my future, and we're a package deal."

"I totally agree," Steph says. "Keep me posted."

"Will do." I end the call and go into the living room to grab my laptop.

Hi Marshall,

Spending that week with you felt good to me too, but it took some time to get over you and I didn't think I'd ever hear from you again. And now here you are. You broke my heart at the airport that day, and I'd only just begun to put it back together after Rob stomped all over it. Watching you close up like that hurt. I know it wasn't your intention because any man who would come to my rescue the way you did in the clearing that day isn't a bad person. But a good man can hurt you too, and that feels even worse. It can't happen again. I need to be clear about that.

There's a lot of truth in what you said about finding the right therapist, and I'm happy you've found someone you're more compatible with. I already told you that one of the reasons I didn't seek therapy after Rob died was that I feared being judged. When I finally talked to you about it that day on the balcony in Mt. Hood, it felt like a thousand-pound weight had been lifted from my shoulders. You're a great listener, and I should have pushed through my hesitation and found a therapist after Rob died, but sometimes it's hard to see the path we should take even when it's right in front of us. The same goes for you. We're all human, and we're just trying to do our best.

Speaking of Graham, please continue the updates about the trackable. I thought it was so touching when you left it at Tumalo in memory of your brother, and now that I know what happened to him, it has even more significance. I hope the motorcycle makes it home.

It's okay if you want to keep sending emails. I'll read them. I'm listening.

Wren

Marshall's next email arrives on the same day my pregnancy app rolls over to a new week, which is not exactly the synergy I'm seeking. It's like shining a light on the fact that I'm thirty-three weeks pregnant and my baby is now the size of a pineapple.

And Marshall doesn't know.

It's not like I can tell him that I've stumbled upon the mommy blogs and that I've categorized them according to their ethos. So far, I've found the Crunchy Moms, the Hipster Moms, the Supermodel Moms, the Competitive Moms, the Zen Moms, and the Hot Mess Moms. I have not found the moms whose deceased baby daddies had secret families (but something tells me it exists), so I feel like an outsider who hasn't yet found her tribe. I guess it remains to be seen what mom category I fall into after my daughter arrives. Clueless but Loving Mom, probably.

What Marshall doesn't know is starting to feel far heavier than my growing belly. I won't be able to wait much longer, but I don't *want* to tell him because I like this new bubble we're creating. Not a vacuum or an ecosystem, but a safe space that thrives on open communication. It's everything I wanted from him, which unfortunately puts the onus back on me.

Now I'm the one who isn't opening up.

But I'm the one who has so much more to lose.

Hi Wren,

I wasn't honest with you when I told you I was on vacation instead of taking a leave of absence. I'm sorry. I should have told you what I was really doing. It was a hard thing for me to talk about, even with my own family, because it felt like a backslide, and admitting I felt worse instead of better would only worry everyone. That's why my sister was so upset the night she tracked me down in Bend. I hadn't told anyone I was leaving town.

I have a client whose name and identifying details I can't share for obvious reasons, but they've been coming to me for almost two years after losing someone in a way that was similar to how I lost Graham—a random, wrong place at the wrong time kind of thing.

I stop reading for a moment. *You were simply in the wrong place at the wrong time. It happens,* Marshall had said when we were sitting in the parking lot of the coffee shop after leaving Wild Iris. I understand now what Marshall meant when he said that Beer Gut and Flannel Shirt would have been more scared of him if they'd known what he was thinking about that day in the clearing. Unleashing his pent-up need for vengeance on a couple of bad men probably felt incredible. No wonder he didn't seem scared. No one would remain unprotected ever again, not on Marshall's watch.

Not if he could help it.

For whatever reason, I was unable to keep my thoughts about Graham locked away that day during my client's session and I just . . . checked out. I didn't even realize what had happened until they started shouting my name and I snapped out of it. It was upsetting to them because I'd always been able to separate my personal and professional lives and give them my full attention. But not that day. That's when I realized I needed time and space and distance to get my head on straight, and the only thing that made sense was a leave of absence. I decided to get out of town, do some geocaching in Graham's honor, and maybe even talk to my brother like he was searching alongside me instead of buried underground (which, by the way, he would hate. We should have cremated Graham and thrown his ashes into the wind. He would have liked that so much better).

The leave of absence was good for me, probably the best thing I've done for myself since Graham died. But part of the reason it was so helpful was because of you. Spending time with you instead of isolating myself, which is what I'd been doing, helped me in a lot of ways. You were instrumental in that even if you didn't know it at the time. When we were on the balcony in Mt. Hood and you shared every aspect of your relationship with Rob, I felt like I was in my office helping a client and that made me feel good. You mentioned not trying to get a free therapy session from me but helping you that day helped me too. I had been feeling a lack of confidence in just about every facet of my life, and you helped me get some of it back. Someone who hadn't been through a life-changing experience of their own wouldn't be as understanding or patient. Maybe they'd find my situation too heavy and frustrating and wish I'd just get over it the way Holly did. But when you found out I'd lost my brother, you never made me feel like I had to act a certain way. You let me be me, even though I could tell you wanted me to open up more. What are the odds that I would run into someone like you?

Marshall

If you ask me, the odds are pretty good.

And maybe the universe wasn't trying to send Marshall to me after all; maybe the universe was trying to send me to him.

Chapter Thirty-two

Hi Marshall,

It's hard to admit when things aren't going as well as people hope they are. It also shows you who's in your corner and who isn't because it takes patience and loyalty to continue offering support when it seems like no progress is being made. Right after Rob died and I found out about his wife and kids, there were times I felt like I was dying inside. But when someone asked how I was doing, my answer was usually, "I'm great, much better, thanks for asking," and I said the words with a smile. It's not that my friends and family weren't concerned and supportive, but I discovered there's a finite amount of time you can take after a loss, and when it's been used up people really want the old version of you to return.

I believe that nothing in life is random, and the odds that you'd run into someone like me were better than you think.

Wren

February turns to March, but winter lingers in Ohio, holding spring at bay and bringing with it a landscape as bleak as my mood. The ground is either buried beneath a layer of white snow or dingy gray with slush that will refreeze when the next icy front rolls through. The anxiety over the difference between taking care of the baby once she's on the outside of my body versus her being tucked safely inside has increased. Meanwhile, the emails from Marshall continue.

Hi Wren,

You already know what happened to Graham, but I never told you about the kind of person he was and what our relationship was like. On the day he died, he showed up at my house around 9:00 A.M., dressed for a hike. He had been living in Guatemala for about six weeks, working odd jobs and crashing in hostels before moving on to the next city, but he hadn't been home in almost a year and a half. Graham was built for the outdoors, and he always smelled like cut grass and dirt and sweat as if all three were permanently ingrained in his skin. My sister Jillian and I had coined the scent "Graham's cologne" because he'd smelled that way most of his life. I pulled him into a bear hug as soon as I opened the door and told him how good it was to see him because we all missed him when he was gone. Graham loved us, but he loved his nomadic lifestyle even more. It was something he needed, and we understood.

A smile lit up his face and he told me it had been too long. Graham's sunny disposition could power a small town. He seldom complained and spent very little time worrying about what came next. When you're the baby of the family, you don't sweat the small stuff. Graham was free-spirited, uncomplicated, and outgoing, but also a bit self-centered because he'd always had to compete with Jillian and me for attention in the way that third-born children always do. My parents also had a much more hands-off style of parenting by the time Graham entered the world.

I wish I could say that my formative years were similar, but my mom has a picture of me wearing a T-shirt that says, I'm the big brother. It was taken at the hospital when they brought me in to meet Jillian for the first time. I don't remember any of this, but I've been told I asked them to send her back. But as I grew older, I always knew that I'd defend her and would never allow anyone to lay a hand on my little sister. Then Graham came along, and my responsibilities doubled. I guess what I'm trying to say is that I've spent my whole life aware of the fact that protecting my younger siblings and keeping them safe would always fall under my watch.

Graham was the most interesting person I knew. Intense intellectual discussions were one of his favorite things, especially those conducted around a campfire or on a beach with the locals of whatever country he was visiting. He was like a sponge that soaked up everything he encountered with an almost insatiable thirst for adventure. He rolled with the punches and his resiliency had no limitations.

I teased him about his hair that day, telling him I was pretty sure that Guatemala had plenty of barbershops. His hair was long enough to skim his shoulders, but my brother pulled it off in a way I never would have been able to. He told me he was growing it out and that a man bun was basically a requirement. All the other backpackers had one, he said, which cracked us up. But Graham never followed the crowd, and I knew he grew his hair long simply because he felt like it. He hated smartphones and the internet in general unless he could log on at a cybercafé for cheap because he needed to book a plane ticket to his next destination. Sometimes he'd even check in with us although never at a frequency that satisfied our parents. They just had to trust that Graham was okay and that no news was good news.

He'd already been to our parents' house before arriving at mine. He still kept most of his worldly possessions there, including the motorcycle that was now parked in my driveway. He'd crash in his childhood bedroom for a week or so and then take off again.

Holly was home that day. As soon as she realized it was Graham standing in the doorway, she shouted his name and then threw her arms around him. Graham wanted to spend the day geocaching, and he asked Holly if she wanted to join us, but she'd already made other plans. He made her promise that she'd meet up with us for dinner and she agreed immediately because she loved Graham like a brother. We said our goodbyes and took off in my Jeep.

We'd covered five miles and found three caches by the time we took a break, both of us sweating profusely and covered in scratches, bug bites, and dirt. I asked him where he was headed after Guatemala, and he said probably Belize but that he wasn't in a hurry to move on. I knew that there was only one thing that could keep my rolling stone of a brother in the same location for longer than a couple of months and asked him what her name was. Katie, he said. She was an ex-pat from Colorado whom he'd been seeing for a few weeks. He told me she'd stolen his heart and that he was going to marry her the minute she agreed to spend the rest of her life with him. I'd been with Holly for six years at that point, so it's another example of how different we were. He asked me about Holly that day, wondering why we hadn't tied the knot yet. I told him I didn't know and then Graham said that was bullshit because I was never unsure about anything. Graham might have been comfortable not knowing what he'd be doing from one month to the next, but I had never lived my life without a plan. He pressed me and I stalled, telling him it was a big commitment. He said that was kind of the point. I told him I loved Holly, but I stressed that marrying her was the kind of decision that would affect me for the rest of my life.

Neither of us knew that Graham only had a few hours left of his.

We didn't know, Wren. I didn't know.

Marshall

I sob for a solid hour after such an intimate exploration of the bond between Marshall and his siblings, and the responsibilities laid at his feet from the moment they were born. The death of a fiancé is devastating enough; losing a sibling is another thing entirely and I'm saying this as someone who doesn't have a brother or sister. Something about that concept scratches at the periphery of my brain, but I'm not sure why.

Of course he feels responsible. No wonder this is so hard for him to talk about. Maybe Holly didn't leave Marshall because he wasn't fun anymore. Maybe Holly left because she knew, on some level, that Marshall had doubts about their future, and Graham's death was the straw that broke the camel's back.

My uneasiness over what I haven't shared grows because Marshall has cracked himself wide open and all but handed me a flashlight. It's what I wanted, and here it is—the quid pro quo I've been waiting for.

Maybe I can employ the same buffering method he's chosen and tell him about the baby in a carefully worded email. *I need to tell you something. I didn't find out about it until I got home. I just thought you should know.*

I'll wait a bit longer. I'm probably feeling the extra pressure because it was such an emotional email. I'll give myself a little more time to make sure that telling him is really what I want to do and to brace myself for his reaction.

But I discover there is something far more worrisome and pressing than what Marshall will say when he finds out I'm pregnant when I go into premature labor six hours later.

It's shortly after midnight when I drive myself to the hospital, which is, unfortunately, the same one where Rob died. When my doctor called me back and asked some questions, she didn't like my answers and told me to head straight to the ER and she'd meet me there. "I don't know if this is labor. It's my first baby," I tell everyone I come into contact with—the woman sitting behind the desk in the emergency room, the triage nurse, and finally my obstetrician.

The contractions are painful and they're coming with frightening regularity. There's a fetal heart rate monitor strapped to my belly and an IV in the back of my hand. I've provided blood and urine samples and had an ultrasound and internal examination.

"You are in labor," my doctor says. "But no reason to panic. Your water hasn't broken and there's no bleeding." I'm right on the line for trying to stop labor or letting me proceed, but my doctor opts for stopping it. "We'll administer steroids to help the baby's lungs mature faster and give you some medication to see if we can keep her in there a little bit longer. I'm going to hold you here until tomorrow as a precaution and then put you on bed rest for the next week or so."

There's not much for me to do after that. Someone comes in periodically to check the readout on the fetal monitor or take my vital signs. I'm not uncomfortable and the contractions have stopped. "Will the father be joining you?" a nurse asks. "We can watch for him when he arrives."

"The who?"

"The baby's dad."

"Oh. No. No one will be joining me." It's a preview of what's to come. Rob won't be with me in the delivery room, and I'll have to constantly answer questions like this. Everything two parents usually do together will look a lot different for me and my daughter.

She colors slightly, sorry to have brought it up.

"There is one," I assure her. "I know who he is and everything. But he passed away right after the conception."

Her expression morphs into one of shocked sorrow. "I'm so sorry. You let me know if you need anything at all," she says, patting my hand.

It's now a little after one in the morning and I'm not going to call my parents or Steph and wake them out of a sound sleep. It's just after ten in Oregon, and I bet Marshall is still up. I can picture him sitting in that big chair facing the window, watching TV or maybe reading a book. My yearning for him has never been stronger, but tonight is not the right time to come clean. I'm too emotional and scared about the baby to risk piling heartache and rejection on top of it.

I place my hands gently on my stomach as if I can protect my daughter from the outside, and I pick up the TV remote. I spend the next four hours channel surfing because I can't sleep. I must remain vigilant, listening for the slightest abnormal blip on the fetal monitor, one eye on the doorway in case an alarm summons a nurse who will charge into the room and break the news that their efforts have failed, and the baby is coming now.

Around daybreak, I call my mother. She doesn't take the news well, but she calms down when I tell her I'm being discharged sometime this morning. I tell her that my doctor has already been in and that whatever they did to stop my labor is still working. "Oh, Wren," she says. "I wish I could be there. It breaks my heart that you're in the hospital all alone." I understand why it breaks hers, but it didn't break mine. Look at me, doing the hard things all by myself.

"It's okay, Mom. I made it through just fine on my own."

. . .

Finally home, I crawl into bed with my laptop and phone. On my nightstand, I've got water and snacks. I spend the rest of the day afraid to get up, and the only time I do is when I have to pee and can't hold it for another minute. I Google every twinge and what it might mean and then I decide not to do that anymore. All the "what if" scenarios are just intrusive thoughts and they're not helping. I place my hands on my stomach. *Just a few more weeks, baby girl. You can do it.*

Steph arrives at dinnertime with my favorite take-out pasta. She stretches out beside me on the bed, and we eat. "You'll be fine," she says between mouthfuls. "I know it was scary, but you're so close to full term."

"I know," I say.

"You're stronger than you think, Wren."

"I know that too. But waiting to jump into the unknown feels more daunting than just jumping. Do you know what I mean?"

"Yes. I felt that way toward the end of my pregnancy too. It'll pass," she assures me.

Rob would know exactly what I mean. I asked him about the Dutch thing once we'd been dating awhile. "How exactly does one teach themselves to speak a foreign language well enough to conduct business? Did you take a class, or did you watch a million YouTube videos or what?"

"I was very motivated, which helped," he said. "I wanted that promotion, and this would guarantee that I got it. There were books and videos and online courses and apps. I did it all. But mostly I jumped into the deep end by never speaking English when I traveled to the Netherlands. I made mistakes and I probably sounded really stupid at times. But no one cared. They were more than happy to correct me, and I never made the same mistake twice. That's the best way to learn anything. Immerse yourself and fake it until you're fluent and it feels natural. No one will be the wiser if you believe you can do it. And eventually, you will."

Right now, impending motherhood feels a lot like flying to the Netherlands, walking off a plane and into a business meeting, and thinking to yourself, *Okay. Let's do this.*

I'm going to do this.

Chapter Thirty-three

Hi Marshall,

Your last email left me in tears. It explained so much and it required a lot of vulnerability on your end. I'm sure it wasn't easy to share those things. Graham sounded like a wonderful person, and his light shimmered through every sentence you wrote about him. Because of your email, I now have an even deeper understanding of—and empathy for—your situation. I may not have any siblings of my own, but I don't doubt for one second that you were an amazing big brother. What happened to Graham wasn't your fault. I truly hope you believe that too.

There's something I need to tell you. I don't know if it will matter because I'm not sure where this is going, but I'm pregnant. I found out the day I got home. It was unplanned, obviously.

I delete the sentences about being pregnant. I want this email to focus on Graham. The next one can be about the baby.

It's interesting what you said to Graham about Holly, and how you pointed out that marrying her would affect your whole life. Marriage is a huge commitment with life-altering ramifications. I don't think there's anything wrong with wanting to be sure. We all need those boxes to be checked. Every last one of them. Marrying someone means you're vowing to love them forever, and forever is a really long time.

Wren

Marshall's parents probably never intended for their oldest child to feel so much pressure when it came to his younger siblings, but he felt it just the same. Society is inherently set up that way. We all know our place in the pecking order, and those who are older will always bear some responsibility for aiding and protecting those who are younger, whether they're our siblings or our friends, or a complete stranger. It's what people are taught to do.

As an only child, I've never been in Marshall's shoes. My parents also never bought into the stereotypes about only children, and they never treated me like one. They never let me think I was the center of the universe, and they raised me to understand that I *was* special, but only to them. The one thing I disliked about being an only child was the lack of a sibling to play with when I was younger and to confide in as I got older.

That's when the thing I couldn't grasp, the thing that's been scratching at the periphery of my brain, finally comes to me, not with a whimper but with an explosive bang.

I might be an only child, but *my* daughter will not be.

I'd accepted Rob's ghost as a permanent fixture that made no sense to try and outrun, not anymore. But I had placed Shayla and her children into a box I vowed never to open. I stuffed them into it along with how I felt about their existence, taped it shut, and put it on a high shelf, tucked out of sight. Done and dusted. It's so totally insane that I actually laugh, because who in their right mind believes that something as juicy as Rob's other family would remain hidden inside the box, never to surface again?

My daughter has two older half siblings, and there's no way I can keep that from her for the rest of her life.

Chapter Thirty-four

Hi Wren,

Holly actually stopped by last night. She'd heard through the grapevine that I was doing better and said she'd been thinking about me since Valentine's Day because it was the first one we hadn't spent together in six years.

When she moved out, she was angry and frustrated with me. Graham's death was hard on her. I've already mentioned that Holly loved Graham and she often stated that she got lucky in the brother-in-law department even though we weren't technically married yet. The fact that we weren't was a huge point of contention between us. When you're a thirty-six-year-old man who hasn't proposed to his girlfriend of six years, people wonder what's causing the hold-up, often out loud and right to your face. Everyone was waiting impatiently for an engagement, but no one was waiting more than Holly. I was ready to get married, in theory, and had been for a few years. But the problem was that I wasn't sure I wanted to marry *her*. The realization had crept up on me slowly and I'd been stewing about it for months. I loved Holly as a person, but I kept her hanging because I was still trying to convince myself that loving her was enough of a reason to proceed even though I knew it wasn't. And then Graham died, and I wasn't thinking about much of anything at all. I was just trying to get through the day.

Holly had given me an ultimatum: either we got engaged or she was going to leave. So I let her go. I let her handle what I wasn't strong enough to do myself, and I mostly felt relieved when she was gone.

She told me the real reason she stopped by was that she needed to know if there was any hope for us. She apologized for not being there for me and for her impatience when it became clear that things weren't returning to the way they were before Graham died. She acknowledged that it was selfish and that she was ashamed of the way she'd placed more emphasis on a proposal than on what I was going through.

She asked if we could try again, and it pained me to look at her hopeful expression, especially knowing what I was about to tell her. I loved Holly for a long time, but I was honest, and I told her I didn't want to try again. I told her we lost something along the way and that I didn't want to look for it anymore. I apologized for not telling her sooner. I told her I knew it wasn't what she wanted to hear.

It was a good lesson, Wren. I shouldn't have let her walk away the first time without telling her what I was thinking and feeling. I shouldn't have let you do it either. I won't make that mistake again. No woman should ever have to question what I'm not telling her.

Marshall

Marshall's confession makes me wonder how many people are in relationships with someone they don't want to marry but love too much to hurt. Marshall didn't want Holly, but does that mean he wants a relationship with me? There's been no reference to "us," but something tells me it's coming once everything else has been shared. Panic rises within me. When I tell Marshall about the baby—and I'm going to, very soon—I'll need to prepare myself for his honest reaction because honesty is all I've ever wanted, even if what a man says is something I don't want to hear.

Knowing that we're both carrying some heavy things but working on them anyway makes me feel like I have a kindred spirit in Marshall. Sometimes, I think of us as fellow fixer-uppers, although that doesn't seem quite right. We aren't in disrepair; rather we are both going through a period of renovation leading us to a transformation.

And the only way out is through.

Chapter Thirty-five

I use an email lookup service to track down Shayla Stephenson's email address. I have no way to confirm that the address provided is current, but I also don't have any other options. I have already scoured the internet looking for Shayla. As I'd already discovered with Rob, Stephenson is too common a last name to give me much, but Shayla's first name isn't one I've come across very often. There was an S. Stephenson that popped up on a social media platform, but the user had utilized every privacy setting available and the profile picture was a sunrise. It *could* be her, but what I need to say is too important and personal to go to the wrong person. And even if it is Shayla, she might not see the message because we're not connected socially. My initial outreach must be successful; it's the only way to get a foot in the door before I attempt to blow it wide open.

Dear Shayla,

My name is Wren Waters. We met very briefly in the hospital after your husband's accident. I would appreciate a few minutes of your time to speak on the phone. Please let me know if we can set something up.

Thank you

My heart is pounding when I click the send button. I have no clue what to expect. My message might be sent straight into the ether, and I'll have no way to determine if it reached the intended recipient. Even if it does, Shayla could ignore it and might block me. It's a waiting game now.

An hour later, Marshall sends a text. The unique tone startles me because I'm used to emails, and it's been a while since he sent a text.

It's a picture of me, and the caption says, I miss you.

The main entrance of the Lost Lake Resort Lodge is behind me. I vaguely remember Marshall gathering the last of our things and insisting he didn't need my help loading the car. I'd told him I'd do one more sweep of the room to make sure we weren't forgetting anything and would be right behind him. When I walked out of the lodge and toward the parking lot, I could see him standing next to the Jeep's passenger-side door waiting for me.

He must have snapped the photo as I walked toward him, though I don't remember seeing him do it.

I glance at the picture again. At the risk of sounding like I'm full of myself, I look radiant. One could say it's the glow of a woman who'd been kissed a lot by someone very good at it.

Another might argue that it's the glow of a pregnant woman.

But I know it's simply what happiness looks like. I may not have noticed Marshall taking the picture, but I certainly remember the joy I felt that day and how it finally seemed that my luck was changing.

I respond to Marshall's text:

I had no idea you took that picture.
I was really happy that day.

He responds a few minutes later:

I was even happier.

I search through all the photos on my phone, hoping I'd snapped one of him when he wasn't looking, but come up empty-handed. I send him a text:

> I don't have any sneaky candid
> photos of you. Not fair. Pay up. ☺

He shocks me by complying, and my heart lurches when his selfie fills the screen. He's sitting in the big chair, the one I pictured him sitting in when I was in the hospital. Today is Saturday and Marshall's wearing a faded T-shirt and jeans and hasn't shaved. There's a coffee cup and a book on the small table beside him. The magnetic pull of his longing smile has me wishing I could climb through the phone screen and straight into his lap. The baby kicks me, hard. *Hey! Remember me?*

You come first, I tell her. *You always will.*

I text him back: What a nice surprise. That's a great picture. I carry the phone around in my pocket for the next hour, but there's no response and I deflate a bit.

But then later that day, he sends another text. No picture this time and it's only one sentence. I can't seem to get you out of my mind today, and I really don't want to.

It shreds me, but in a hopeful way. If I took a selfie right now, Marshall would see that same longing smile on my face that I saw on his. I close my eyes and let myself remember the way he smells and how I felt when his arms were around me—protected and as if I mattered.

I want to text him back and tell him I can't get him out of my mind either. I want to say, *What does it mean? What are we doing? Where do we go from here?* But I know what his text means. It means he wants to try again. It means he wants to know if I do, too.

Every fiber of my being shouts, *Yes!* But his answer will depend on how he feels about the one thing I haven't told him.

Tell him now, Wren. Tell him you really need to talk to him and just say it. You've done hard things. You can do this.

I can, but I don't want to, because coming clean with Marshall means risking another goodbye, this one potentially permanent. I reflect on my dilemma, and for the first time I feel a tiny shred of compassion and forgiveness for Rob mixed in with the anger and sadness. I don't think Rob was an evil person. Selfish, yes. Rob wanted what he wanted, but he didn't act with malice. He just wanted to have his cake and eat it, too.

Clearly, so do I. The longer I go without telling Marshall about *my* secret family—party of two—the longer I can remain in this hopeful, happy space. Yes, I'm strong. Yes, I have the self-awareness to know that what I'm doing is deceptive on a multitude of levels. But I also want more time to reminisce about the joy I felt when we were together and to bask in the fantasy of a happily-ever-after with Marshall. It's been such a horrible year.

I text him back: I can't get you out of my mind either.

Now I'm really playing with fire, because I'm pretty sure I know what we're doing, and his reply comes immediately. I should have never let you go. I regret it every day. You check every single box, Wren.

And there it is, the confirmation of my hunch.

The emails are for Marshall, teaching him how to open up about his past and get comfortable with being vulnerable. A way to let me in that works for both of us.

But the texts are for us.

The texts are about the future.

That night, I have another very vivid pregnancy dream—a nightmare, actually, the worst I've ever experienced. I'm on a train speeding through the countryside of a foreign land where I do not speak the language. Unlike Rob, I have not taken any classes or watched any videos, so I can't understand what the people seated around me are saying. My daughter is with me, buckled into her stroller. I have at least five suitcases with me as well as a diaper bag and purse and I have no idea how I'm going to carry everything.

Beer Gut and Flannel Shirt are also on the train, and the calculated expressions and sinister glances they share leave me rooted to my seat in terror. There is nowhere to escape from the threat, and I must fight.

Once, when I tried to kill a wasp that had flown into my apartment through a small hole in the screen, I failed to kill it on my first attempt, the rolled-up magazine in my hand delivering a glancing blow that served only to anger it and send it buzzing toward me with renewed fury. I put more force behind my second attempt, and the wasp's body became a gruesome smear that took some scrubbing to remove from the glass.

Beer Gut and Flannel Shirt are so much bigger and angrier than that wasp. Any action I take must be enough to eliminate them permanently.

They are filled with bloodlust, and this time Marshall will not be able to intervene on my behalf. They know it and so do I. When the doors open, I dash through them, clipping my left shoulder on the frame in my rush to escape the train car and put distance between myself and the men who are more than ready to finish what they started that day in the clearing. It is only when the doors slam shut behind me that I realize I haven't brought my baby with me. I watch Beer Gut's and Flannel Shirt's faces redden in fury and then I watch in horror as they stride toward the stroller with purpose. I wake up screaming, drenched in sweat, my heart racing. I can't breathe, and even though I've never had a panic attack, I think I might be having one now.

The baby kicks me with brutal force, as if she's mad that I've awakened her. Can she feel my terror? Does she sense that her host is freaking the hell out? I lay my hands on my belly and practice the breathing methods I learned in my childbirth class; I hope they help me when I'm in labor more than they're helping now. It's two in the morning and I feel like a child who wishes she could run into her parents' room and jump into bed with them.

I wish I weren't alone.

I wish I could talk to Marshall so I could tell him about my dream. He'd know exactly what to say to talk me down from this ledge, though I'd have to keep the parts about the baby to myself. Then I realize it's not that late in Oregon, and there's a good chance Marshall is still up and I won't be rousing him from sleep. Before I think too much about what an *awful* idea this is, I fumble for my phone on the nightstand and fire off a text. Can I call you?

He responds a few minutes later. Of course. Are you okay? What's wrong? Do you want to FaceTime instead?

I do want to FaceTime. Talking to Marshall is what I want but seeing him is what I need. I'm lying on my side under the covers, my pregnant belly hidden. After clicking off my bedside lamp, I text him back. Yes.

My phone is propped up on the pillow next to me, and I lose control of my emotions as soon as the call comes through and his face fills the screen. (Seriously, I'm really getting tired of the tears. Before my life took an unexpected turn, I wasn't much of a crier.) He's sitting in that same damn chair in his living room, and he reaches for the TV remote and pushes a button, muting whatever he was watching.

"What is it? What happened?" The concerned look on his face is my undoing. He seems troubled and like he cares deeply about my answer, and I don't feel quite so alone now.

"I had a nightmare. It was intense and so *real*. I was traveling to a place I'd never been and the two men you saved me from in the clearing were there. They were angry. I somehow knew and so did they that you couldn't save me this time. When the train doors opened I ran and I was so happy that I'd figured out how to escape them." I stop talking and take a breath because the words are spilling out without pause. "The train doors shut, and I realized I'd left my . . . my bags behind and didn't have my wallet or passport or clothes or anything. And the men were going to take all of my things before I could figure out how to get back on the train." Now that I'm talking about it, it doesn't sound that scary and certainly not like it warrants the meltdown I'm having. But it would if I told him it was my baby they wanted.

"They wanted to hurt me, but they couldn't, but I was still helpless and lost in a strange place. It was dark and I was alone," I say instead of telling him the truth—that I know what the dream meant and that I don't need Google's help to interpret it. I'm afraid of what not having an extra set of hands will mean when my daughter arrives and that keeping her safe is my responsibility alone. That I'm struggling with not having a partner to stand beside me when things are hard and frightening.

"I know it's scary but it's normal for traumatic events to appear in our dreams in different capacities. You're safe. It wasn't real."

"I know. I'm okay, really," I say, giving my eyes a quick wipe with the back of my hand. The baby's kicks have settled down. "I feel better now that I've talked to you. It was just a very vivid dream."

"Yeah, they can be."

"Do you dream about Graham?" I ask.

He doesn't hesitate. "Yes. They're horrible. But I'm not having them as often." He smiles. It's a sad smile, but it's tinged with hopefulness, like maybe the dreams will eventually stop.

"Thank you for listening. I'm okay now." Surprisingly, I'm already feeling drowsy. Marshall's words have had the same calming effect on me they've always had, and that means more to me than anything he can do with his mouth or his hands. A man who is there for me emotionally is the secure foundation I've been searching for, the one upon which lasting love can be built.

"Of course. I'll check on you tomorrow. Sleep tight," he says.

After we hang up, I think about the reappearance of Beer Gut and Flannel Shirt from a different angle, and my rage trades places with my fear. If anyone ever tries to harm my daughter, I'll be the one to save us and they'll be nothing but a gruesome, unrecognizable smear on the window.

There was one mom group I didn't give much thought to—the Mama Bear Moms. I think I'll fit right in.

Chapter Thirty-six

My due date arrives without fanfare at the end of April. "We made it," I say to my daughter. "Good job."

I am as big as a house.

Not really but it feels that way every time I change position in bed or try to get out of a chair too quickly. I don't care, because I'm thankful my daughter decided to hold off on making her entrance into the world. I'm ready now. Her gray and pink nursery awaits; she can come anytime.

Despite the texts Marshall and I are now exchanging every day—including the one that mentions him buying a plane ticket so he can come for a visit—I have somehow convinced myself that waiting until the baby is born is the best way to handle telling him. My stress level is too high, I justify. I have plenty to worry about without adding to it. Taking a little more time won't change the outcome. Either he'll be okay with it, or he won't.

Even Steph didn't call me on my bullshit when I told her, which only validated my procrastination. "I can understand where you're coming from, Wren. You'll want to go into the birth as clearheaded as you can. It's a big change." I think what she meant was: *This baby is about to rock your world in ways you can't even imagine, and that's the only reason I'm cool with you tabling Marshall temporarily.*

My mom flew in yesterday. "What if I'm overdue, Mom? First babies don't always show up when they're supposed to."

"I took two weeks off, and if I need to take more I will. It'll be fine."

"Okay," I say.

"Wren. I know you're nervous, but I will be in that delivery room no matter what. So will Stephanie. You won't have this baby alone. I can promise you that."

That night, at bedtime, I have a hard time settling. I can't get comfortable, I'm too hot and then I'm too cold, and my lower back is killing me. I'm hungry but I can't eat much because the pressure of the baby on all my organs, including my stomach, isn't leaving a lot of room for food. Steph *did* give me the heads-up on this stage, and so did all of my other friends who have given birth. By the time you're full-term, you will be done with *everything,* they told me.

When I finally doze off, I have another dream. In this one, I'm in the car with Rob and he is screaming at me, which is something he has never done. We are flying down the road, and I've just told him that I'm pregnant.

"Why, Wren?" he shouts. "Why would you do that? Did you do it on purpose? What in the fuck am I supposed to do now?" My mild-mannered boyfriend is lashing out at me like a wounded animal that's been backed into a corner. Dr. Jekyll has morphed into Mr. Hyde and it's terrifying in both its suddenness and its intensity.

"I didn't mean to," I say. "It was an accident." But in the dream, I'm fully aware that I have just sprung some very unwelcome news on a man who was lukewarm about having children, and I feel nothing but guilt and shame.

Rob is not paying attention to the road. He's only got one hand on the wheel; the other pounds on the dashboard in tandem with the frustrated sounds he's making. I've never seen this side of him and I cower, pressed up against the passenger-side door.

"Did you even think about how this might affect me?" he screams. "Or did you only think about yourself?"

"I wasn't thinking about anything. It was an accident," I say again.

"Yeah, you weren't thinking about anything," he sneers. "How stupid are you?"

"Take me home," I say. We were already heading there but my apartment is *my* home and when we reach it, Rob will not be coming inside.

"What do you think I'm doing?" he says, and the coldness, the cruelty in his voice destroys me. "Do you actually think I want to spend time with you after some bullshit news like this?" We sail through the intersection, and in this dream iteration of the accident that took Rob's life, he is the one who runs the stop sign and we are T-boned on his side by the car that has the right-of-way. The sound of skidding tires and crunching metal explodes around me.

I wake up gasping for air, every muscle tense from the anxiety of bracing for an impact that never came. This dream was the flip side of the one I had where Rob and I were married and he was ecstatic to meet his daughter. I firmly believe that my subconscious served up this dark version because it would have been closer to the truth if Rob were still alive. He wouldn't have screamed at me or used those words the way he did in the dream, but he might have *felt* all of those emotions on the inside. Kept them stuffed down where he kept all the other frustrations about his double life—if he had them at all. The dream highlighted the fact that I never really knew Rob and that an unplanned pregnancy might have sent the whole façade tumbling to the ground like a house of cards. I never had the chance to see how far Rob might have gone to handle this unexpected development, and there is absolutely no reason to dwell on it now. He's gone, I'm having the baby, and it no longer matters what Rob would have thought about any of it.

But it does matter what Marshall thinks, because soon I will be springing this very unexpected news on *him*. The baby that feels like a silver lining to me might feel like a heavy anchor to him and will require a special person who's willing to take on that weight and see it through to the end.

I am done with these pregnancy hormones and the horrifically vivid dreams they produce. I'm worn out physically, emotionally, and mentally. But I needn't have worried about my mom coming too soon, because when I get out of bed to relieve my aching, over-full bladder, my water breaks.

Chapter Thirty-seven

It's a Tuesday and Steph is at work when my mom calls to let her know that it's go time. "I'm on my way," she says. Like my mother, Steph has been on standby and has cleared her schedule to be there for me. I'm in excellent hands, and I should feel calm, supported, and centered.

Instead, I feel horribly off-kilter. My daughter is much easier to care for when tucked safely inside my body. Once she's out, she'll discover that I don't know what I'm doing, and it will be my responsibility alone to figure it out.

The contractions are wildly more painful than the ones I experienced in premature labor, especially since my water has already broken. This is the real deal. Steph and I utilize all of the pain-mitigation methods at our disposal—the whirlpool tub, sitting on a giant ball, and walking when I'm able. For someone who hates to be embarrassed, I have already been in several situations—and some variation of nakedness in all of them—that would have mortified me in the past, but just like Steph predicted, I don't care. The nurse comes in to check my progress around three in the afternoon. "You're doing great, Wren. Six centimeters."

I was only at three the last time she checked. "I'll take that epidural now," I gasp. Steph takes over, making sure everyone understands my wishes.

"The anesthesiologist is on the way," the nurse assures me.

"Maybe someone can stand in the hall and watch for them," I say once the contraction ends and I can speak again because it feels like Freddy Krueger is trying to use his knife fingers to claw his way out of my uterus from the inside. Everyone laughs even though I am dead serious, but no one has to go into the hall because the anesthesiologist breezes into the room two minutes later. "Hi. I love you so much," I say.

More laughter, like maybe he and the nurse have heard this a time or two. My mom books it out of the room because she can't handle big needles any more than she can handle blood. "I'll be right back," she says. "Just going for coffee."

They make me sit up and swing my legs over the side of the bed, which does not feel comfortable at all. Steph stands in between my legs and I put my arms around her neck and lean forward, rounding my back. Do I fear the needle that's about to slide into a small space next to my spinal cord? No, I do not, and five minutes after they tell me I can lie back down, the pain blissfully disappears. The anesthesiologist leaves; my mom waltzes back in with a cup of coffee.

"Wow, your timing is perfect," Steph says.

"I guarantee you she was waiting in the hall," I say.

For as wonderful as the epidural makes me feel, there's a downside, because my labor has stopped progressing. I doze as the next few hours tick by slowly. Steph keeps herself busy by using my phone to send text updates to our group chat. She relays the encouragement from our friends and promises to let them know the minute the baby is born. It takes a village, isn't that how the saying goes? Maybe I'm not so alone after all.

Finally, the nurse checks me again and announces that I am fully dilated and can start pushing with the next contraction. I can't feel anything, so a nurse watches the monitor and tells me when to push. It's just like my dream, except that Rob isn't holding one of my legs. Steph holds one and a nurse holds the other. My mom is up by my shoulders.

I'm resting between pushes when my phone rings. I am so focused on bringing my daughter into the world that this barely registers. "Wren?" says a nurse I swear I've never seen before, because now that the birth is imminent, my room is suddenly filled with lots of new people. "It's a FaceTime call from someone named Marshall. Do you want me to answer it?" I have completely forgotten that it's 9:00 P.M. on Tuesday which is what Marshall and I decided on for our next FaceTime call.

"Noooooooooo!" Steph and I shout in unison.

"Got it," she says, and silences the call.

I give one more mighty push with everything I've got, and my doctor says, "Congratulations. Your daughter is here." She places her on my chest. "Who wants to cut the cord?" she asks.

"I do," I say, and I don't feel sad that Rob isn't here to do it. I feel empowered that I *can*. Once the cord is clamped on either side, someone hands me the scissors and I cut. I look down at my daughter. For the first time in far too long, my emotions do not spill forth as tears. I am dry-eyed and composed, and I've never felt stronger.

I have just landed in a foreign country where I don't know how to speak the language and yet I somehow, instinctively, know what to do. I can hear the doctor and nurse talking about the successful delivery of the placenta and a few other post-birth things, but I don't pay much attention. I'm much more interested in staring at my daughter. Light blond downy fuzz covers her head, and her eyes are bluish green. She looks exactly like her father, but I don't feel angry or bitter because she is all mine.

"Way to go, Mama," Stephanie says. My mother is still crying too hard to speak.

"If anything other than a baby came out of me during the delivery, I do *not* want to know. Understood?"

"Understood," Steph says.

"Mom?" the nurse says. For a split second, I think she's attempting to help my mother get control of herself, but then I realize she means *me*.

I am a mom.

"Yes?" I ask.

"Can we have her name?"

I thought long and hard about what to name my daughter. I've always loved the name I chose—it's classic and elegant, but it's also the kind of name she'll need to grow into. Until then, I'm going to call her by the nickname I've decided on. I'll teach her how to fly, and then one day she'll leave the nest, because everything I've taught her will have prepared her for the day she'll climb high and soar.

"Her name is Isabelle Waters Stephenson. But I'm going to call her Birdie."

The next morning, I text Marshall to apologize for missing his FaceTime call and ask if we can talk today at 2:00 P.M. my time instead. It will be noon in Oregon; maybe he can spare a few minutes while he's eating lunch.

Sure, no problem. Are you okay?

Yep. Just wasn't able to pick up last night. I have something I need to tell you. Just call when you're free.

Now that Birdie is here, I find myself wanting to come clean with Marshall in a way I didn't when I was still pregnant. Rob might have kept me hidden, but nothing will ever keep my daughter in the shadows of my life.

I've had a shower, and while parts of my body are beyond *tender*, mentally I feel pretty good. My daughter is healthy, and I've done what I didn't think I could do. A hormonal shitstorm is brewing, but right now it's like being in the eye of the hurricane. The birth is behind me, and I'm relatively calm thanks in large part to the hospital staff whose only goal is to take care of us. Birdie is asleep in the bassinet next to my bed, and I'm sipping on a fountain cherry 7UP that Steph dropped off. My mom is at my place making sure I'll have everything I need for when Birdie and I are discharged tomorrow morning.

It's now or never.

The FaceTime call comes in at 2:03. "Wren. You said you were okay," Marshall says as soon my image fills the screen and he realizes I'm in a hospital bed. "What's going on? Are you hurt?"

"I'm not hurt. I'm fine, really. I had a baby last night. A daughter." The color drains from his face. "She's not yours," I say quickly. "She's Rob's. I found out the day I flew home. I know it's a shock, and I should have told you as soon as we started talking again. I'm sorry." I guess Steph's not the only one who can unhinge her jaw like a snake, because Marshall's is on the *floor*, and his eyes are as wide as saucers. My news has rendered him speechless. "Please say something."

"I . . . I don't know what to say. You had a *baby* last night?"

"Yes. I know it's a lot to wrap your head around. It certainly was for me."

"You're okay, though?" he asks.

"I'm okay. It was an uncomplicated birth and she's healthy. I couldn't ask for more than that."

"That's good. I'm glad you're both okay." His blank expression is in stark contrast to what must be going on inside his brain, because Marshall is a highly contemplative man, and I can almost hear the whirring.

"Listen, I know this is a lot and I'm still trying to get a handle on it myself. You don't have to say anything right now. I just wanted you to know. I'm sorry, I have to go." I end the call and flop back against the pillows, feeling spent but relieved.

Chapter Thirty-eight

I receive an email from Marshall around midnight. Birdie is asleep in the crook of my left arm, and I'm scrolling on my phone with my free hand. I'm exhausted, but every time I fall asleep a nurse comes in to check on me or it's time to feed Birdie again or I have to go to the bathroom.

Marshall's email is probably a very carefully worded explanation about how a baby just isn't something he's got the capacity to take on right now, which is understandable. Birdie and I are a package deal, and any man will need to consider the implications before starting something with me. But I open the email without hesitation, because nothing I can say or do will change the way he feels. This is something only he gets to decide.

I scan the first few lines and there's no mention of the baby at all—just Graham.

Hi Wren,

The last thirty minutes of Graham's life play on a loop inside my brain. It's not constant like it once was, but it will never stop playing completely. When Graham and I got back into my Jeep after hiking back from the last cache we found that day, we were thirsty, tired, and exhausted. I remember groaning when I sat down in the driver's seat because every muscle in my body reminded me that I'm closer to forty than thirty. Graham was hurting, too, but it was a good kind of pain, you know? We decided we'd go back to my place, get cleaned up, grab Holly, and go out for a burger and a beer. Graham joked that we might need some ibuprofen to make that plan happen.

I was low on gas, so we pulled into a convenience store off the highway. I could see through the glass windows that it was empty other than the woman behind the counter and a man standing on the other side of it. Graham was now complaining that he was hungry *and* thirsty, and I figured a gas-station snack and some bottled water would tide us over.

We can pump our own gas everywhere now, so I chose the option to pay at the pump. I meant to pay inside and grab the water and some chips or candy bars while I was in there. Graham poked his head out of the car and asked me to grab him a Coke along with the water. I was still punching buttons on the gas pump and hadn't even gotten the nozzle into my tank yet. There are so many questions—do you want a car wash, do you have any fuel saver points, do you want a receipt? That kind of thing. And since I'd accidentally hit the pay outside button, I told Graham to go in, that it would be faster because he'd be back at the car by the time I was done filling up. Graham complained that he was really stiff and sore now that we'd stopped moving and I told him that taking a walk inside the building would loosen those muscles back up. I'm the older brother, I joked. Get in there.

Graham grumbled a little, but he was smiling in a way that told me he really didn't mind. I've told you how good-natured Graham was. He just rolled with the punches and walked into that gas station like I'd told him to.

The pump had barely clicked off when I heard the gunshots. Three of them. I remembered the woman working behind the counter and the man who had been standing in front of it, and I knew before I turned around that I'd sent my brother into the middle of something that had unfathomable consequences.

It's my fault that my brother isn't here. Grief was something I could tackle, and I've spent a lot of time working through it. But the hardest work I'm doing in therapy centers around my guilt and shame. I've come a long way, but the events of that day will be with me for the rest of my life and will bleed into other aspects of it, including my relationships.

I understand why you didn't tell me about the baby. I'm sure it was a shock to you after everything you'd already been through. You didn't know I would come back into your life. I reached out to you again because of the progress I'd made in therapy and the realization that I'd let you go and wished I hadn't. And that maybe it wasn't too late for us.

I like kids. I want kids. Falling in love with a woman who has a child won't send me running, but my actions ended my brother's life that day, Wren. The choices I made that day will influence every decision I make for the rest of my life, the way Rob's duplicity necessitates honesty and transparency in relationships for you. I don't know if I have the mental fortitude to balance your autonomy with the responsibility I'll feel for keeping the woman I've fallen for, and her child, safe. It's something I'll need to think about for a while.

Missing you,

Marshall

I'm sobbing when the nurse comes in to check on me. "Everything okay?" she asks, and it's a blanket question meant to identify the real issue. Am I in pain? Is it the arrival of the postpartum hormonal hurricane now that I'm no longer in the peaceful eye? Am I exhausted, thirsty, or hungry? It could be anything. I'm not going to tell her that I'm feeling Marshall's shame and guilt so acutely that I fear I may never stop crying. "Just tired," I say.

"I can take the baby to the nursery if you'd like," she says.

"That's okay. I'm fine with keeping her with me." Birdie is still asleep in the crook of my arm, but I wipe her face because some of my tears have landed on her.

Marshall's response was not what I expected, but it all makes sense now, why Marshall reacted so strongly when I offered to go inside the convenience store at Crater Lake when he was pumping gas and he said no, that he would. And every time we stopped for gas, I'd offer to go inside and get whatever we needed and every time, his answer was the same. *It's okay. I'll get it. You stay in the car.*

I thought the baby would be a deal-breaker from a relationship standpoint. It's no secret that men aren't exactly clamoring to date single mothers, and that's understandable. It's a big responsibility and there are lots of potential ramifications—positive and negative. But this tug-of-war between love and responsibility, and what it might look like long-term, is something unique to Marshall, and only he can determine if it's something he can handle. He might decide that it's too much for him and that he can't.

Carefully, I place Birdie into her bassinet and reply to his email.

Marshall,

My heart breaks for you, but I hear you. I understand what you're saying. I think we should take a step back for the next couple of months and put our communication on hold. I don't have any maternity leave since I'm freelance, and my life is about to get very hectic and stressful. I'll be fine—just need time to learn this new language I've never spoken. Motherhood is daunting.

Your plate is full, too, and my unexpected news has only added to it. Take as much time as you need. All I ask is that whatever decision you make, it needs to be final. If you want to walk away from this (and again, I understand completely why you might), I don't want to hear from you months later when you've had a breakthrough and feel like you're finally ready. I can't do that again. It's not that I don't think time can heal us and change our perspectives. I know it can. But I've got a daughter and a life to plan. I don't want any gray areas. I'd rather have brutal honesty and a clean break, and I will be just fine.

I want you to be part of my future because I've fallen for you too. But you have to do what's right for your life, and I'll accept whatever decision you make. Whatever you choose, please know that you were instrumental in helping me to heal, and I'll never forget that.

Missing you too,

Wren

Chapter Thirty-nine

Birdie and I are discharged the next day even though I would be quite content to live at the hospital for a few more weeks, surrounded by knowledgeable professionals waiting in the wings to lend a helping hand. But alas, it doesn't work that way.

At home in the cozy little couch nest I fashioned out of blankets, I spend hours holding my daughter, counting her fingers and toes, and talking to her. I feel overwhelmed, but it's not as scary as I imagined it would be. My mom and I spend most of our time sitting in the living room and talking while I feed Birdie. She jokes that it's her job to keep *me* fed, and she plies me with all my favorites, including the chicken and dumplings she's been making for as long as I can remember.

We have lots of hours to fill, and I tell her about Marshall. It's not that I've been trying to hide him from her, but I feel like it's finally the right moment to tell her about my time in Oregon.

"Wren," she says. "I had no idea. He sounds wonderful."

"He is," I say. "He really is, Mom. But I'm not sure what will happen now. I didn't tell him about the baby until last night."

Her delighted expression dims a little, although she tries to hide it. "Oh."

"Yeah," I say. "It's not just about me anymore and it changes things."

She deflates further when I tell her what happened to Graham and how Marshall blames himself. "He was truthful when he told me he wasn't sure if he was up for the responsibility. I appreciate his honesty."

My mother's practical nature kicks in when she says, "You asked Marshall for time and it's clear that he needs it too. Give him a chance to absorb and work through it. It's a lot, but don't decide for him in your head. You might be surprised."

"I've had a lot of surprises lately," I say. "I don't know how many more I can take." But Marshall's acceptance of my situation would be a pleasant one compared to the other life-changing, rug-pulled-out-from-under-me jolts I've experienced in the last year.

I tell her about Shayla, too, explaining why I want to talk to her and that I've now sent seven emails to the address that might not be correct but probably is. "She's ignoring me but hasn't blocked me yet, probably because she doesn't want me to know that she's receiving the messages. I'm not giving up on this," I say. "It's important, and I'm going to keep trying. For Birdie."

My mom smiles at me. It's the same smile she's given me all my life whenever I encountered something hard but didn't give up. It's the kind of smile that says, *I know something you don't, and you're on the right track.* "The things that have happened in the last year are almost incomprehensible, Wren. But you're going to be a wonderful mother."

It takes one to know one.

Before my mom flies home, she leaves me with one more gift. My parents have paid for four weeks of help from a woman named Lori who's a cross between a postpartum doula and a mother's helper.

"Mom, this is too much," I protest. *I don't deserve it.*

"It isn't too much," my mother says. "Your dad and I could buy you a bunch of baby gear you'd undoubtedly put to good use, but nothing beats having someone to help you, which is the one thing you don't have."

An extra set of hands means I can stay caught up. I earn a good income, but I'm a solo enterprise, which means no one is swooping in to back me up while I take time off. I scheduled two social media posts from my hospital bed and have been working ever since. I'd already made one big mistake when, due to my sheer fatigue, I posted the right social media content on the wrong client's business page, and the only reason I didn't lose their business was that I all but threw Birdie into my mom's arms and immediately deleted the post and replaced it with the correct one. But if my mom hadn't been there to pinch-hit, my error might not have been rectified so quickly. My parents' generosity means I can remain caught up and maybe hold on to my sanity in the process.

Lori arrived the same day my mom flew home to Florida, and she showed up every day after that at 8:00 A.M. and stayed until 4:00 P.M. She filled in the gaps and did the things my mom used to do, and I was eternally grateful, because the early weeks when I would have been alone have been the hardest. Without help, I would not have been able to work without interruption or rest during the day, which gave me the ability to handle the sleepless nights, when it was just Birdie and me, without totally falling apart.

I still feel like I don't know what I'm doing, but with each overwhelming and exhausting day that passes, I'm one day closer to figuring it out.

Chapter Forty

My friends throw me a baby shower when Birdie is six weeks old. I'd already had a family shower when I was eight months along, thrown by my aunt Molly, who lives in Dayton, and I was humbled by the generosity of my relatives. I can't help but suspect that everyone felt sorry for me because of the whole dead-baby-daddy-who-was-also-married-to-someone-else thing.

I've been on my own completely for a couple of weeks now, and so far, so good. A lot has changed since those early days, and I feel like I've found my groove. I can't remember what it's like to sleep through the night and that won't be happening until Birdie starts doing it herself, but I'm used to it. I'm able to squeeze in my work while Birdie's napping or chilling out in her bouncy seat, and I can't help but think, *Maybe I've got this*.

Having a child has done wonders for my perspective on life. No matter what happens with Marshall, I've got Birdie and she has me.

Steph is hosting today's shower at her home, and she walks toward me holding a tall flute of champagne that lacks even a hint of orange juice to dilute it. I just nursed Birdie and she's been whisked away to continue making the rounds of my friends, who are taking turns holding her.

"Everything still humming along now that Lori's gone?" Steph asks.

"I'm doing okay," I say.

"Feeling good physically?"

"Everything seemed mostly back to normal at my six-week checkup." All I can say about that is women's bodies are truly amazing.

"Still flying to New York next week?" Steph asks.

"That's the plan," I say.

"You don't want to wait a little longer before you go?" she asks.

"I don't want to go at all. I tried to do this the easy way, but Shayla won't respond to my emails, so I guess we're doing it the hard way."

I may not want to do this, but I'm going to.

For Birdie.

Chapter Forty-one

Traveling alone with an infant is a fresh kind of hell, and I am basically a Sherpa. My friend Lisa offers to drive us to the airport, and she holds Birdie while I take advantage of curbside check-in and watch as all the gear I brought is tagged and whisked away. That just leaves me with Birdie—whom I attach to my chest in her wrap carrier once I'm checked in—and the backpack-style diaper bag that I'm wearing on my back, which is plenty. Even so, I'm proud of my ability to navigate Birdie and myself through the TSA line without too much difficulty, although by the time I'm done with all the filling and emptying of bins, I'm sweating profusely. I swing by the bathroom closest to our gate and pee one last time, Birdie still strapped to my chest the way I practiced at home. When I'm done, I have to stand sideways, parallel to the sink, and wash my hands one at a time, but I get the job done. Then I put Birdie in a fresh diaper and cross my fingers. Thankfully, our flight leaves on time, and Birdie sleeps for most of it. Our two-hour layover gives me plenty of time to feed Birdie and grab a sandwich. We settle in on the hard plastic chair at our gate, and Birdie fusses for a good thirty minutes before conking out. Then our flight is delayed, and it gets pushed back further every thirty minutes or so.

I begin to rethink my choice to fly alone with a baby.

I walk laps near the gate, trying to settle Birdie, who is fussing again. Finally, we board, and it's an hour past sunset when we land in Rochester, New York. I call an Uber that deposits us at our destination, a Holiday Inn Express. The bellman helps unload my gear, and Birdie and I check in and go up to our room. My decision to end our day of travel in a hotel proves to be a good one, because Birdie and I need to be well-rested for what's to come. I feed her, change her, and get her settled in her travel bassinet. Thankfully, she falls asleep easily.

The next morning, I take my time feeding Birdie and then bathe her in the bathroom sink. I line it with a towel and cradle her with my left arm while washing her with my right. I dress her in a pink plaid one-piece outfit with a matching hat and booties. She immediately fills her diaper, but when I check, I'm pleased to discover it's not a blowout. I change her diaper, feed her again, and place her in her car seat, where she falls back to sleep.

I shower quickly, because even though Birdie was asleep when I put her carrier on the bathroom floor, she is now awake and screaming. I put on the new outfit I packed for myself—a pair of loose black pants and a button-front shirt that are both a size bigger than my pre-pregnancy clothes. The outfit makes me feel more like my old self, which is fitting, because I'm trying to pick up where I left off before Rob died. Or maybe I'm just Wren 2.0.

Older, wiser.

Mother.

I turn on the hair dryer, the noise lulling Birdie back to sleep, giving me time to apply some makeup and do my hair. When I'm finished getting ready, I feed Birdie again and we stay in the room until our noon checkout.

There are a few taxis parked out front when Birdie and I arrive downstairs in the lobby, and I'm able to install the car seat in one of them much quicker than I did in the Uber last night. My heart is pounding as I give the taxi driver the address.

"Here goes nothing, Birdie," I say.

The taxi driver assists me in removing Birdie's stroller from the trunk and I click her car seat into place on top. I wedge the travel bassinet—folded flat and zipped into its carrying case—and my backpack into the stroller's storage area underneath. Slowly and awkwardly, I make my way toward the door with one hand on the stroller's handle and the other on the handle of my wheeled suitcase. The concrete isn't completely smooth, so I bump along trying to keep both wheeled items moving forward in synchronization.

When I finally reach the door, I ring the bell. I've decided to use the element of surprise to my advantage because I think the outcome will be better. I'm sweating again, but it's only partially due to the amount of stuff I'm lugging. My nervousness reaches a fever pitch, and I take deep slow breaths as we wait. Finally, just when I think no one is coming, I hear the sound of approaching footsteps. The door opens and Rob's widow, Shayla, looks at me, her eyes narrowing and her forehead creasing in confusion. "Can I help you?"

"I'm Wren Waters. We met once, in your husband's hospital room. I'd appreciate a few minutes of your time."

She looks at me more closely. Looks at the stroller and the top of Birdie's head. Back to me. Back to the stroller. "You have *got* to be fucking kidding me," she yells, and then slams the door in my face.

Chapter Forty-two

I take a deep breath and ring the doorbell again. I have come here to say my piece, and dammit, I'm going to say it. I have a quest to complete, and Shayla is a part of it whether she likes it or not. I stop ringing the bell and start banging on the door. I continue even when my fist starts to ache. The door finally opens, and Shayla's face is beet red. "I have absolutely nothing to say to you," she shouts. "Get off my property!"

"I'm sure you don't have anything to say, but I *do.*" Her eyes grow wide, and I can feel the anger coming off her in waves, as if it contains actual heat. She's wearing a tennis skirt and matching top, and a visor holds her short blond hair back from her face. My presence on her doorstep is certainly not how she envisioned spending her time on this mild June Saturday. "My mother taught me it wasn't polite to show up at someone's home unannounced, but you haven't responded to my emails, so here I am."

Rob might be gone, but Birdie is still connected to the life he tried so hard to keep from us, regardless of what Shayla thinks about that. Our children's shared DNA is an invisible thread that will connect them for the rest of their lives. People are still asking why I gave Birdie Rob's last name. "No one would blame you if you didn't," they said. First of all, I gave Birdie my last name *and* Rob's. Second, Birdie will share Rob's last name with her half siblings, and those children are the reason I am here.

The way Shayla flicks her eyes away from me when I mention the emails tells me that she definitely received them and probably hoped that I'd give up and go away. In the past, I might have. But this is the present and I'm a different person than I was a year ago.

"If you think I'm going to hand over a single dime, you are vastly mistaken," she says.

"I'm not here for any money."

She rolls her eyes. "No, I'm sure you aren't," she says, and her sarcastic tone pisses me off but also fortifies me.

"If you can stop talking and start listening, I'll be more than happy to tell you why we're here," I say. She exhales loudly and looks as if she's pondering my statement—if only to get rid of me— when a child's voice yells out, "Mom?"

She whips around. "Someone's at the door," she shouts. "I'll be there in a minute." She turns back to me and says, "We have a busy day planned. You've got five minutes."

"I didn't know that Rob was married, and I certainly didn't know he had a family. I didn't know about any of it. You can choose not to believe that, but I have nothing to gain by lying. I am truly sorry for your loss and the loss your children have suffered. But that's not why I'm here.

"Rob didn't know I was pregnant. It was unplanned and the baby was conceived the night before he died. I don't know how he would have juggled another child and it doesn't matter now. But someday, Birdie will be old enough to comprehend that her dad died when I was pregnant with her, and she'll have questions about her heritage. I plan on telling her all the wonderful things I remember about Rob because she deserves to hear the good parts. But she will also grow up with the knowledge and pain of never knowing her father. As she gets older she may want to know about the grandparents on her dad's side—Rob told me they were deceased, I don't know if he was telling the truth about that—"

"That's true," Shayla says. Her tone has softened but not by much.

"—and she might also wonder why there are no aunts, uncles, cousins. Why her family seems to consist of only her and me. I want to get out ahead of it so that Birdie never has to feel as blindsided as we did. Depending on how old she is when she starts asking, I'll tell her. And someday, when she's mature enough to hear all of it, I'll tell her everything. Maybe she'll have compassion for her father and forgive him for the mistakes he made. Maybe she won't. I don't ever want Birdie to be ashamed of where she came from, and I won't hide it from her because if I do, her curiosity about all those empty branches on her dad's side of the family tree might prompt her to go looking for answers on the many websites that will analyze your DNA and tell you who you're related to. And that might lead her straight to your son and daughter. Is that how you want them to find out? If you tell them yourself, they'll never have to feel like we did—shocked, devastated, and hurt. Maybe *they'll* have compassion for their father. Maybe they won't."

"They don't need to know," Shayla says. "That is not their business!"

"But it is," I say, "whether you want them to know it or not. These three children are all down to one parent. Maybe you think the odds of them losing the only one they have left are low, but there's no guarantee someone won't run a stop sign and plow into one of *our* cars. Someday, our children might be grateful for whatever family they can cobble together. Maybe they'll even find solace in it. The best-case scenario is that you and I grow old and gray, and the kids never have to feel like they're adrift, wishing and searching for some semblance of a family to hold on to. But a lot can happen as the years go by."

Shayla looks as if I have slapped her. "We are done here. I've given you enough of my time."

I reach into my front pocket and withdraw one of my business cards. "At least keep my contact information and maybe show me the common courtesy of a reply the next time you receive an email from me. And for what it's worth, your loss was much more significant than mine, and I can't even fathom the depth of your pain. I'm not sure how you've all gotten through it."

She takes the card and shuts the door. She doesn't slam it this time, but there's a finality to our exchange that's hard to miss. I order an Uber and have to stand awkwardly at the end of Shayla's driveway waiting for it to come and pick us up. The day started overcast, but the sky gradually darkened and the temperature dropped. It starts to rain, and it's the only time I'm not okay with it. Birdie, thankfully shielded by the roof of the car seat, has awakened and is looking up at me like, *What exactly are we doing here, Mom?*

"I'll tell you someday when you're older," I say as the rain falls on me. I have no umbrella, because I simply couldn't fathom having one more thing to carry. The Uber is still fifteen minutes out. My mind and body feel heavy with defeat, but I tried my best and if Shayla won't meet me in the middle, there's not much more I can do.

"Wren," a voice says from behind us. I whip around, startled by the sound. Shayla is standing halfway down the driveway. "Please come inside," she says. "I don't want you to stand in the rain."

It seems I may have gotten that foot in the door after all.

Cautiously optimistic, I follow Shayla, leaving the stroller on her porch, which has an overhang, and placing my suitcase and diaper bag on the floor just inside the front door. "Do you drink tea?" she asks as soon as I take a seat in the chair she motions me toward.

"Yes. Thank you," I say.

"Milk? Sugar?"

"Just milk."

I cancel the Uber.

This is Rob's home, I think to myself while Shayla fetches the tea. There's a gallery wall directly across from me. The pictures of Rob's and Shayla's life, the family they made together, hang in various stages; their wedding, and then a picture of them on the beach holding drinks—their honeymoon possibly—next to one with fall leaves and pumpkins. Another one with a Christmas tree. Then the pictures switch to Rob and Shayla and a baby wearing a blue outfit, followed by pictures of them with another baby, this one wearing pink. They are smiling proudly, as if they are the first people to ever bring another life into the world.

I know that smile, that feeling.

Shayla returns with the tea and sets a mug down beside me. "I'm sorry," she says.

I know that it's meant to be a blanket apology for the door slamming and everything she has said since my arrival. "It's okay," I say, accepting it. We say vicious things when we're wounded, and Rob's actions have given Shayla a gash that goes clear to the bone.

"What is her name?" Shayla asks.

"Isabelle. But I call her Birdie."

"She looks just like him," she whispers.

"I know."

She sighs. The visor is no longer on her head, her plans dashed first by me and then by the rain. She looks absolutely defeated. "I thought about what you said. That your daughter might find Robbie and Rowan someday. I hadn't thought of that." She lets out a rueful sound. "I don't know how in the hell that escaped me. Probably because I'm still dealing with what Rob's death has done to these kids. They remember him and they miss him so much." Her eyes fill with tears. "They are still grieving. You said you weren't sure how we've gotten through it and the truth is, we haven't. I don't know that we ever will. I am so angry and sad and the kids just seem lost."

"Yes," I say, because I am familiar with the mingling of those two emotions. At least Birdie will be spared any real memory of her dad, which would only make the loss of him hurt more.

"We didn't have a bad marriage, but the travel didn't do us any favors. Rob loved his kids, but he didn't love the day-to-day grind of caring for them. He left that to me, and over time I grew to resent the freedom he had. He didn't like that I resented it. I thought one day when the kids were older and didn't need so much hands-on care we might rekindle what we had lost. I never imagined he might not be there waiting for me, for us, or that he might have met someone. Asked her to *marry* him."

"The lengths he went to are almost incomprehensible," I say. "But we both know those lengths were real. I want you to know that I had doubts about the relationship. There was always something missing that I couldn't put my finger on. I felt like he was holding something back, and now I know it was the part of his heart that belonged to you and the kids. He was never going to give it to me." It is the only gift I can leave her with, and Shayla begins to cry. *You and the kids still mattered to him.*

"I wish he could have been a better man," Shayla says. "For me and his children." She doesn't specifically mention Birdie, but she doesn't have to.

"Well, they have us," I say.

"They have us," she agrees.

"Thank you for letting me explain why I've come today. It was really important to me, and someday, it will be important to Birdie." I order another Uber and we finish the tea while we wait.

Shayla's daughter, Rowan, appears in the doorway. She looks a lot like her mother. Same nose, same full lips. But her eyes are Rob's—greenish blue. "We finished the show," she says shyly, trying to catch a glimpse of Birdie.

"Would you like to see the baby?" I ask. Rowan nods and comes closer. She kneels by Birdie's car seat.

Shayla looks at me. "She loves babies. Can't wait until she's old enough to babysit."

The sound of thundering footsteps comes from somewhere at the back of the house and Robbie bursts into the room. He looks so much like his namesake. He ignores Birdie and me and flops into Shayla's lap. "The show is done. I'm hungry."

She ruffles his hair and smiles. "You're always hungry. We'll have a snack in a minute."

Watching Shayla with her children, knowing they have experienced a deeply painful loss at such a young age chokes me up and my eyes fill with tears.

I get a notification that my Uber driver is approaching. "My ride is almost here," I say. "Thank you for the tea and for inviting us in."

"You're welcome. I have your card," she says. "When it's time, we'll figure things out. You and me."

A tear plops onto Birdie's face, and I wipe it away with my thumb. "Yes. We will." I turn to go and then I turn back around. "Shayla?"

"Yes?"

"I don't want any money from you. I meant that. I just wanted to talk. Birdie and I are doing fine on our own."

Chapter Forty-three

Once we're home, the closure I've been chasing since the day I sat at Rob's bedside in the ICU and learned what he'd been hiding finally arrives. Rob's horrendous duplicity made me feel stupid and like there was something wrong with me, and I allowed that to bleed into other areas of my life. But I'm not stupid, and my only misstep was falling in love with the wrong man. I don't know what other challenges the universe has in store for me, but I do know that my success rate for getting through the tough times is currently sitting at one hundred percent.

The only way out is through, and here I am.

A week later, I receive a text from Marshall, and the unique tone delivers that same old Pavlovian hit of hope. If I could wrap barbed wire around my heart, I would. But I'm also strong enough to withstand whatever he's about to say. I reach for my phone with stoic pragmatism.

Are you free right now? Not busy
or in the middle of anything?

I'm not busy. Do you want to call me? I can talk.

I can't control the outcome of what's sure to be our most important conversation yet, but even if this doesn't go the way I'd
hoped it would, my quest remains complete.

I just need you to buzz me in.

I'm still trying to figure out what he means when my phone rings,
and instead of Marshall's name on the screen, it's the notification I
get when someone needs me to grant them access to my building.
Marshall is . . . here?
In Dayton.
Birdie is asleep in her wrap on my chest when Marshall knocks
on my door. When I open it, he looks at me the way you look at
someone who's been *through it.*
With tenderness.
With compassion and understanding.
Then he gives me one of those full-wattage, heart-melting smiles,
and I start crying. Very gently, he wraps his arms around me and, by
extension, Birdie. He places the softest, sweetest kiss on my mouth.
Then he looks down at Birdie. "What's her name?"
"Isabelle. But I call her Birdie."
"She's as beautiful as her mother."
"Are you sure?" I ask. He knows what I'm asking.
"Yes." He says it with conviction.
"Okay." I close my eyes and exhale. *Thank you, universe. I'll try
never to doubt you again.*
Not a fling.
A future.
"Come in," I say, shutting the door and suggesting we move to
the couch. "You didn't have to fly all the way here. I would have
read your email, or taken your call."

"I know you would. I like to think of myself as a patient man, but it feels like I've been waiting an eternity to see you again. I couldn't wait anymore, not one single minute."

I'm about to ask him how he knew where I lived, but he probably used the same method I used when tracking down Shayla's home address. For a fee, the internet will give you anything you desire.

"What made you decide?" I ask. *What made you choose us?*

"Therapy. Lots of therapy," he says. "But also, friends and family. Kent and I were out on my boat one night, and he reminded me that I'd been dealt a raw hand and that Graham and I were in the wrong place at the wrong time. But then he pointed out that maybe you and I were in the right place at the right time and if I could just get out of my own damn head, I'd realize what a gift it is to find a good woman because I'm a good man who deserves happiness just as much as the next person. He said if you made me happy, then for the love of God, I should just roll with it. It's the most helpful thing Kent's ever said to me."

"But it's not just about me. It's about her too," I say, glancing down at the top of Birdie's head.

"That's where my sister Jillian came in. After we lost Graham, we started getting together for dinner once a month. She's busy with two kids of her own, but there's nothing like the loss of a sibling to make you immediately clear space for the only one you have left. Jill understood my fear about the added responsibility that a baby would bring to the relationship, but she was also frustrated enough to give it to me straight. 'Stop acting like you have to save everyone,' she yelled. 'You can't and you're going to drive yourself insane. Bad shit happens, Marshall. Get over yourself.'"

"She's right," I say. "You can't save everyone and it isn't your responsibility to do so. But for what it's worth, I think you're an incredible man. Maybe you couldn't be Graham's hero or save the poor woman who died with him. But that day in the clearing, you were my hero. And you always will be."

"Hearing you say that means a lot to me, Wren." He reaches for my hand and squeezes it. "I also told Jillian I'd had clients who were in relationships with single parents and that it didn't always end well. A lot of men act like the children of single mothers are a burden, but what if things go well and they end up caring deeply for the woman *and* her kids only to lose them all if the relationship doesn't last? Then what?"

I'm happy to hear that Marshall has pondered the potential outcomes, and examined them through different scenarios. But neither of us has a crystal ball.

"Then Jillian reminded me that people come into our lives and sometimes we lose them. Or they lose us. But Graham would never turn down the chance to pursue something he wanted because he was afraid of the pain he'd feel if he lost it. Our brother never met a challenge he couldn't face head-on. He was fearless, and I'm not talking about all the times he bungee-jumped off some rickety bridge with a fraying rope tied around his ankles or jumped into a river even though the locals told him there might be piranhas. I might lose you someday, Wren, which means I'd lose Birdie, too. But I might not, which means I'll have worried about it for nothing. And if I do lose you both, I've worried twice. So I'm not going to worry about it. The best way to honor Graham's memory is to live life the way he did. Fearlessly."

We need therapists to help us reach the conclusions and catharsis that elude us, but sometimes what we really need is to listen to our family and friends. They know us almost as well as we know ourselves.

"I missed you terribly," I say. "And I'm so happy you're back."

"Well? What do you think?" I ask later that evening when we're settled in a booth at Skyline Chili. Marshall dips his spoon back into the bowl and takes another bite. "Okay, Skyline Wanderer. This is some damn good chili."

I laugh and say, "I told you it was."

We finish our meal and are waiting for the check when I tell him I flew to New York to confront Shayla. He looks surprised, and then his expression shifts to one of admiration as I tell him everything that transpired. "I want Birdie to know where she came from. Someday, she might find great comfort in knowing she's got half siblings."

"That was a smart move on your part to get out in front of this," he says. "Kids are resilient, but what you did could really help them down the road someday."

"It wasn't an easy conversation, but I'm happy with the way things turned out. I liked Shayla. Maybe someday we'll even consider ourselves friends."

We're sitting on the balcony of my apartment building waiting for the sun to set. Birdie is sleeping and the sun has already begun to dip lower. The sky is a swirl of pink and orange that feels serene and beautiful and hopeful. "Life is so heartbreakingly amazing," I say. I don't have to explain what I mean. Marshall knows.

He smiles at me. "It's a wild ride."

I know that everything that happens in our lives—good, bad, and all the stuff in between—colors them and makes us who we are. But it also gives us the ammunition to make changes in how we view things.

I'm changing the way I view things.

You can slap a smile on your face, you can even enjoy yourself and have fun when you're hurting inside. But that doesn't mean you aren't working hard and healing. And one day, if things go the way you want them to, you realize that the scales have tipped and the weight of the sadness you feel is finally lighter than your happiness.

Marshall turns to me and takes my face in his hands. The kiss he gives me awakens all the feelings I've put on hold for so long.

"Is this okay?" he asks.

"Yes," I say, because I know what he's really asking. "Better make your move, though. I have no idea how long Birdie will sleep before she needs me again."

I don't have to tell him twice. He takes me by the hand, and I lead him inside and down the hall to my bedroom. Marshall is slow, gentle, patient, but I know by the sound of his breathing that he's holding back and would rather go harder. "I'm not made of glass," I say.

"Yes, you are," he whispers.

Somehow, we manage to finish what we started without interruption. I lie in Marshall's arms afterward, my cheek pressed to his chest, lulled by the beating of his heart until I fall asleep.

Later, when I hear Birdie on the monitor, I get up to attend to her. When I return, I lie on my back next to Marshall thinking about the events of the day and waiting for sleep to claim me again. He stirs but doesn't awaken.

Then he reaches for my hand in his sleep as if he's searching to make sure I'm still here, and the day ends so much better than it began.

Chapter Forty-four

My plane touches down in Portland on an overcast day in late September. Birdie and I are staying for ten days, and my excitement has been building for a while now. Marshall insists on parking the Jeep and fetching us from inside the airport, and by the time I retrieve our bags and turn around, there he is, striding through the double doors. I throw myself into his arms as we embrace, standing there for far too long, the crowd milling around us, but it feels so good to be in his arms that I don't care.

"What's the word, Bird," Marshall says. Birdie gurgles up from her stroller and shakes her little frog toy at him. "Thanks," he says, reaching for it and pretending to play with it before handing it back to her.

In case you're wondering, yes, I do know how lucky I am.

Marshall has made multiple trips to Ohio since his inaugural visit, tweaking his schedule and flying in as early as possible on Friday afternoons and back out as late as possible on Sunday nights. This arrangement felt very lopsided, but Marshall insisted that he should be the one to get on a plane because it's easier for him to make the trip than it is for me to travel with a baby. I don't disagree. But I have felt the pull of autumn in the Pacific Northwest because that's where it all started for Marshall and me, and the urge to return has only grown stronger. I long to see the fall colors on the leaves of the trees surrounding the lake. I long for lazy boat rides on a Sunday afternoon. I long for the sound of rain on the windows of Marshall's living room while I'm curled up on his lap in the big chair. My longing for all of this has grown stronger for another reason as well—I feel happiest when Marshall is beside me.

Once we're home from the airport, Marshall brings in our luggage and I follow him to the den where Birdie will be sleeping. She's outgrown the travel bassinet, but I've replaced it with a travel crib that I've taken to Florida several times while visiting my parents.

I stop in the doorway, Birdie in my arms, too stunned to speak. There's an actual crib in the corner where the desk used to be. The desk is still there, but it's on the other side of the room now, as if an invisible line has been drawn to separate the two spaces, with room for a baby on one side and a workspace on the other.

"It's okay, isn't it?" Marshall asks. "Jillian went with me to pick it out. She said it was a good one. Very safe. I was going to tell you so you wouldn't have to bring the portable one, but I wanted you to have a backup in case Birdie didn't like it."

"It's more than okay," I say, my voice thick with emotion. "It's perfect."

You can tell a single mother over and over again that the relationship is real and that you are all in. Or you can show her by buying a crib and assembling it in the room that used to be your office. Rob showed me what a selfish man looks like. I'm grateful that Marshall constantly reminds me what a selfless man looks like.

What a shame it would have been not to have the opportunity to see the difference.

The next day, once I've attended to Birdie and we've eaten breakfast and gotten dressed, Marshall says, "How do you feel about a boat ride? I've got something to show you."

The sky is overcast, but the temperature is in the mid-seventies. Perfect weather for taking the boat out. "I'm intrigued. Sure, let's go."

Marshall's boat has every size life jacket they make, including the one his sister used for her kids when they were babies. He grabs it from the boat, and we work together to put it on Birdie. "I won't be going fast and for the most part, we'll be in the no-wake zone," he says.

He boards the boat first and reaches his hands up for Birdie. Once she's safely in his arms he extends a hand to me, and I step on. Looking at Marshall holding my daughter in his arms like a treasure he must protect at all costs feels indescribable.

"Put this on, Wren," he says, motioning toward a life jacket on the seat across from his.

I do as he says, and then, satisfied that he has given our safety his full attention, he hands Birdie back to me. I hold her on my lap as we slowly cruise around the lake. She must love the gentle motion, because she immediately falls asleep.

"Are we going to Kent's?" I ask. Maybe Marshall wants to take me there to visit so that we can introduce Birdie to him. But then I remember that Marshall said he has something to show *me*.

"Nope." He hands me his phone. The geocache app is open, and I watch the GPS arrow moving in the same direction we are. "We're doing a lake cache?" I ask.

He looks at me and grins. "You said you always wanted to."

I keep watching the arrow and a few minutes later I say, "That way," and point. He turns the boat in to a small cove out of the main boat traffic. "Almost there," I say.

A minute later, he cuts the engine and drops the anchor. I can tell by the app that we are right on top of the cache. "Where is it?" I ask, thinking that there will be a buoy or something to indicate the cache's position.

"Look down," Marshall says, pointing into the water. As if reading my mind, he holds out his arms for Birdie, and I place her into them. Then I look over the side. I don't see anything at first, but when I move to the front of the boat and scan the depths, I can just make out a canister floating straight up a foot or so beneath the surface, weighted to the lake bottom by a chain attached to something heavy. I turn back around. "I see it! How am I supposed to get it into the boat?"

"I guess you'll have to jump in and pull it up," he says, laughing when he sees my shocked expression.

"You didn't say anything about getting in," I say. "Isn't the water too cold? And I'm not wearing my swimsuit."

"That's because I'm kidding," he says. Carefully, gently, he hands Birdie back to me and grabs a net for scooping up fish. He stretches out on the bow of the boat and leans over, as close to the water as he can get. Then he uses the handle of the net to lift the chain and pull the canister up so he can reach into the water and grab it. The whole thing comes up—canister, chain, and the rock that was holding it in place. His forearm is wet to the elbow.

The dark gray canister is about the size of a one-liter water bottle and is made of the same rugged material as my phone case. Birdie and I sit down, and Marshall loosens the lid and hands the canister to me. I'm pretty sure I know what's inside. I reach into the canister and pull out the little motorcycle toy. "It's here. It made it home." Graham would never come home, but the trackable Marshall left behind in his honor at Tumalo State Park did.

I place the motorcycle in his palm, and he closes his fist around it. Then I put my arms around him, Birdie in between us, and hug him gently the way he hugged me when he showed up on my door-step. Neither of us says anything; we don't need to.

As we motor slowly back to Marshall's, he says, "Friends and family have an open invitation during boating season. There will probably be some people stopping by later. If you don't want that, let me know and I'll put the word out that today isn't a good day."

Having never been introduced to a single member of Rob's fam-ily while we were dating, I *do* want this. "I'd like to meet them," I say. "Today is a great day."

They start arriving in the early afternoon. Kent arrives first and gives me a big hug. His wife, Joelle, is with him, and they ooh and aah over Birdie. Marshall has brought some extra chairs out and placed a big cooler full of ice on the deck. "Sit down," he tells them.

His parents show up half an hour later. His mom has brought several appetizers, and his dad puts a six-pack of beer in the cooler. After the introductions are made, I slip inside to feed and change Birdie. When I come out of Marshall's bedroom, his mom is stand-ing in the kitchen putting cookies on a plate. Her name is Joan. I offer to help, but she waves her hand and tells me she's got it. "Marshall has told me so much about you," she says with a big smile.

"It's been quite a year," I say, which feels like the world's biggest understatement.

She pats my hand. "It sounds like you've handled it just fine. And now you have that beautiful baby."

I like her. It's easy to see where Marshall's kindness comes from, because the apple didn't fall far from the tree.

A few of Marshall's friends drop by throughout the day. Some of them, like Kent and Joelle, live on the lake, and others are friends Marshall has known since his college days. His sister, Jillian, and her husband, Ben, stop by with their kids, and Marshall tells his brother-in-law that the keys are in the boat and to have at it.

Jillian offers to hold Birdie so that I can make a plate. "Thank you. Can I refill your wine while I'm up?" I ask, noticing her empty glass.

"Please," she says. "That would be great."

I return with the wine and sit down next to her with my plate. "You know, it takes a special woman to help heal a heart she didn't break," Jillian says. "I haven't seen my brother this happy in a long time. Thank you for that."

Her words fill me with warmth, and I turn to her and say, "It takes an equally special man who's willing to help raise a child he didn't make."

She raises her glass and so do I. We clink them and that's the moment I gain the sister I've always wanted.

Nighttime brings meat thrown on the grill with a sizzle, another round of plates filled, and a group boat ride at dusk. Those who are left all pile in—Marshall's parents, Birdie and me, and Kent and Joelle. We cruise around the lake and it's fully dark by the time Marshall cuts the engine and glides the boat into place at the dock.

The day has been overwhelming in the best possible way. Marshall worked tirelessly to make it that way, to anticipate my needs so that I never felt out of place and could truly enjoy myself.

He has done everything he could to show me that Birdie and I belong.

Chapter Forty-five

Birdie wakes up early on our last day. It's almost as if she wants to wring every last second she can out of our dwindling visit. As our time together has drawn to a close, my emotions have been all over the place. Marshall noticed, of course, and I was honest about my feelings. "I'm not sad," I protested with tears running down my face. "It's just been a great visit."

It's still dark out, but I sit down at Marshall's desk chair and feed Birdie without turning the light on. My weepiness is gone, replaced by the knowledge that we can return, and that Marshall will be getting on a plane to Ohio in just a few short weeks. When I lay Birdie back down in the crib, she falls asleep again but there is no chance that I'll be able to.

Marshall intercepts me in the hallway on my way to the kitchen. "Hey," he says. "I already made the coffee. Let's go drink it on the deck."

We pull on sweatshirts and go outside. As we watch the sun begin to rise in the east, I remember the sunrise at Crater Lake and how emotional it made me feel to witness such beauty. This one is even better. Sunlight dapples the water and I hear the faint sound of a boat motor in the distance as the lake wakes up. Then Marshall turns to me and says, "I don't think I can do the long-distance thing anymore."

My heart sinks. Is that why we're having coffee on the deck? So he can share his honest thoughts? "It's a lot for you," I say. "But we can come here. You don't always have to be the one who gets on a plane."

"What I mean is that I can fly to Ohio one last time, rent a truck, and help you pack up your things. Then you and Birdie can come here to live with me." He squeezes my hand. "We don't have to make any other decisions right now. It's just that I love you and I'm happier when my birds are here in the nest."

It wasn't the first time he'd said "I love you," but it was the first time the words had sounded like something other than a personal declaration of his feelings toward me. This time, "I love you" sounds like *Let's build a life together.*

"Is that something that would make you happy? Moving here?" he says.

Thinking about what would make me happy is something that's been on my mind a lot lately, too. I could be happy on my own because I'm happy with myself. I've made it through the worst year of my life, and I did it by putting in the work. By feeling every emotion fully, even the ones that were so hard to feel.

And so has Marshall.

I think back again to something he once said about us: better together.

I think we can amend that now: the best.

Nothing is holding Birdie and me back from making the move. My parents haven't lived in Ohio in years. I love my friends, but we don't see each other as often as we'd like because we're busy living our lives and there's no shortage of ways we can keep in touch regardless of where we're living. My wanderlust, my desire to Airbnb myself around the country, has faded because it's not just about me anymore.

Birdie makes me want to put down roots and see what grows.

Marshall interprets my silence as reluctance. "You said you liked the rain," he says, as if the weather is ammunition he must exploit to convince me.

I smile and squeeze his hand. "I do like the rain. And I love *you.*"

The man sitting next to me, his arm around my shoulders, will not deny me access to anything. Not his head, not his heart, not his life. He's shown me that time and time again. And he treats Birdie like his own. At this moment, I feel nothing but yearning for this strong man I hope I'm sitting next to for the rest of my life. It's so deep I can feel it in my bones.

In my mind, I zoom out as if I'm flying, looking down at him and the sparkling water of the lake below. I don't need a sign from the universe telling me what to do, because I know without a doubt that Marshall is the softest, safest place for me to land.

So I do.

Acknowledgments

The Trail of Lost Hearts is my tenth book, which seems fitting as I finished the book a few months after celebrating my tenth anniversary of being published. Like Wren, I also believe in trusting the universe to send us exactly what we need, and I needed this book and the way it made me feel while I was writing it. Writing a novel will always be hard work, but there are times when the writing process has felt very joyful—and this was one of those times. *The Trail of Lost Hearts* poured out of me and it was exactly the book I needed to write because it was the one I wanted to read. I am still in awe that I get to spend my days doing what I love and that readers message me to say how excited they are to read my words. "Thank you" doesn't even begin to cover it. If you're reading this right now, please know that your support and enthusiasm helped make a writer's dreams come true.

To my editor, Leslie Gelbman. You are a true partner and a kindred spirit. Thank you for pushing me to be the best I can be. You have my utmost respect and affection.

To everyone at St. Martin's Press. Words cannot express my appreciation for your continued support and enthusiasm. Special thanks to Jennifer Enderlin, Lisa Senz, Brant Janeway, Marissa Sangiacomo, Katie Bassell, Kejana Ayala, and Grace Gay. I'm so happy to be a part of your world and a player on your team.

Jane Dystel, Miriam Goderich, and Lauren Abramo of Dystel, Goderich, and Bourret. You are truly the trifecta of literary-agent awesomeness. Thank you for all you do.

To Tammara Webber. I'm not sure how to thank you for your cheerleading, your sage advice, and your spot-on feedback as I wrote this book. You fanned the flames of my flickering creativity until it became a forest fire. The universe knew what it was doing when you became my critique partner many moons (and books) ago. I sure am lucky.

To Stephanie Cox of The Bookish Boy Mom. Thank you for your feedback on this manuscript as well as the stellar skills you bring to the management of my social media accounts. I couldn't do this without you. I think it's also worth mentioning that you and Elysse Wagner of Compulsive Reader's Book Blog (a fantastic book cheerleader in her own right) *both* hail from Dayton, Ohio. It just so happened that I needed a hometown for Wren (not to mention some input on that Skyline Chili), so Dayton it is! Boom. Done.

To Barb Petersen-Fox. Thank you for reading the manuscript through the lens of your professional experience as a therapist. Your feedback is greatly appreciated! To Hillary Faber. Thank you for going in blind and reading one of the many revision drafts (and for loving it).

To my children, Matthew and Lauren. Thank you for never getting frustrated with my constant pleas for your patience and understanding as I worked through the many stages of writing a novel. You are my two greatest gifts in life and watching you grow into young adults is the hardest job I've ever loved.

Thank you to anyone who has ever come to one of my signings.

Looking out into a sea of faces after worrying that there might be only one face—or worse yet, no faces—and seeing you there truly fills my heart with joy.

To the wonderful individuals who have written to me on social media or emailed to let me know how much one of my books has touched you—I am simply in awe that you took time out of your day to let me know.

To Ashley Spivey. You embody grace under pressure. Your continued championing of my books (as well as the entire author community) despite the challenges you've faced in your personal life is above and beyond anything I've ever seen. Your tireless endeavors and your amazing Spivey's Club group are so instrumental in spreading the word about authors and their books, and one of these days, I'll figure out how to thank you properly. In the meantime, please know that my appreciation is endless.

Special thanks to the bloggers and bookstagrammers who have been so influential in my ability to reach readers. You work tirelessly every day to spread the word about books, and the writing community is a better place because of you. Jamie Rosenblit of Beauty and the Book, Kristi Barrett of A Novel Bee, Susan Peterson of Sue's Reading Neighborhood, Andrea Peskind Katz of Great Thoughts' Great Readers, Hannah at Bookworms Talk, Sarah Symonds of DragonflyReads, Sarah Sabin of Mama's Reading Corner, and Stephanie Gray of The Book Lover Book Club. Your gorgeous pictures and posts are every bit as beautiful as your kind words and support. Thank you from the bottom of my heart.

To the members of my Facebook readers' group, On Tracey's Island. I love that you're still in my group despite my long periods of radio silence. I'll try to do better.

To those who discover and champion my foreign editions, it is thrilling to see your praise and to understand just how far around the globe my stories have traveled.

I want to express my sincere appreciation to the book clubs

who choose my titles, the booksellers who hand-sell my books, and the librarians who put them on their shelves.

My heartfelt gratitude goes out to all of you for helping to make *The Trail of Lost Hearts* the book I hoped it would be. Words cannot express how truly blessed I am to have such wonderful and enthusiastic people in my life.

And last, but certainly not least, my readers. Without you, none of this would be possible.